I0823931

MONSTER *in the* MOONLIGHT

BERKLEY PRIME CRIME TITLES

BY ANNELISE RYAN

A Death in Door County

Death in the Dark Woods

Beast of the North Woods

Monster in the Moonlight

MONSTER *in the* MOONLIGHT

ANNELISE RYAN

BERKLEY PRIME CRIME · NEW YORK

BERKLEY PRIME CRIME
Published by Berkley
An imprint of Penguin Random House LLC
1745 Broadway, New York, NY 10019
penguinrandomhouse.com

Book design by Elke Sigal

Library of Congress Cataloging-in-Publication Data

Names: Ryan, Annelise author
Title: Monster in the moonlight / Annelise Ryan.
Description: New York : Berkley Prime Crime, 2026. |
Series: A monster hunter mystery ; book 4
Identifiers: LCCN 2025035690 (print) | LCCN 2025035691 (ebook) |
ISBN 9780593953570 hardcover | ISBN 9780593953594 ebook
Subjects: LCGFT: Detective and mystery fiction | Novels | Fiction
Classification: LCC PS3568.Y2614 M66 2026 (print) | LCC PS3568.Y2614 (ebook)
LC record available at https://lccn.loc.gov/2025035690
LC ebook record available at https://lccn.loc.gov/2025035691

Printed in the United States of America
1st Printing

The authorized representative in the EU for product safety and compliance is Penguin Random House Ireland, Morrison Chambers, 32 Nassau Street, Dublin D02 YH68, Ireland, https://eu-contact.penguin.ie.

To Scott,
for all your help,
support,
and love over the years.
And for your tolerance.
Especially that.

MONSTER *in the* MOONLIGHT

PROLOGUE

Lydia Palmer pulled onto the shoulder of the road, wincing at the noise her exhaust system made and quickly shutting down the engine to silence it. The old car coughed and sputtered before complying and she pleaded with it to hang in there a little longer, as if it could somehow hear and obey her.

The darkness surrounding her was faintly mitigated by the pale silvery light of a high full moon. It cast the branches of the surrounding trees, which had yet to fully leaf out, in a ghostly black-and-white tableau. The windows of the houses she'd passed as she drove down the road had all been dark, their inhabitants either asleep or away. A glance at her cell phone told her it was a few minutes past two thirty a.m.—the perfect time. It was far enough past the midnight witching hour, late enough for the diehard barflies to have staggered home and fallen into bed, and early enough that daily workers wouldn't be up and about yet. She tucked her phone into her pants pocket and climbed out of the car, closing the door as quietly as she could.

She stood there a moment, watching and listening, hearing nothing but the hoot of a distant owl and the trills of spring peepers. Satisfied, she went around to the back of the car and opened the trunk, taking out a small trowel, a shovel, and a flashlight before easing the trunk lid down until it was just shy of latching. Shoving the trowel into the back pocket of her jeans, she held the flashlight in one hand and the handle of the shovel in the other.

There wouldn't be much traffic, if any, at this hour on a weeknight, but she was still hesitant to use the flashlight, fearful it might attract attention. Or bugs. Moonlight enabled her to navigate along the shoulder, but once she descended the embankment and entered the narrow, rutted path that ran between the two dense thickets of trees edging this section of Bray Road, darkness enveloped her. Still, she stumbled along for several more yards to distance herself from the road before she turned the flashlight on. She skimmed the light over the surrounding trees. The way it danced over the bare branches and the dead remnants of last year's vines still twining their way across the ground and up the trunks made it appear as if the trees were moving. For one scary moment, Lydia imagined the trees as malevolent creatures closing in on her, the dead vines reaching out and writhing until they trapped her and squeezed the life out of her.

Her foot caught on a root protruding from the ground, and it snapped her back to reality. She shook off the horrifying image, and after taking a beat, she continued, wisely employing the shovel as a walking stick. When she saw an opening in the trees up ahead, she turned the flashlight off, stuck it in a pocket, and waited a moment while her eyes adjusted to the darkness.

Twenty yards later, she emerged along the edge of an open field containing the dead remnants of last year's crop of feed corn. The field extended out to her left as far as she could see and ran up to a distant copse of woods far ahead. To her right, some twenty yards away, was a split-rail fence separating this field from one containing freshly turned clods of soil. The fence also followed the rear tree line of the woods to her right, snugging up close enough in some spots that the branches hung over the top rail. She aimed for this corner of the two fields, carefully navigating the hardened cornstalk remnants.

When she reached the fence and slipped between the wooden rails into the plowed field, she trembled with excitement. Leaning back against the corner post, she checked her surroundings. She'd been here on two other nights already and nothing much had changed, at least not in this portion. Still using the shovel as a walking stick, she followed the fence line farther back into the plowed field, moving away from the woods and the road. Periodically she checked for the landmarks she'd noted on her previous trips. She also counted her steps, not because it helped her navigate but because it reassured her to do so. Minutes later she arrived at the hole and finally put the shovel to its intended use.

While her previous efforts had proven fruitful, the dry ground remained hard and resistant. She had initially hoped the loose, turned soil in the field would make it easier, but there had been no rain for several weeks now and the chunks of churned-up dirt were hard as rocks, the ground beneath difficult to penetrate.

"Figures," she muttered, glaring at the hole, and bemoaning how nothing ever came easy for her.

Her breath created tiny clouds of mist in the chilly night air, but after less than an hour of digging, she was hot, sweaty, exhausted, and had only one new coin to show for her efforts. She leaned on the shovel and eyed her progress: a hole some four feet square and now about two feet deep. It was slow going not just because of the hard-packed ground, but also because she needed to stop every so often to examine the dirt she'd removed as well as the walls and bottom of the hole.

She climbed out of the hole, shrugged out of her jacket, and draped it over the top rail of the fence a few feet from where she was digging so she wouldn't fling any dirt on it. Then she leaned against the fence for a moment to take a brief break. Her mouth was as dry as the soil she was trying to dig. Why hadn't she remembered to bring any water? She'd forgotten it last night, too, and somehow in her furtive preparations for tonight's exploits, she'd overlooked it again.

Not enough sleep. Too many distractions. But if this pays off, things will be looking brighter soon.

With a weighty sigh, she went back to it, and as she was about to drop into the hole, a flash of reflected moonlight caught her eye. Bending down, she picked up a shiny object, sucking in an excited breath when she realized it was another coin. She scraped the dirt off and examined it more closely with her flashlight, exhilaration coursing through her when she saw the date on it. Shoving it into her pocket with the first one she'd found and the one from last night, she grabbed the shovel, prepared to resume her digging with renewed vigor.

She slipped down into the hole, raised the shovel high, and brought it down hard to loosen the soil at her feet. On her third such effort, the loud *crack* of a breaking branch from the woods between the field and the road made her freeze with the shovel poised in the air.

She heard another crack . . . and then another. Had someone seen her car parked along the shoulder and stopped to investigate? She hadn't heard a car out on the road, but realized the sounds of her own exertions might have drowned it out. Not to mention all the electric vehicles out there these days. They made hardly any noise at all, unlike her car, which could be heard approaching from half a mile away.

After a minute or so of silence, she decided the sound must have come from an animal, a deer perhaps or maybe a coyote. Then she heard another noise like a stealthy crunch of footsteps, and her sweat-slicked skin prickled with goose bumps. The night took on a weighty, uncomfortable silence then and Lydia had a strong sense of something watching her . . . perhaps even stalking her.

Her eyes surveilled the neighboring cornfield, her heart pounding loud in her ears as she scanned back and forth along the line of the trees, searching for any motion. With her free hand, she reached to her back pocket for the trowel, only to realize it was several feet away on the ground outside the hole where she'd used it to sift through the dirt around the perimeter. Instead, she hoisted the shovel midway down the handle and held it out in front of her, blade first. If an animal predator was stalking her, the shovel would hopefully keep the animal at bay.

After waiting an interminable length of time, she slowly lowered the shovel and began to relax, though she wondered if she should pack it in and come back tomorrow night to try again. Next time she'd remember the damned water, bring an entire jug of it not only for drinking but also to wet the ground and make it easier to dig. She'd just about convinced herself of this plan when an inner voice cajoled her to keep at it a little longer. There was too much at stake and there had to be more. After all, she'd already struck gold, so to speak.

She caught a flash of movement off to her left and saw a coyote trotting over the clumps of dirt, heading toward the woods at the back of the field. Had that been what she'd heard moving through the trees a moment ago? Coyotes often ran in packs, but she'd seen only the one and she knew they were typically shy around humans.

She decided to go back to work, give it one last push.

A lone howl broke the silence of the night.

Not a coyote. A wolf.

She scrambled out of the hole and once again surveilled her surroundings. As she bent down and grabbed the shovel, she sensed something behind her and whirled around, shovel at the ready. What she saw made her gasp, and the shovel dropped from her hands.

She was hit hard and fast in the center of her chest. She windmilled her arms, her feet scrambling to try to stay upright. Then her heel caught on one of the larger clumps of dirt and her ankle twisted painfully, making her fall backward toward the fence. Her neck hit hard on the edge of one of the rails, triggering a brief flash of intense pain, a lightning bolt that shot from her shoulders to her toes before disappearing. Her view shifted and rolled for a few seconds until it eventually settled on the sky overhead, the full moon shining down through wispy, scudding clouds. She tried to holler, more out of fear than pain, but found she had no breath and couldn't make a sound. Nor could she move a muscle. Except for her eyes. She shifted her gaze to her left, blinked, and then did it again, expecting the image she now saw hovering above her to change. Because what she saw was impossible. It couldn't be real.

Her heart juddered much the way the engine in her car had earlier. Darkness closed in like it had when she'd first stepped between the trees, but this time there was no adjusting to the dimming light. She was beyond seeing, beyond feeling, beyond movement, her brain only able to register sound. The last thing she heard was so disturbing, so unbelievably horrible, she welcomed the all-encompassing void that followed.

Moments later, an eerie howl echoed through the night air, baying at the full moon shining down from above.

CHAPTER 1

I was showing a customer a necklace with two opposing silver dragon heads that came together in a heart shape over a red amethyst teardrop when the cops arrived. My dog, Newt, sat beside me and got my attention by whining and wagging his tail, creating miniature fur balls that rolled across the floor like tiny tumbleweeds. He raised his nose and started sniffing madly, compensating for his near blindness. I turned to see why he was so excited, at first noticing only dust motes dancing in the beams of late-afternoon sunshine streaming through my front windows. I made a mental note to have Rita and Devon do some serious spring cleaning.

Then I saw the two people who had arrived and understood Newt's excitement. My reaction was equally enthusiastic, and if I'd had a tail, I probably would have been wagging it, too.

He's here.

I glanced over at the checkout counter, where Rita had just finished processing a payment for someone, and saw her arch her eyebrows with interest. I gave her a look to summon her over and she nodded, the loose, wispy white hairs in her ever-present sloppy bun creating an undulating halo around her head.

Jon Flanders, or Flatfoot Flanders as Rita had taken to calling him, stopped a few feet away and gave me a tentative smile. He looked good, his blond hair cut short on the sides, but a longer lock in front hung boyishly over his forehead. His blue eyes twinkled, making me think he was happy to see me. Or was that simply wishful thinking on my part?

Jon was here! My heart felt like it might burst, and the reaction surprised me a little. I knew I'd missed him of late but perhaps I hadn't realized how much.

The man with Jon, who I guessed was also a cop based on his military haircut and ramrod posture, was dressed in jeans, a white shirt, and a suit jacket. My excitement at seeing Jon was somewhat tempered by this second man's presence because this wasn't at all how I'd imagined our eventual reunion in the gazillion scenarios I'd run through my mind over the past few months. It was supposed to be a private, romantic setting, an opening—or rather a reopening—of the lines of communication between our minds and our hearts, not a ménage à trois.

"Oh, my niece just *loves* that necklace!" Rita cooed, moving in and smoothly taking over with the customer. The rhinestones on the lanyard attached to her eyeglasses caught some of the sunbeams and reflected little dots of light around the room like a disco ball. Her enthusiasm was all for show. Rita didn't have a niece. I excused myself and walked over to the newly arrived duo.

"It's good to see you," I said to Jon, mildly irritated by the tentativeness I heard in my voice. Newt had no such reservations. He was all over Jon, wagging his tail furiously, nosing one of Jon's hands, and whining with excitement.

Jon returned my greeting with a brief nod and then did the introductions. "Wyatt Moorhead, this is Morgan Carter. Morgan, this is Wyatt Moorhead. He's a detective down in Elkhorn."

"Nice to meet you, Detective Moorhead."

"Please, call me Wyatt."

Jon said, "Can we go upstairs and talk?"

Okay, apparently this visit was all business. And when Jon mentioned where Wyatt was from, it gave me an inkling of what the business might be about.

"Sure," I said.

I stepped past the two men and led them up the stairs to my apartment on the second floor, with Newt following. The late-afternoon sun was putting on a stunning display here as well, thanks to a wall of westward-facing glass. Unfortunately, it also highlighted all the dog hair and dust that had settled on my glass-topped coffee table, granite countertops, and wood floors. And then there were the dried drool spots courtesy of Newt. I had dusted, vacuumed, and mopped it all just yesterday morning but it was a never-ending battle. I loved my dog, but he was kind of a slob.

I directed the men to the living portion of the open-concept space and headed for the kitchen.

"I could use a coffee," I said over my shoulder. "Can I get you guys something? I have water, coffee, tea, some pink lemonade, and if you're so inclined, some nice IPAs."

"I wouldn't mind some water," Wyatt said.

I glanced over at Jon expectantly. "Same," he said without looking at me.

"Jon tells me the mummified body seated by your front door is real," Wyatt said as I started a single cup of coffee in my Keurig machine.

"Yep, that's Henry," I explained. I got each of the men a bottle of water from the fridge and carried them into the living room. "Henry was part of the Alaskan gold rush, but he fell into an ice crevasse and was frozen for many years. Some Inuit found him. Then Native Americans had him, and eventually my father bought him. The ice started the mummification process and I'm not sure if something or someone else finished it. All I know is, he's been a mascot here at Odds and Ends practically since the store opened. And he saved my life once."

Wyatt's eyebrows shot up, but I chose not to clarify further. My mind was too busy thinking about other things.

My coffee was ready, and I grabbed it and settled into a chair across from the men, somewhat amused they had chosen to sit side by side on the couch. Newt flopped down on the floor at my feet, ready for one of his many daily naps. I took a sip of my coffee, using the activity to study Wyatt over the top of my mug. He was an attractive man, tall and well-built with broad shoulders. His eyes were a brown so dark, they looked black, and he had a hair color to match. A hint of a five-o'clock shadow graced his cheeks. I pegged his age as somewhere in his early forties.

"So, what's up?" I was trying to sound casual even though my heart was pounding so hard, I could see a small pulsating light in one corner of my vision. Before anyone could answer, I quickly added, "Wait. Let me guess. This has something to do with the Beast of Bray Road."

Wyatt's eyebrows shot up again and I couldn't resist a smile.

"It does," he said. Then his eyes narrowed with suspicion. "Did you hear something about it?"

"You mean, something new?"

Stories about the Beast of Bray Road were legendary in parts of Wisconsin. There had even been a low-budget horror movie made about it—a slasher flick I recalled viewing with my parents several years ago, which, in hindsight, had been a bad idea.

"There's been a possible attack," Wyatt said. "It happened three nights ago, and a couple of nights before, a witness saw a strange creature eating an animal he thought looked like a dog. And a farmer who lives nearby is missing one."

"I don't watch the news much," I admitted. "But I didn't think you'd seek me out for my knowledge of police investigative techniques, so when Jon mentioned you were from Elkhorn, I kind of guessed what it was about. There have been sightings and incidents involving the beast in other locations, but Elkhorn is famous for it . . . or was a few decades ago. Maybe 'infamous' would be the better word."

Wyatt nodded, looking solemn. "I've heard about your other recent cases. Word gets around in the law enforcement community, and I knew Jon here had worked with you on those, so I asked him for an introduction."

I glanced over at Jon, who was studying the writing on his water bottle label like it was evidence at a crime scene. It occurred to me then that he wasn't here because he'd wanted to see me or because he'd missed me. He was here because of a professional obligation. The realization hit hard. Seeing him had triggered emotions in me I hadn't expected—longing, joy, an aching need I didn't fully understand. Had seeing me done anything for him? I wondered. Was his apparent reluctance to look at me a good sign or a bad one?

"You want me to investigate this possible attack as a cryptozoologist?" I asked Wyatt.

"I do." He sounded tentative and his smile morphed into a wince. "But it's a bit of a delicate situation because my boss thinks what you do is . . . um . . . well, to put it bluntly, some kind of hocus-pocus. No offense."

I shrugged. "None taken. I've heard worse."

This wasn't unexpected, though I had to wonder why the police were involved at all. The field of cryptozoology was filled with charlatans and fakers whose only interest was in bilking gullible people out of their money. I was one of the few in the field who took the work seriously and had no goal other than finding the truth, whether it confirmed the existence of a cryptid or not. Most times, it didn't. And that was okay. While some folks might not care about a cryptozoologist poking around the location of a supposed sighting, law enforcement officials, as a rule, did. And not because they feared wasting money on me because I never charged for what I did.

"I'm not sure why you need me or for that matter why the police are involved. Was the animal the beast supposedly killed the mayor's beloved pet or something?"

"I'm sorry. I haven't been clear," Wyatt said. "There have been two separate incidents. The sighting of the creature eating a smaller animal happened two days before the possible attack. And that attack resulted in the death of a local woman."

His blunt answer set me back on my heels. Despite the creature's frequent comparisons to a werewolf and its reputation for fierceness, stories about the Beast of Bray Road had never involved it killing a human, at least not in real life. In movies, on the other hand. . . .

Before I could respond, Jon stood, ran his palms down his thighs, and said, "You two can continue this discussion on your own. I've made the introductions for you, Wyatt, and if it's okay, I'm going to head back. I don't want to miss the last ferry of the day."

This was a gut punch. I'd been so happy to see Jon after weeks of nothing but text messages and the occasional awkward and all-too-brief phone conversation. I desperately wanted to talk, to feel him out, to sort through the complex issues currently keeping us apart. If he left now, I wouldn't have the chance, but I felt helpless to stop him.

I stared into my coffee cup, eager to hide the hurt and devastation I knew must have been showing on my face. Wyatt stood, and as the two men shook hands and shared their parting words, I fought back tears.

Jon saved me from having to look at him by striding past me and flinging a casual "I'll show myself out" over his shoulder.

I briefly considered begging him to stay, but I was seized by a sort of paralysis that kept me mum. *Another time,* I told myself. It could wait.

But could it? Should it? The deaths of my parents two and a half years ago had made it painfully apparent to me that time was never guaranteed. I hated this limbo. Rita had suggested I was too stubborn for my own good and I was starting to think she was right. Seeing Jon had made me realize how much I wanted him back in my life on a regular basis, whatever it took.

As I heard the door to my apartment close behind him, I promised myself I would call him as soon as I finished with Wyatt Moorhead. After all, how hard could it be to come up with some sort of compromise?

Did I mention I can be pigheaded at times?

CHAPTER 2

Wyatt, seemingly oblivious to my emotional state, began a dry, clinical recitation of the events surrounding his case.

"We were called out to Bray Road around three in the afternoon this past Thursday, April twenty-third, for a deceased person in some woods. The body was located a couple hundred yards from the road, give or take, but not far from a narrow, rutted path that runs between parallel groves of thick woods. This path serves as an access road for farm equipment because beyond the wooded sections there are two fields. The farmer who owns one of them saw a bunch of buzzards circling in the area and went to investigate, thinking it might have been the body of his dog that had gone missing. Instead, he found a dead woman, fully clothed, lying on her back a few feet inside woods bordering a cornfield. There were several visible wounds on her body, most notably a large tearing type of injury to the left side of her throat. Her car was parked out on the road along the shoulder and there were some curious scratch marks on it."

"Curious how?"

Wyatt handed me his phone. I stared at a picture of what looked like claw marks—four lines running vertically down the driver's door. I zoomed in and saw shiny metal in the scratches, suggesting they were recent.

"There are others," Wyatt said. He reached over and swiped to the next picture, which showed four similar lines running down the hood of the car, though they appeared more ragged and were interrupted rather than continuous. He swiped again and I was looking at similar scratches across the trunk.

"They look fresh," I said.

"Fresh enough that we found chips of paint on the ground beside the car."

I reverse-scrolled and studied each of the pictures again before handing Wyatt back his phone. "Tell me more about the victim."

"The woman was found on her back, and she had already stiffened with rigor by the time we arrived. The medical examiner said the cause of death was a broken neck high enough to have caused instant paralysis of everything below, including her respiratory muscles."

The horror of such a death washed over me. "Time of death?"

"Estimated to be about twelve hours before we found her, or around three in the morning, give or take an hour."

Interesting.

Wyatt asked, "How much do you know about the Beast of Bray Road?"

I knew a little bit, though I'd not spent as much time on it as I had on other cryptids. My parents had done minimal research on it in the past, and I knew there had been stories about it in the news media off and on over the years. But I also knew there were bound to be legends and rumors I hadn't heard and wouldn't be able to find easily without talking to the locals. Wyatt might be a good source for those, and I decided to let him give me a lesson. Besides, I wanted to figure out what he knew, what he'd heard, and where he fell on the belief spectrum.

"Tell me what you know about it," I said, flipping his question back at him.

Wyatt appeared pleased. "Sure. I'm not an expert but I've brought myself up to speed on the subject recently. Let's see. . . ." He squinted at the ceiling for a few seconds before continuing. "Best I've been able to determine, the Beast of Bray Road has been a local legend ever since the first reported sighting back in 1936, though that story didn't come out until other sightings were reported decades later when Linda Godfrey wrote about the spate of sightings around Elkhorn. Are you familiar with her story?"

"Some. I know she was a newspaper reporter who was assigned to write up something about the local reports and she eventually did her own research and collected enough stories to write a book about it. I think my parents have her book somewhere though I confess I haven't read it."

"You should. Godfrey poses some interesting theories."

"Did her witnesses all think the Beast of Bray Road was a werewolf?" I asked.

"Most, but not all, describe some type of dogman or other man-wolf combination. But there was also a contingent that claimed it was a Bigfoot. Despite the differing opinions, there are striking similarities in the descriptions. It's typically described as being at least six feet tall, furry or hairy—sometimes gray, sometimes brown—with the build of a muscular man but a head more like that of a dog. Its eyes are shiny and glow either red or yellow depending on who you talk to, though personally I think this might simply be eyeshine. Some people have said it runs on all fours, others claim it stands on two legs, and still others have spotted it squatting or sitting on its haunches like a man might.

"The carcasses of mutilated animals—deer and livestock—have sometimes been found in areas where the beast has been sighted, suggesting it's a carnivore. And that ties into our report of a missing dog. Plus, there's another farmer on Bray Road who recently reported one of her goats missing."

"Have any fresh carcasses been found in the area?"

"You mean, aside from the human one?"

I winced.

"Sorry. That was in poor taste," he said with a sheepish grin. He ran a hand through his hair and then shook his head. "I did find some rib bones. I suppose they looked like they could have been from a dog or a goat."

Newt, still sleeping at my feet, suddenly raised his head and pricked up his ears. He let out a little whine and I patted him and told him it was okay. Reassured, he dropped his head back down, resting it on one of my feet. They say the average dog understands more than one hundred fifty words, but I swear Newt knows twice that many. Sometimes, I think he can spell most of them.

"Have the bones been analyzed yet?"

"I didn't collect them."

"Why not?"

"The usual. Lack of funds. My boss wouldn't be happy knowing I submitted animal bones to the crime lab. Besides, they weren't where the woman's body was found."

I thought about this for a moment, wondering what, if anything, the bones might prove, and decided they were of little evidentiary value.

"Did you find any blood in the scratches on the car?"

"Nah, just flaking paint and some dirt."

Those scratches bothered me for reasons I chose not to share with Wyatt yet. I wanted to see what else he might tell me first and he needed no encouragement to continue.

"Some other things I've learned recently," he said. "It seems our beast has some distant cousins. There's a creature called the Bluff Monster, and some think it might be the same animal as our beast because there are similarities in the descriptions. Comparisons have also been made to Minnesota's Wendigo and the Dogmen of Michigan."

"You really *have* done your homework," I said with a smile, genuinely impressed. He grinned. "However, I would be remiss not to point out that while the Wendigo does share some characteristics with your beast, it's typically described as having large antlers. Has anyone described anything like that?"

"Not that I'm aware of."

"And I believe the Bluff Monster is considered to be a Bigfoot-type creature, more simian in build and nature."

"True." Wyatt's grin widened. I thought he might have been offended by my gentle clarifications, but he seemed to be enjoying them instead.

"That leaves the Dogmen of Michigan. I think they're probably closer to your beast than the others since both creatures are thought to be canine cryptids."

"I agree," he said with a definitive nod. "Jon was right. You know your cryptids."

Hearing this secondhand version of a compliment from Jon both surprised and pleased me. It made me blush and I quickly took a drink of coffee to hide my reaction.

"It's in my blood," I said, setting my cup down. "Both of my parents were cryptozoologists, though they were often considered amateurs or hobbyists. I grew up traveling the world with them while they hunted for cryptids, listening to them discuss the rumors and helping them research the facts. I think I'm more grounded in science than they were because I have degrees in biology, zoology, and skepticism."

Wyatt chuckled at that.

"I believe there was a B movie made about the Beast of Bray Road some years ago, wasn't there?"

Wyatt rolled his eyes. "Gawd yes. A low-budget horror flick. Very low-budget."

"It also portrayed the beast as a werewolf."

"It did, yes. I suppose it appealed to a certain audience, and it put the beast on the map for a while, but the way the beast was portrayed in the movie was bloodier and much more violent than any of the actual reports."

"You think your werewolf is a benevolent creature?"

"Not anymore. Not that I ever did. And this recent death changes all that, assuming a werewolf is to blame."

"You sound like you believe werewolves are real."

"I believe these people saw something, though I'm not convinced it was a werewolf, or a dogman, or any of those other things."

"What do you think it was, then?"

"If I had the answer to that, I wouldn't be here talking to you," he said with a grin.

"Fair enough. You said your victim was several hundred yards off the road in some woods. What was she doing out there at three in the morning?"

His eyes grew big and he waggled his fingers in the air. "That's part of the mystery," he said, pronouncing the word "mystery" in an over-the-top, eerie, woo-woo tone that almost made me laugh. I held it back because I wanted him to think I was taking the matter seriously. But was I? I mean, come on . . . werewolves?

Then again, was the idea of a blood-crazed creature that was part man, part wolf any crazier than the ideas of Bigfoot or the Loch Ness Monster? Honestly, if the mystery of what this poor woman had been doing in the woods hundreds of yards from the road at three in the morning hadn't piqued my interest, I think I would have turned Wyatt away without a second thought.

"Is it possible your victim might have been involved in an assignation out there in the woods?"

Wyatt looked momentarily surprised by the question, but then understanding spread over his face and he laughed. "For a second there I thought you were suggesting her assignation was with the beast."

"No, I know this isn't a Disney movie. But I am puzzled as to what anyone would have been doing out there in the middle of the night. Might she have gone out there to meet a lover?"

Wyatt assumed an equivocal expression and then shook his

head. "Why would anyone in their right mind hike through the woods for a romp when there was a perfectly good car parked along the shoulder of a relatively deserted road? The back seat would surely have been more comfortable than the ground."

I supposed he had a point. *Moving on.*

"Could your victim's body have been carried into the woods?" I asked. "Or could she have been forced there by someone and then killed?"

Wyatt shrugged. "I suppose it's possible, but it strikes me as unlikely. There is evidence she was dragged—her shirt was rolled up and there was debris from the cornfield under it and in her hair. But we've had a rainless spring so far and the ground out there is very hard and very dry. There were no footprints or drag marks other than some displaced ground debris."

"No witnesses? No screams heard?"

He shook his head. "Bray Road is typically dead that time of night." He grimaced as he realized his wording might have been a bit imprudent. "There was the witness who said he saw a creature eating some kind of animal near where we found the rib bones, but that happened two nights before."

"How did he describe the creature?"

"Tall, hairy, pointed ears, big teeth, standing on two legs at times."

"Was he on the way to Grandma's house?" I teased. Wyatt ignored this, so I moved on. "The witness said hairy? Not furry?"

Wyatt thought for a moment and then nodded. "Pretty sure he said hairy, but I'll check the report when I get back to make sure."

"Will I be able to talk to this witness?"

"I don't see why not. But keep in mind, his story is tainted by darkness and alcohol."

"Got it. Did you look around the area where this supposedly happened?"

"I did, twice. Once right after it happened—more out of curiosity than anything—and again two days later when I realized the woods the creature appeared from were adjacent to the woods where we found our victim's body. I did find something that might corroborate the guy's story."

I arched my eyebrows in question.

"It was a dog collar in the field where he claims he saw the creature."

"Was the collar bloodied or shredded?"

Wyatt shook his head.

"Do you know for sure the collar belonged to the missing dog?"

Wyatt shook his head again, looking abashed.

"I don't suppose your witness got a picture of this creature?"

Wyatt made a face. "He did but it's not going to help much."

A picture always ups the ante, and I felt a tiny trill of excitement even though I knew odds were, it would be dark, fuzzy, out of focus, or all of the above. Still, a girl can hope.

"Show me."

CHAPTER 3

Wyatt had a copy of the photo on his phone, but as I feared, it was a disappointingly dark and blurry shot of a shadowy shape some distance away, silhouetted by the light of the moon. There were few discernible details—for all I could tell, it could have been a picture of an oddly shaped bush or a small tree—but the longer I stared at it, the easier it became to imagine I saw a head with a long snout and pointed ears atop a tall body. Despite my scientific approach and need for indisputable proof, I do have a vivid imagination, especially when it comes to cryptids.

It didn't matter, though, because Wyatt had sufficiently piqued my interest already. Though to be honest, I was more intrigued by the question of why the dead woman had been out on a deserted road in the middle of the night than I was by the possibility of a werewolf lurking about. Even so, I wanted to talk to the guy who claimed to have seen the werewolf, and Wyatt had assured me he'd arrange for that to happen.

I made immediate plans to travel to Elkhorn the following day, letting my employees, Rita and Devon, know I would be leaving and wasn't sure when I'd be back. They were getting used to these unplanned, last-minute excursions, as this was my fourth investigation into a possible cryptid in recent months. Fortunately, they were both eager and capable of running the store in my absence.

I spent an hour or so packing, some of this time devoted to thinking through what I needed to bring along for Newt and some of it spent contemplating what toys I'd bring along. Anticipating the possibility of some nighttime stakeouts, I threw a flashlight, a headlamp, and my night vision binoculars with the built-in camera into my backpack, along with a thermos, a canteen, some dog treats, and a collapsible water dish for Newt. It was late April, and while the days might be pleasant enough, the nights would be cold with frost likely by morning. Keeping this in mind, I made sure to pack plenty of warm clothing, including a hat, gloves, and some wool socks. Then I threw in some chemical hand and feet warmers for good measure.

Just as I finished packing, Rita popped into my apartment with some minor questions that struck me as odd because they were things I felt certain she already knew. The real reason behind her visit was revealed when she handed me something as she was about to go back downstairs. It was a neck chain with a small Lucite disk on it that had some kind of plant material sealed inside.

"What is this?" I asked her, puzzled.

"It's wolfsbane." She flushed and looked away as she said it.

"Wolfsbane? Meant to ward off werewolves?"

She gave an ambivalent nod of her head and avoided looking at me. "It's been on a shelf downstairs for years."

"I didn't think you believed in any of this stuff, Rita. How many times have you told me I'm wasting my time looking for cryptids?"

"I don't believe in them, but I know hunting for them brought your parents a lot of happiness and I've seen it do the same for you. And if it makes you happy, you should do it."

"Okay, but why the wolfsbane?"

"Because one thing I do believe in, at least on some level, is the existence of evil in this world. And while I really don't think it will manifest itself as a werewolf, where's the harm in hedging your bets?"

"Fair enough." I smiled and put the necklace on, feeling oddly warm and fuzzy toward Rita.

"I don't suppose Jon is going to join you on this excursion?"

My mood plummeted. "No, I'm not sure Jon is going to join me for much of anything anymore."

"Did you talk to him?"

"How? He's had a million excuses for why he can't come visit me here or invite me to his place over on the island, our phone conversations are rare, short, and exceedingly impersonal, and he said he didn't want to be with me because of the risks I take."

"He has a painful past. He's hurting."

"So am I."

"Well, here's a thought," Rita said irritably. "Stop taking stupid risks."

I scowled at her. "It's part of the job, Rita," I insisted.

"Is it? Are you sure about that?" She rolled her eyes and headed for the stairs, tossing a parting shot over her shoulder as she descended. "Try not to get yourself killed, okay?"

I spent the rest of the evening attempting to block out my conversation with Rita and my thoughts of Jon. Instead, I busied myself writing out a loose plan of strategy for what I'd do once I got to Elkhorn, and then searching for any information my parents had had on the Beast of Bray Road. Their cryptid files, maintained in our apartment's third bedroom, which they had commandeered as their office, were extensive. For those not in the know, the room appeared to be a cluttered, chaotic mess of overstuffed file cabinets and bank boxes full of magazines, articles, and notes stacked along the perimeter walls. But I'd spent hours of my childhood and young adult years in that room, sorting, searching, reading, and filing according to my father's quirky system. I knew where to go.

Sadly, I didn't find much. Unlike other cryptids such as Bigfoot, Nessie, chupacabra, and the like—all of which had dedicated, full file cabinet drawers—the Beast of Bray Road files, along with the book Wyatt had mentioned, occupied a single folder less than an inch thick.

The book's author, Linda Godfrey, had been assigned by her paper's editor to investigate the rash of reported sightings back in the eighties and nineties. Godfrey had gone into the assignment a skeptic and come out the other end a self-proclaimed cryptozoologist who didn't necessarily believe these witnesses had seen a werewolf but was convinced they'd seen something unusual. Exactly what that was, however, remained a mystery. I flipped through the book, skim-reading some of the more intriguing first-person accounts, and then set it aside with the intent of exploring it in more detail later.

The folder didn't contain any scientific information, but there were news clippings about a couple of first-person reports and some general information on werewolf folklore. I tried to read them but I couldn't get Jon off my mind. My thoughts kept wandering back to his visit earlier, trying to interpret every word, action, and nuance of his behavior. When I found myself reading the same paragraph multiple times without comprehending what it said, I knew it was pointless to keep trying. I threw all the info into my laptop case so I could take it with me in the morning.

I knew sleep would prove elusive if I didn't talk to Jon, so I made the call before I could talk myself out of it, hoping to put my whirling thoughts to bed along with the rest of me.

I half expected he wouldn't take the call and was mentally reciting the voicemail message I would leave when he answered.

"Hi, Morgan."

"Oh. Jon. Hi," I stammered, mentally kicking myself for sounding not just tentative but stupid. I shook it off. "It was great getting to see you today. Thanks for referring Wyatt to me. I think he'll be fun to work with."

Fun to work with? Good grief, girl. Is that the best you can do?

"I'm glad you like him," Jon said. "I figured what he wanted would be right up your alley."

"It's intriguing, especially when you consider most of the theories about the Beast of Bray Road center around the idea it's a werewolf. A bit far-fetched but worth looking into. I'm heading for Elkhorn in the morning."

"Of course you are."

Did I detect a hint of snark in his comment or was I imagining it? "I'm sorry my work makes you uncomfortable, Jon, but I love doing it. It's in my blood."

He let out a sigh that carried all the weight of our issues with it. "I understand that, Morgan," he said, "and I explained to you why it's uncomfortable for me. Not what you do per se, but rather how you do it. You go through life with this reckless abandon and the risks you take affect me in ways that have honestly surprised me. When I think about what could happen to you, it makes it hard for me to breathe. That's on me. My personal dysfunction is as much to blame here as yours is, and on some level, I understand why you do what you do."

"No risk, no reward," I blurted out. It was an aphorism I'd heard my parents utter dozens of times, but it sounded cavalier and inconsiderate to my ears now. I desperately wished I could take it back.

An uncomfortable silence settled between us—an insurmountable wall built from our individual dysfunctions. It divided us as definitively as the shipwreck-littered waterway known as Death's Door, which separated Jon's island home from mine on the mainland. I fought back tears and finally managed to say, "I really, really want to make this work, Jon. I miss you, and if I could take you with me on every one of these trips, I would. But your job makes it impossible, and I know if I gave up my cryptid work for the sake of our relationship, I'd be stifling a crucial part of myself. We'd both be miserable."

"I'd never ask you to do that. I *haven't* asked you to do that."

"I know." The tears I'd been holding back spilled over. "I miss you, Jon."

“I miss you, too, Morgan. I don’t think I realized just how much until I saw you today.”

My emotions had a stranglehold on my throat, and I wanted to end this conversation before my tears turned into an all-out blubbering episode. I managed to squeak out, “’Night, Jon,” and disconnected from the call.

Then I cried myself to sleep with Newt at my side.

CHAPTER 4

I got an early start the next morning, leaving just as the sun was coming up. Newt, excited to go on a new adventure, sat in the back seat, lazily wagging his tail, head out the open window, tongue lolling to better absorb the myriad smells breezing by. I drove to Sturgeon Bay and then toward Green Bay, where I picked up Interstate 43 down to Milwaukee and eventually into Elkhorn. I'd calculated it to be a four-hour drive, but it took me just under five. Newt likes exploring new places, so I tend to make frequent stops where I can let him walk.

As I got closer to Elkhorn, I recalled some of what I'd read in Linda Godfrey's book the night before. While her retelling of people's encounters with the beast were terrifying, they were never deadly, at least not for the people involved. There were some mysterious deer and livestock deaths reported—though no dogs—but in most cases, the creature was said to have retreated from humans rather than attacked them.

There was one notable exception, a particularly scary story describing how the creature had run alongside someone's car as they tried to get away, and it had managed to keep up with the vehicle for more than a mile even though the driver was going fifty-five miles an hour. And there were also reports of scratches on vehicles that were found after the drivers had supposedly been pursued by the creature.

When it came down to the individual descriptions, they all bore some similarities, though whether from actual experience or the rapid spread of gossip was hard to tell. Most described the creature as hairy or furry, standing six to seven feet tall, and possessing a canine head like a German shepherd's. There was some debate as to whether the creature was a biped or a quadruped, as both postures had been observed when the creature was at rest and also while running. Most people reported a glow to the eyes, but because the majority—though not all—of the sightings had occurred at night and included some type of artificial light source, this could easily be explained away as eyeshine.

As for why the sightings had occurred where they did, it was anyone's guess, though Godfrey's stories in the local paper had triggered similar reports from surrounding areas. While the heyday of these sightings was in the eighties and nineties, Godfrey's articles had resulted in a phone call from a newspaper editor in a neighboring town who said his father, Mark Schackelman, had seen the beast back in 1936. Schackelman had been a night watchman for the St. Coletta Institute, a Catholic institution for people with special needs located in nearby Jefferson County. The institute, which in the pictures looked as creepy as any horror movie madhouse from the early 1900s, had been built on land containing Native American burial mounds. Part of Schackelman's job was to walk the grounds each night, and on one occasion, he spotted a creature matching the descriptions that would follow half a century later. Schackelman said the creature was sitting atop one of the burial mounds, digging furiously, and it ran off when Schackelman got close. But he spotted it again the following night in the same place, doing the same thing. According to Schackelman's son, his father had never mentioned the experience to anyone outside of the immediate family and it was clear that whatever he'd seen had terrified him.

After Godfrey's first article had appeared in the local weekly paper, reports began to surface of animal mutilations and the killing or disappearance of area livestock. Some theorized there was a satanic cult operating in the woods of Walworth County, and the beast was a Satan worshipper wearing a mask and animal pelts.

It was all the stuff of nightmares, but as I drove the country roads past picturesque farms and bucolic fields bathed in warm sunlight, it was hard to imagine a bloodthirsty werewolf lurking about.

I checked into the motel room I'd reserved online the night before, in a Hampton Inn just outside of town and conveniently located by a Starbucks, a Kwik Trip, several fast-food restaurants, and a marketplace with a grocery store, ensuring easy meal planning. The motel allowed dogs, though the clerk checking me in gave me a bit of side-eye when he saw how big Newt was.

I'd just started unpacking when Wyatt Moorhead rang me on my cell phone.

"Hi, Wyatt."

"Is this the intrepid werewolf hunter and her trusty sidekick?"

I chuckled. "It is. Have you got all the motels staked out so you'd know when I arrived?"

"You're here?" He sounded genuinely surprised, though I remained suspicious. His timing was a little too convenient.

"I am. I just checked in at the Hampton Inn off Highway 67."

"Excellent choice. Are you ready to go? Because the guy who saw the dog-eating werewolf is free until three o'clock. He works second shift."

I glanced at my watch, saw it was nearly eleven thirty, and said, "Sure, but I need half an hour to get settled in my room."

"How about I pick you up in thirty, then?"

"That works, though I'd prefer to take my own car. In case you didn't notice when you were in my apartment yesterday, Newt is both a shedder and a drooler, and he goes with me anywhere I go. For the sake of your car, it's best if I take my own. I can follow you, or you're welcome to ride with me if you don't mind the occasional furnado with a bit of slobber."

"Furnado?"

"It's self-explanatory if you ride in my car with the windows down."

"Ah. Gotcha. Your car will be fine."

"We'll meet you out front at noon."

I finished unpacking and then got Newt set up. I was relieved to see my room had a faux-wood vinyl type of floor rather than carpet because Newt and rugs are a bad combo. While this floor would make the mess easier to clean, it wouldn't lessen it any, so I put down a large towel I'd brought with me before setting out

Newt's food and water on top of it. In keeping with his nature, Newt went straight to it, making a sloppy, wet mess and managing to exceed the boundary of the towel a time or two.

I was hungry, too, and I grabbed a bottle of water and one of the sandwiches I'd packed in my cooler, setting them on the table while I put the remaining items into the room's mini fridge. I'd barely managed to eat half of my sandwich before a text from Wyatt announced his arrival. I replied, saying I'd be out in a few minutes, tossed the other half of my sandwich in the fridge, cleaned up the mess around Newt's bowls, and grabbed the leash.

As I exited my room, I nearly collided with a dark-haired woman passing by in the hallway. Most people who are surprised by a dog the size of Newt tend to be afraid and back away, but this woman immediately oohed and aahed over him, bending down to his level and scrubbing his ears. Newt closed his eyes in ecstasy.

"What a beautiful beast!" she said. "What's his name?"

"Newt."

"Pleasure to meet you, Newt." She patted him on the head, straightened, looked at me with a pleasant smile, and said, "You have a nice day."

"You, too," I said.

We continued along our separate ways though Newt glanced back at the woman a couple of times with a longing look on his face.

Wyatt was in the parking lot leaning against his car and I said, "Newt just ate, and I need five to let him do his business. Walk with me and tell me more about this witness of yours."

We walked down a grassy area alongside the motel and Newt made quick work of his needs. By the time we were in my car and pulling out, I knew that our witness's name was Paul McNamara, that he worked at the local hospital as a lab tech, and that he'd moved here from Georgia about two months earlier.

"Why did he move here?" I asked.

"His parents live in town and his dad, who's in his fifties, was recently diagnosed with some kind of early-onset dementia. Paul moved here so he'd be close by to help them."

"Are they from here originally?" Wyatt shook his head, which prompted my next question. "Do you think Paul was familiar with the story of the Beast of Bray Road prior to his sighting?"

Wyatt shrugged. "He said he wasn't. He grew up in Illinois, in a Chicago suburb. His parents moved to Elkhorn two years ago because Paul's father was offered the position of CEO at the local hospital, the same one where Paul works. The elder McNamara's symptoms started not long after he took the position, and progressed rather rapidly. He has since resigned. Paul's mother doesn't work, but I got the impression they're well-to-do and money isn't an issue."

Money wasn't an issue for me, either, as I had inherited my parents' millions when they died. While I realized and deeply appreciated the profound advantages my wealth afforded me, I'd have given it all back in a heartbeat if it meant my parents could be alive again. I couldn't help but wonder if Paul McNamara's father would have been willing to make a similar trade if he could divest himself from the tragic diagnosis he'd been given. Life can be so unfair and arbitrary at times. Not to mention strange. Like a werewolf running around southern Wisconsin.

"Do we have time to do a quick drive down Bray Road first?" I asked. "I'd like to see it, and if you can point out the spot where Mr. McNamara had his sighting, it might help when we talk to him."

Wyatt glanced at his watch. "Sure. It won't take long. The road is only four miles in length, and it hooks into Highway 11 on the other end, so we can loop around."

Like so many small towns scattered throughout Wisconsin, Elkhorn is a charming example of early Americana with hints of the German and Scandinavian origins of its founding people. There was an eclectic variety of home styles, a small downtown area filled with boutique-style shops and cozy cafés, and a periphery that quickly gave way to farmland. There was little to no suburbia, just an abrupt shift from urban landscape to fields filled with dairy cows.

It was a pleasant enough day, and I lowered the windows as we navigated the main street through town, taking in the tantalizing aromas of baked goods and various other cooking smells. Moments later we were passing by last year's cornfields while the scents of fresh dirt and manure filled the air. We came up on a sign on our left directing us to Bray Road and I turned onto it, somewhat disappointed at how ordinary it looked.

I drove past open fields, pastures with horses and cows, a turnoff, and the requisite farmhouses. About two and a half miles in, the houses were fewer and set farther back from the road, the woodsy groves were large, and the road became shaded. The atmosphere felt eerie at that point, but I wasn't sure if it was real or if my imagination was getting the better of me.

"Pull over up there by that grassy field," Wyatt said. He pointed off to the right. "This is the field where Paul McNamara saw the creature. It came out of those woods up ahead. The picture he took was from across the road, close to the shoulder on that side."

I studied the location, and when I felt I had seen enough, I said, "Okay. Next."

"The sites are only a quarter mile apart," Wyatt explained as I pulled back onto the road. Less than a minute later, he indicated I should pull off again. "There's the start of the path leading back to where the body was found." He was pointing to an opening between two groves of trees. "It's private property but you could drive it if you want since I'm with you."

There was a **NO TRESPASSING** sign nailed to a tree near the start of the rutted lane, and the drop from the shoulder down to it was steep. "Let's come back later and walk it," I said. "I want to experience it the same way the victim did."

"At three in the morning?" Wyatt asked.

An involuntary shiver shot down my spine. "Let's start out doing it in the daylight," I said.

CHAPTER 5

Before pulling back onto the road, I plugged the address Wyatt gave me for Paul McNamara's house into my GPS. I'd planned to leave Newt in the car with all the windows down once we got there, but Paul was expecting us, and when he saw Newt, he insisted I bring him inside. We followed Paul down a hallway and through his kitchen to a lovely patio topped with a pergola that looked out onto an expanse of grassy yard. It was backed by a small pond where geese were milling about, drawing Newt's attention.

Paul had a patio table with a built-in fireplace, and he lit it up. The heat it provided was just enough to eliminate any hint of chill in the air.

"I've given Ms. Carter a brief summary of your experience out on Bray Road," Wyatt said once we were settled. "She specializes in cryptids. Do you know what that is?"

Paul gave a hesitant nod. "It means 'animals that aren't real' or something like that, right?"

"Close enough," I said. "Cryptids are creatures thought to exist despite no scientific proof to support it. The cryptids most people are familiar with are the Loch Ness Monster and Bigfoot."

"Okay," Paul said. "I'm guessing a werewolf qualifies as a cryptid, then?"

I smiled at him. "It does," I said a bit tentatively. "Though werewolves, goblins, vampires . . . those sorts of creatures are more in a fantasy realm."

"Well, if seeing is believing, then the Beast of Bray Road is no fantasy because I saw it with my own eyes. I never believed in vampires and goblins, but I'm rethinking the existence of werewolves after what happened. Whatever it was out there, it looked terrifying. You can see for yourself. I managed to get a picture of it though it's not very clear."

He took out his phone, swiped the screen, and handed the device to me. I'd hoped the original might be clearer than the one Wyatt had shown me, or offer up some small detail that would prove helpful, but no such luck. I handed the phone back, thanked him, and smiled again, bigger and friendlier this time, hoping it would warm him to me since I was about to question the veracity of his claim.

He must have sensed this because he immediately went on the defensive. "I know the picture isn't great, but I saw the creature clearly enough."

"It was quite dark, wasn't it?"

"Sure, but there was a full moon. Or close to one, anyway."

Despite his defensiveness, he didn't seem angry. Still, I decided to hold off on suggesting that alcohol or confirmation bias might have played a role. I didn't want him to become withdrawn and shut down.

"Tell me what you heard, what you saw, and any other details you remember."

"I heard several things. First was a howl off in the distance, like a wolf. Then I heard something crashing through the trees alongside the road from the same general direction. Something big. And it was coming toward me. Then I heard grunting noises and the sound of hard breathing, like an animal exerting itself."

"Any sounds of a struggle?"

Paul considered this for a few seconds, screwing his face up in recollection. "No," he said tentatively, then with a shrug, "Maybe?" He sighed. "I don't know."

His willingness to admit his interpretation of things might have been colored by emotion or prior suggestions was encouraging. I liked the way he had thought about his answer before giving it.

"When did you first see the animal?" I asked.

"As soon as I crossed the road." No hesitation this time. "In fact, I wasn't even all the way across. I wanted to put some distance between me and those woods, but I was afraid it might come at me from behind. When I looked back, I saw it bursting out of the trees into a grassy field. I turned to watch it and backed the rest of the way across the road. It ran for, oh—I don't know—maybe twenty yards or so? And then it stopped and started eating whatever animal it had carried out of the woods."

"How did it emerge from the trees? Was it on four legs? Two?"

"Four." Again, no hesitation.

"And how did it carry the other animal?"

"In its mouth. It shook its head violently, the way dogs do when they catch a smaller animal."

"After it emerged from the woods, did it stay on all fours?"

Paul shook his head. "Hell no. It rose up on its back legs and stood there, holding the dead carcass in its front legs, or arms, or whatever you want to call them. I could see the poor animal hanging down."

This detail hadn't been evident in the picture he took, perhaps because of backlighting from the moon. "Are you sure it was a dog? It couldn't have been a raccoon, a coyote pup, or a goat perhaps? Something like that?"

Paul's face screwed up in consternation and I saw glimmers of doubt there. "I'm pretty sure it had four legs," he said finally. "Beyond that. . . ." Another shrug.

"Okay. Good. That's helpful. What happened next?"

"The creature stopped eating and sniffed at the air. I was afraid to move, not wanting to draw any attention to myself." He paused, swallowing hard. His fear as he recalled this moment was genuine, palpable. "Then it turned and stared straight at me. I was afraid to so much as breathe, convinced if I moved an inch, it would come after me. I held my breath so long, I began to feel lightheaded and then I started panic breathing. You know, gulping in air. The last thing I wanted to do was pass out and end up helpless."

"How scary it must have been for you," I said with genuine empathy, knowing exactly how it felt to have a panic attack. I'd had more than my share over the past three years.

Paul nodded, swallowing hard again, and I noticed Newt had

gone over to him, sensing his rising tension. Newt settled a chin on one of Paul's legs and Paul automatically began stroking Newt's head with one hand. Newt's presence had an instant calming effect on Paul, much the same way it always did with me. He's magical that way.

After a moment, Paul continued his story, his hand still stroking Newt's head. "I was afraid the creature could smell me because it kept its nose up, sniffing the air." He paused and grimaced. "Though how it could pick up any scent beyond its own stink is beyond me."

"You smelled it?"

"Oh, yeah," he said with a shudder. "It was a musty kind of odor at first, but different from anything else I'd smelled out there. It was kind of like the smell you get when you leave a bunch of wet towels in the laundry basket for too long, but more pungent because there was also an underlying stench of decay or rotting meat. And I don't think it was from the animal it was eating because it looked . . . well, fresh. Bloody."

Bile rose in my throat, more from the idea the victim animal might have been a dog than from Paul's description of the smell. Fresh and bloody helped explain why Paul could see it but the camera didn't. Reflections of moonlight on the poor creature's bodily fluids might have highlighted aspects for the human eye. I made a mental note to take another look at the picture later with this in mind and logged the odor information away. Then I prompted Paul to continue.

"What happened next?"

"It squatted and began to eat."

"Squatted?"

"Yeah, it sat back on its haunches kind of . . . like this." Paul gently eased Newt's head off his leg, got up from his seat, and proceeded to demonstrate. Newt cocked his head to one side and eyed him curiously.

"How long did it stay like that?"

"Not long." As soon as Paul settled back into his seat, Newt resumed his prior position. "I finally dared to back away some more and I think it caught the motion. It stood, sniffed the air again, and then carried the carcass back into the trees. Thank goodness." He rolled his eyes in relief. "Best I can figure, I must have been downwind from it."

"When it left, it carried its kill in its mouth?"

Paul nodded.

"It was on all fours?"

He nodded again.

"Could it have been a bear?"

"I don't think so," Paul said with a hint of hesitation. He looked down at Newt, patting the big, furry head. "The ears looked pointed, it was thinner than a bear, and it appeared to be mostly bald with just spikes of hair here and there. The body looked muscular, almost human, when it stood on two legs. And the head looked more . . . doglike." He stared at Newt the whole time he talked, almost as if comparing the image in his mind with the live animal on his thigh.

"What time was it when all of this happened?"

"I'm not sure. I didn't look at my watch, but I got back to town a little after four in the morning, so I'd guess it was around three-ish?"

"How is it you happened to be out there on the road at that time of night?"

"Well. . . ." A flush flooded his cheeks. "I'd gone out drinking with some peeps from work. I'm kind of new on the job and wanted to make some connections, but most of them left early. I was going to leave, too, but then I was invited to be part of a dart team at the bar. I used to play in a league back in Georgia, so I decided to hang and maybe make some new friends that way."

"How did that go?"

"Good at first. Or so I thought." He sighed and ran his free hand through his hair. "The beers kept coming, the guys playing darts got to talking about the Beast of Bray Road, and I called bull on the whole thing. One thing led to another, and the next thing I knew, I was with these two guys, and we were driving out to Bray Road after the bar closed. They challenged me to walk the road at night under the full moon and swore they'd make a believer out of me."

Paul paused and shook his head woefully, giving Wyatt a guilty look. "We had no business driving anywhere because all three of us were drunk on some level. I don't know why I agreed to go with them but I'm guessing the alcohol had something to do with it. I was having fun, and it seemed like a harmless lark at the time. Anyway, the guys parked on the road, and we all got out and walked along the shoulder for a way—I'd guess maybe a half mile or so—without seeing anything. Then again, we were laughing and talking so loudly, I doubt anything would have come near us. At some point, one of them pointed off to the side of the road and said, "There it is!" in this panicked voice. Of course, I looked where he was pointing, and next thing I knew, I was shoved down into a ditch alongside the road. My ankle twisted, and though I tried to keep my balance, I fell into some bushes. By the time I managed to untangle and right myself, those yahoos were running down the road, laughing their butts off." He blushed again. Gullibility can be a humbling trait.

"How mean, not to mention juvenile," I said.

Paul nodded and smiled. "I don't know. Maybe it was some kind of initiation ritual. Maybe I had it coming. I did rib them pretty hard about the idea of a werewolf lurking about, though I'm on the verge of becoming a believer now. Anyway, I started walking toward town and hadn't gone much more than a quarter mile when I saw the creature. After it disappeared back into the woods, I kept walking, though I spent a lot of time looking over my shoulder."

"Did your friends ever return for you?"

"They did not," he said with a pained smile. "Fortunately, a sheriff's deputy drove by, saw me limping down the road, and offered to drive me the rest of the way into town. When I told her what I'd seen, she laughed it off, but I insisted on making an official report because I was freaked out and worried the thing was dangerous. Turns out, I was right."

I cocked my head to one side and drew my brows together in a silent question.

Paul glanced sheepishly at Wyatt before continuing. "The hospital grapevine has been buzzing about the woman who was found dead out there four days ago."

"Sounds like you're lucky you didn't end up dead as well," I said.

"Yeah." His expression softened. "Those guys who drove me out there . . . I don't think they meant any real harm. It was just a joke, a stupid prank. And in a way, I'm glad they did it, because if they hadn't, I never would have seen that thing."

"How drunk were you?" I asked in my best nonjudgmental tone. If I thought Paul might have taken offense at the question, I was quickly disabused of the notion.

"Like I said before, I was feeling no pain when we first got out there and started walking the road. And I can't say for sure how drunk the driver of the car was because I wasn't counting his drinks. But I can tell you that after thrashing around in the bushes and then trying to walk on an ankle twice its normal size, I was sober enough when I saw that thing."

"And you'd never heard of the Beast of Bray Road before this happened?"

"God, no. I've looked into it since after overhearing one of the cops say folks think it's a werewolf." He shook his head vehemently. "I don't know what it is," he concluded. "But it's scary as hell and apparently has an appetite for fresh meat."

CHAPTER 6

I had parked in the street in front of McNamara's house, and after getting Newt into the back seat via the passenger-side door, I nearly got hit by a car coming down the road as I stepped from between my car and the one parked behind me. It was my fault; I should have been more careful to look first, but I was distracted thinking about Paul McNamara's story, and the offending vehicle was a gray hybrid—silent and hard to see. The woman driver—though I supposed it could have been a long-haired man—swerved to miss me and continued on her way, seemingly unaffected. I, on the other hand, felt my heart in my throat.

"That was close," Wyatt said from the passenger seat as I got behind the wheel. "I grabbed the plate number if you want it."

I shook my head. "It was my fault. I wasn't paying attention. I need to send a message to someone. Mind waiting a minute?"

"Of course not."

I typed out a quick text message to Devon asking him to see what he could dig up on our witness, Paul McNamara. Wyatt cocked his head and eyed me sideways as I tapped the screen, but I made sure to tilt my phone to keep him from reading what I was typing.

"What's your take?" he said when I was done and had slipped my phone into my pocket.

"How big is the missing dog?"

"Medium, I guess. Maybe thirty, forty pounds? I've only seen pictures of it."

"And the goat?"

"Not sure, though the other goats on the farm are about as big as a medium-sized dog."

"Do you know what color either animal was?"

Wyatt looked perplexed by the question, but he went ahead and answered. "The dog was a light blond color. The goat was black, I think. Why?"

I flexed my hands on the steering wheel as I contemplated my answer. "Thirty to forty pounds is a lot of weight to be flinging about like that. It suggests the predator was large and powerful. If the dog had light-colored fur, you'd think it would show up in the picture Paul took, though I realize it might have been dirty or bloody. I'm sure Paul saw something unusual out there, but the combination of darkness, alcohol, and his confirmation bias makes it all questionable. The howl he heard could have been made by a dog, an ordinary wolf, or even a coyote. What I found interesting is the odor he picked up on. Smell is a keen sense, an evocative one, and people who sight cryptids rarely mention smells. If Paul is right that the animal being eaten was a fresh kill, it wouldn't have stunk yet. Most carnivores prefer fresh meat to decaying carrion, though it's not guaranteed. And the shaking behavior Paul described is a common killing tactic employed by canine carnivores, including wolves. Big cats, on the other hand, tend to bite deep into the neck to pin and paralyze their prey. It's hard to conclude anything definitive from Paul's description or his picture and honestly I question how well he could have seen the animal the creature was chewing on from across the road in the dark."

"There was moonlight," Wyatt reminded me.

"Yeah, silhouetting the creature according to Paul. Let me see the picture again."

Wyatt pulled it up on his phone and handed it to me. Now that I had a better idea of what to look for, I could just make out slight variations in light and dark on the belly of the beast that could have been in the shape of another animal. "Could have" being the operative phrase. I handed him back his phone and started my car.

Wyatt slipped the phone in a pocket, slapped his thighs with both hands, and said, "Okay. What next?"

"I want to go back out to where Paul saw his creature and where . . ." I couldn't recall the poor victim's name. "Where the woman's body was found. Did you ever tell me her name?"

"Don't know if I did. It's Lydia Palmer. Go up to the stop sign and hang a left."

I made the turn and then asked, "Does Lydia Palmer have any family?"

"Just a son, Dylan, who's twenty."

"I'd like to talk to him, if I could. You don't have any idea what Lydia was doing out there in the middle of the night?"

"Not really. I talked to Dylan right after it happened, but he was understandably upset. He's had a rough time of it these past few years and this was the icing on an already difficult-to-swallow cake."

"How so?"

"He was in a car accident four years ago that left him paralyzed from the waist down and he's been wheelchair-bound ever since."

"No father in the picture?"

"Ervin Palmer. He died in the same accident that paralyzed Dylan."

"How sad. Is Dylan going to be able to make it on his own?"

Wyatt shrugged. "I think he's relatively independent and he has an aide to help him out, which is good, but I don't know if the aide is private pay or through insurance. That might change things. I don't think Lydia was particularly well-off money-wise, though I've heard she did have a life insurance policy for twenty-five thousand."

"What happened with the car accident?"

"Hard to know. Ervin was driving, and his blood alcohol level was three times the legal limit. The accident was unwitnessed, and Dylan claims he doesn't remember anything about it. Best we could figure from the evidence at the scene, Ervin lost control and went off the road, and the vehicle rolled a couple of times. Neither of them was wearing a seat belt and both were ejected from the car."

We were once again driving through downtown Elkhorn and I noted the library when we passed it, pinning it on a map in my brain because I knew I had some research I wanted to do there. I'd somehow failed to notice it on my prior drive through town, which was surprising because the building occupied an entire block.

Wyatt pointed to another building on our right that bordered the town square park.

"That's the local government building, where the city police are located," he said. "Our office is just outside of town not too far from the turnoff to Bray Road."

On the next block, he pointed to a gigantic white stone edifice—a rectangular arch with two tall Corinthian columns in the middle—that looked like the front of a building. Turned out, that was exactly what it was. I'd briefly noticed it earlier but hadn't seen the cute little park behind it.

"It's the front of the old First National Bank building, which stood there from 1865 to 1915," Wyatt explained when I asked. "They retained the facade when the rest of the building was taken down and now it's a historic landmark with a nice little green space beyond. The park behind it is rather unimaginatively called First National Bank Courtyard."

I slowed to get a better look, only to get a honk from behind urging me on. I made a note to come back and explore it more another time.

Minutes later we were headed out of town and the sign for Bray Road appeared again.

I turned onto the two-lane blacktop and drove more slowly this time with Paul McNamara's story in mind, taking in the narrow shoulders, the woods and shrubbery, and the shallow ditches. Low-hanging clouds scudded across the sky, casting moving shadows on the ground and creating pockets of light and dark, warmth and shade.

As we passed an intersecting road on our right called Hospital Road, Wyatt said, "If you were to turn here and go a mile or so it becomes Sitler Road, which then dead-ends on County NN. Turn right again and it will bring you out by the hospital and the sheriff's office, which also contains the court and jail."

"Good to know."

When we got close to Paul's spot, I pulled as far to the right as I dared, and parked on the narrow shoulder, which still left my car a foot or more in the road. A gray car passed by slowly, and once I saw the road was clear, I got out and leashed Newt. It was cool enough for me to leave him in the car, but I wanted to make use of his amazing nose.

"Paint the picture for me again," I said.

"Sure. Paul was headed in the opposite direction we are, but on this side of the road until he heard the noise. Highway 11 is about a mile and a half straight ahead, and the trip back to town the way we came is a little over two miles. The creature emerged from these woods into that field up there on the right and by then Paul had crossed to the other side of the road."

The area Wyatt indicated was a copse of trees that extended about a hundred yards ahead of us and stretched as far back from the road as the eye could see.

We walked along the shoulder for a few feet before I crossed a shallow ditch into the grassy field where the creature had supposedly dined on a small animal. I kept Newt leashed for the time being but let him lead the way with his nose to the ground, sniffing madly. Suddenly, he stopped, sat down, and whined.

I examined the weedy grass in front of us and saw where it had been trampled flat. A rust-colored stain a few feet away contrasted with the otherwise green-and-brown surroundings, some new grass, some old. Newt raised his nose to the air, nostrils twitching, and then looked back at me. He whined again. A gentle breeze lifted my hair off my face, bringing with it a faint scent resembling spoiled meat. I dropped Newt's leash, told him to stay, and walked up closer to the discolored spot. I'd seen dried blood on grass and dirt before and was willing to bet that was what had stained the area in front of me.

A trail of more flattened growth led to the edge of the woods, seeming to melt into the border of trees. I turned to look for Wyatt and saw he was standing on the shoulder of the road watching. I was surprised he hadn't followed me.

"Afraid the beast is going to get you?" I teased.

He chuckled. "Not at all. I wanted to let you experience it on your own."

"Remind me again. How long ago was Paul's sighting?"

"Six days now."

"And Lydia was killed two days later?"

"Correct."

"Has it rained during any of those days?"

"Nope. Not a drop. In fact, we're experiencing a rather significant drought. There hasn't been any real rain since February. The only reason anything is growing out here is because of snowmelt. Relief is in sight, though. The forecast is calling for a big storm to come through later this evening."

I eyed the trail of flattened grass leading into the trees. "Did you follow this into the woods?"

"I did. Nothing there."

I considered venturing in to see for myself but decided it could wait. If I felt strongly enough about it, I could always return on my own. "And where did you see the rib bones?" I asked.

"Just to your left, about fifteen yards over."

I walked that way, scanning the ground, and finally found one small bone that looked like a rib. It was old, weeks if not months. And it looked like it might have come from a raccoon or a large possum. I did an about-face, picked up Newt's leash, and headed back to the car.

"Couldn't find the ribs?" Wyatt said.

"I found one, but it was old. Definitely not fresh."

We drove on down the road until we reached the area where the rutted trail led between the trees. I pulled as far over onto the shoulder as I could, though I couldn't get onto the grass completely without parking at a steep angle along the edge of a ditch. I let Newt out on the road and leashed him.

Wyatt led the way across the ditch and onto the narrow, rutted path running between the two sections of woods. The path was closely bordered on both sides by woods, and I imagined it would be a tight fit for whatever farm equipment typically used it. About a hundred yards in, the path curved to the left and I caught glimpses of a large, open area through the branches of trees that hadn't fully leafed out yet.

The walk was surprisingly pleasant. The air was cool and scented with the mossy smells of spring and evergreens, and the ground was hard and dry, though the old ruts worn into the ground, along with the occasional surface root and dried vine, made it necessary to watch where we stepped. While it was an enjoyable trek at the time, I couldn't help but wonder how difficult it would have been to navigate it in the middle of the night, even with the light of a full moon or a flashlight.

After we cleared the curve to the left, the trees gave way to an open field covered with the stubbled remnants of last year's corn crop. Off to our right about fifty feet away, a split-rail fence marked off another field where the soil had been tilled and left in large clods scattered over the ground. The fence extended down the side of this field to a distant tree line several hundred yards away, while the front portion of the fence followed the back edge of the woods on our right.

Wyatt turned left and we followed the tree line there for twenty feet and then ducked into the woods. I saw something bright yellow flutter and realized it was police tape used to cordon off the area. It struck me as overkill—pardon the pun—given how isolated the site was, not to mention that anyone or anything could have come out here with no one being the wiser. I stopped, told Newt to sit and stay, and then walked up to the perimeter tape.

The ground here was a bed of dead leaves, pine needles, and dirt. The same rust-colored stain I'd observed at the location of Paul's sighting could be seen here but this time I couldn't smell anything, even though the blood here was supposedly fresher and the stain considerably larger. Newt, on the other hand, kept sniffing the air and whining, sniffing and whining.

Wyatt stood silently by my side for several minutes. Finally, he said, "We found her face up, both arms flung out to the sides. The blood here came largely from her neck wound, spreading out and seeping into the ground around her, most of it to the left of the body because the wound was on that side of her neck. The autopsy revealed her carotid artery had been severed, but we didn't find any evidence of arterial spray, suggesting death from the broken neck had occurred beforehand."

"Death before the throat injury would have been a blessing," I said, and Wyatt nodded. "Did you find any type of knife or other sharp object at the scene?"

"Nope. As I mentioned before, the wound looked jagged, more consistent with a tearing injury. And there were several lines of torn tissue, like a claw might create."

"Interesting."

"An animal hair was found in the wound. The lab said it appears to be ursine."

"So, it was a bear attack," I surmised with a shrug.

"Maybe, but she also could have picked up the hair through accidental contact while walking through the woods or from being on the ground. We get black bear sightings now and again and there's evidence of both deer and bears rubbing on the trunks in these woods. In fact, we found several similar hairs stuck in the bark of a tree right over there." He pointed off to his left.

"That makes sense," I said. "It was an early, warm start to spring, and black bears would have been coming out of hibernation, the males as early as mid-March and the females in early to mid-April. They tend to be torpid when they first emerge but after a week or so they get more active. And hungry."

"Yeah, that's all well and good but a podcaster somehow got wind of the autopsy results and has been saying that the injuries appear to have been made by some type of claw and that the scratch marks on the car are more canine than ursine because bears tend to leave five claw marks, not four."

"Not always but let me guess why the podcaster said this. It suggests it could have been a werewolf attack."

Wyatt smiled grimly. "The guy didn't come right out and use the word 'werewolf,' but he did suggest the killing might have been at the hands, or rather the claws, of the Beast of Bray Road, effectively resurrecting werewolf rumors that died down decades ago. Times are different now, and with the internet, news travels fast. The conspiracy theorists are already crawling out of the woodwork, and if history is any indication, it won't be long before we'll have rumors flying around town like a fleet of UFOs."

That made me chuckle.

There was some normal ground color amid the darker staining, spots where the weight of Lydia's body had apparently prevented any blood from getting onto the ground. I thought I could make out the vague contours of a head and an arm, and Wyatt confirmed my suspicion.

"Her head was up there, toward the back edge of the woods, feet down here, toward us."

I nodded and circled around the police tape a couple of times, working my way closer to the cornfield. When I emerged from the trees into the midafternoon sunlight, I was forced to blink several times as my eyes struggled to adjust to the brightness. I squinted at smashed and flattened remains of the cornstalks, shaking my head and trying to make sense of this location. What could have possessed a woman, or anyone for that matter, to venture out here in the middle of the night? It boggled the mind.

"It gets to you, doesn't it?" Wyatt said from over my shoulder.

I started, not realizing he'd followed me. His approach had been silent. Had the same thing happened to Lydia Palmer? Had some creature stalked her, sneaking up with great stealth before attacking?

I did a slow spin, noticing there wasn't a house or any other man-made structure anywhere in sight. It was utterly—and frankly, eerily—quiet save for the rustle of tree branches in the breeze. No birdsong, no industrial or automotive noise, no hum of overhead wires or low-flying planes, nothing. I took out my cell phone and checked the signal strength. It showed me one bar for a second, but then it flickered and disappeared.

I turned to Wyatt. "Cryptids aside, the thing about this case that intrigues me the most is trying to understand what Lydia Palmer was doing out here. It would have been strange enough if she'd come here during the day, but in the middle of the night?"

"No idea," he said with a half-hearted shrug. "I've looked over her social media, her laptop, and her phone. Her computer was password protected but Dylan was able to guess what it was. If there's a clue anywhere, I didn't find it."

I walked back under the canopy of trees and stared at the area inside the perimeter tape. "Describe the injuries she had again. I know you said the gash on her throat appeared ragged, but I'm interested in the directionality of any other injuries."

"There was a deep, downward slashing wound on her abdomen, beneath a ripped part of her shirt. Four parallel lines." He paused and narrowed his eyes in thought, pulling at his chin. "And I think I told you already that her shirt was rolled up in the back."

"Right. You mentioned she might have been dragged." I looked down at the area where her body had been but couldn't see any evidence of drag marks. Or any marks of any kind for that matter. The ground appeared dry and largely undisturbed aside from the horrible, dark stain, though there seemed to be fewer dead leaves inside the perimeter tape. That seemed odd, given they were everywhere else. "Dragging can be an indicator of animal behavior," I said. "Some species like to cart their kill off to a spot more private and isolated, like a den. Or sometimes they drag kills to feed their offspring. Of course, it could also be a human killer, though why would they drag her all the way here from her car?"

Wyatt looked dubious.

"Any evidence of Lydia participating in online dating? Or any dating for that matter?"

"Nope. No rumors or sightings of her with anyone around town. Though Dylan did mention there was a guy who works at the library named Lester Hofheyzer who he thought was sweet on Lydia, but I don't think they were dating. Dylan made it sound like it was a one-way street. He said his mom thought the guy was nice but, um, 'quirky' was the word he used."

"I've had worse dates," I said, only half joking.

"You and me both," Wyatt countered.

"Let's head back," I said. "I'd like to get a look at Lydia's car so I can examine those scratch marks if possible."

"No problem. It's still in our evidence garage over by the station. I can show it to you now if you want, or you can look at more pictures of it I have at my desk."

"I'd prefer to see it in person. And can you arrange a talk with Lydia's son? I want to get a better idea of what this woman's life was like. Was she interested in cryptids? Was she out here because she was doing her own hunt for the Beast of Bray Road? Maybe this guy at the library can tell us what type of books she checked out."

"That's quite an agenda," Wyatt said, leaning back and looking comically overwhelmed.

"It's all part of my process. Can I also see the official coroner's report?"

"As long as you promise not to go public with anything it contains unless and until I say so."

"You have my word."

"I don't have the official report yet but expect it anytime. I'll let you know. Anything else?"

I gathered from Wyatt's tone this question was meant to be sarcastic and rhetorical. Foolish man.

"Yes. I don't suppose you'd let my employee Devon have a look at Lydia's laptop and phone. He's a whiz at that sort of thing."

Wyatt's lips pursed into a moue of disapproval. "Until we have an official cause of death for Lydia Palmer, I can't release them. And then they become the property of her son."

"Devon can access them remotely. No one needs to know."

"I'm going to pretend I didn't hear that," Wyatt said with a frown. "And we looked over her electronics. There was nothing there."

"Devon is good. He might be able to find things your guys missed. And he doesn't take credit for what he does, other than hitting me up for bonuses. All that will go to you."

Wyatt scratched his head again and stared off into the trees. I could tell he was considering my request and I decided it would be best not to pressure him on it.

I walked over to Newt, who was still sitting like a good boy right where I'd left him. His tail started wagging, brushing aside leaves and pine needles and clearing a fan-shaped area behind him. It stirred up a cloud of aromatic, woodsy smells.

"Think about the laptop and phone," I said to Wyatt as we

made our way back to the car. "For now, let's tick off some of the other items on my list, and when we're done with those, we can come back to it."

Wyatt followed silently behind me, agreeing to nothing. Regardless of his decision about the laptop and phone, I planned to have Devon scour through Lydia Palmer's social media and as much of her online footprint as he could find. Maybe he could dig up something that would make some sense of this case because so far all I had were lots of questions.

CHAPTER 7

I made a U-turn on Bray Road, ticking off someone in a gray car who barreled past us with a blare of the horn.

"I think I saw that same gray car pass us earlier when we were at Paul's site," I said to Wyatt as the vehicle disappeared down the road.

"It's probably someone who lives here on Bray Road."

Sure enough, we passed the gray car as it pulled into a driveway about half a mile down the road.

The recurring sight of any vehicle made me paranoid, worried my ex might be stalking me again. David Johnson—the man I had spent six months of my life with, the man I had once been engaged to, the man who had murdered my parents—was on the loose somewhere. He'd disappeared when my parents were killed, but in recent months he'd been contacting me via letters sent anonymously, though I knew they were from him, and the occasional phone call. I had even come face-to-face with him briefly during my last case.

Jon was determined to track him down, or at least he had been prior to our time apart. I had no idea if he was still looking for David, who was a master of disguise and identity theft, or if he'd abandoned the cause much the same way he'd abandoned me.

Jon's past was as tragic as my own. His wife and young son had been killed by a drunken driver three years ago and it had nearly destroyed him. It was why he took issue with my cryptid work or, rather, with the risks I often faced with my cryptid work. He had told me my disregard for my own safety was something he didn't think he could live with because he didn't want to risk another loss like the one he'd experienced with his wife and son.

I understood this, but it seemed the only alternative to our breaking up was for me to give up my cryptid work and that was a trade I wasn't willing to make. At least not yet. Though given how badly I'd missed Jon in my life of late, I was once again questioning the wisdom of my choices, especially after seeing him yesterday.

I followed the directions Wyatt had given me earlier and turned on Hospital Road. Minutes later we emerged on County NN by the hospital.

"All of our autopsies are performed here at the hospital in the basement morgue," Wyatt explained. "The impound garage holding Lydia's vehicle is located just ahead on the left across the highway from the courts building and sheriff's department."

"Must be nice having everything located so close together," I said.

"It is," he agreed.

We parked outside the impound garage and I followed Wyatt

through a door with a punch lock. Lydia's car was close to the entrance, an older model blue Ford Fusion that showed its age. The exterior sported dozens of chips, dents, and dings, the tires were bald, the wheel wells and lower doorframes were rusted, and the passenger-side mirror was missing. Either Lydia hadn't cared about maintaining the vehicle or she'd been too financially strapped to do so. My money was on the latter.

In addition, there were the exterior scratches supposedly inflicted by our werewolf. They appeared consistent—four gouges evenly spaced apart—and ranged in length from about a foot for the one running down the driver's-side front door to nearly three feet for another down the length of the front hood. When I stood on my tiptoes to get a better look at the roof, Wyatt informed me there were no scratches there.

I drew Newt's attention to the scratched areas. He sniffed at them briefly but quickly grew disinterested.

The interior of the car, while also suffering from age, was neat as a pin. Not a scrap of dust or dirt marred the dash, the seats, or the floors. The front seats had some stains and tears in the cloth and the carpet on the driver's side was threadbare, but seat covers and mats had been used to try to hide the worst of the damage.

With Wyatt's permission, I triggered the trunk release and went around to the back of the car, noticing the handicapped plates. The scratches here were relatively straight and went from just past the hinge to the edge of the trunk lid. I ran my fingers over them, feeling the slight gouge they'd made in the paint. The inside of the trunk was empty except for a few smears of fine dirt, and the carpet was torn in several places.

"I believe Lydia put Dylan's wheelchair in here whenever they went anywhere," Wyatt explained. "That's probably what caused these marks." He pointed to a series of silvery scrapes and rubs along the edges of the trunk opening.

"Did Lydia have any defensive wounds?"

Wyatt's brows drew together. "No," he said. "But I don't think she could have defended herself with the broken neck because she would have been paralyzed."

"Right. How is Dylan getting around without his mom or the car?"

"I think the caregiver lives in and he has a car."

"That's fortunate. Any chance of getting to speak with the son today?"

Wyatt nodded. "Let me give Dylan a call and see if he's up for a visit."

I glanced at my watch, saw it was going on three thirty, and nodded.

We piled back into my car and Wyatt called Dylan Palmer as we sat in the lot outside the garage. I couldn't help but overhear parts of the conversation.

"Dylan said we can come by in an hour or two. He'll call when he's ready. He's very curious about you," Wyatt said unnecessarily once he'd finished the call.

"And you lied to him."

Wyatt flushed. "More a withholding of some of the truth."

This so-called withholding of the truth consisted of Wyatt referring to me simply as an outside consultant. This was something I'd run into a lot lately: bureaucrats and other interested parties not wanting to admit they hired a cryptozoologist and trying to walk a fine line between the lure of a potential cryptid hanging around and the possibility it might be snacking on tourists for lunch.

This thought, rather obliquely, made my stomach rumble. It was loud enough that Newt turned his head to the side and eyed me curiously. I had no doubt Wyatt had also heard it, but he was kind enough not to say anything. I, on the other hand, went straight to the elephant in the room.

"Since we have some time to kill, can you recommend a place to get something to eat?" I asked, rubbing a hand over my noisy belly. "I scarfed down half a sandwich when I first arrived in town but it's all I've eaten today and I'm starving. I don't need fancy, just decent."

"We specialize in not fancy here," he said jokingly. He glanced up at the sky, which was rapidly clouding over, causing the temperature to drop several degrees. "How about some great soup and another sandwich? I know a little place I can take you to. They also have an amazing selection of baked goods for dessert."

"I don't want to keep you from your duties. Or your family." Wyatt wasn't wearing a wedding ring, but I didn't want to jump to conclusions.

"No worries. I've been divorced for three years now, my parents have died, and my brothers live out of state."

"No special someone in your life?"

He shrugged. "I'm seeing someone . . . kind of. But she's at a convention in Chicago all week."

"Kind of?"

"It's a long story."

"Well, isn't it lucky then that we happen to have some time to kill?"

CHAPTER 8

Wyatt's eatery was tucked between some charming shops downtown, a little hole-in-the-wall with outdated décor and a cozy atmosphere. The food was delicious, effectively warding off any blues triggered by the storm building outside. Wyatt's brief info dump about his life—romantic and otherwise—intrigued me, and after we ordered, I grilled him for more specifics. I learned he had two brothers, both older, one in Minneapolis, the other in Arizona. His father had died of cancer two years ago at the age of seventy-eight and his mother had followed a year later with a heart attack.

"Honestly, I think she died of a broken heart," Wyatt said. "She and my father were married for fifty-one years, and they adored one another. Mom never got over Dad's death and her decline the following year was swift and rather horrifying to watch."

I shared with him how my parents had met hunting for

cryptids—specifically the chupacabra—and how they, too, had been a match made in heaven.

"My childhood was definitely unique," I told him. "Because I traveled so much with my parents, I was homeschooled by my mom and the occasional tutor. As a result, I met folks all over the world but had hardly any friends at home."

Wyatt then shared that one of his brothers, Nate, was a lawyer, the other, Kevin, was a pediatrician, and that his decision to become a cop had been a disappointment to his parents.

"I managed to redeem myself a little when I married Sarah because she's a doctor, but then the divorce put me back at square one. My parents doted on their grandchildren, and they hated that Nate and Kevin lived so far away. But kids weren't in the cards for me and Sarah."

"Relationships are hard, aren't they?" I said, thinking of me and Jon.

"They certainly haven't been easy for me, particularly with the work I do."

"The hours?"

"That's part of it, but it's also the work itself, the things I see and do. My ex, Sarah, struggled with the danger of the job, and she'd get upset when I told her about hairy situations I'd faced on a shift. She's an ER doctor, so she knew what could happen and wanted me to change careers. But I love what I do, despite the danger. Maybe even because of the danger. I don't know." He shrugged. "Anyway, things improved a little when I made detective, but by then it was too late. Hannah, the woman I've been seeing for the past year, thinks I'm too closed off. She gets upset with me because I don't talk about my work, but I learned not to with Sarah. Besides, it's hard to get someone to understand the subtle nuances of some situations when they don't know the job and haven't experienced it."

"I can relate," I told him with a grim smile.

I'd had several people try to get me to talk about my parents' deaths over the years, but I had no desire to speak about it. Not only was it traumatic for me to recall the image of them lying there with their throats slashed, but the memory left me awash in feelings of guilt and regret because I'd been the one who brought the murderer into their lives.

Wyatt eyed me thoughtfully. "I may be talking out of school here," he said, "but when I asked Jon to arrange an introduction, he said seeing you would be difficult. Something in his voice clued me in to his true feelings for you and it piqued my curiosity. He seemed—I don't know—wounded somehow. Not mortally but close to it."

This revelation made my face flush hot, not from embarrassment but from sorrow. I knew I harbored no small amount of blame for the problems in my relationship with Jon and it broke my heart to know I'd hurt him.

"Maybe it's the detective in me but I decided to poke him a little to see if he'd open up," Wyatt continued. "It didn't take much to get him talking about his history with you."

This surprised me and made me cringe a little. Jon knew how hard I worked to keep my public and private lives separate and yet he'd apparently spilled his guts about us to this stranger. I didn't like where this was headed, and it was about to get worse. Not to mention a bit, well, weird.

"What exactly did he say?" I asked. Despite trying to hide my annoyance, I heard it come through clearly in my voice and knew Wyatt had, too.

"He told me about what happened with your parents."

No, no, no. Jon wouldn't do that.

"Care to elaborate?" I said, shooting eye daggers at him. I was notably prickly at that point, aiming my anger with Jon squarely at Wyatt. Later, when I looked back on this conversation, I would marvel at just how deftly Wyatt had handled me. Freaking detectives. They're like shrinks but with more of a gotcha mentality. And I would soon learn Wyatt was a double whammy.

"I can only imagine what an awful situation it must have been for you," Wyatt went on, his expression sincere and empathetic. "It would be hard enough to lose one's parents in such a horrific manner, but then to find them like that . . . how traumatizing it must have been. And probably still is. Toss Jon's tragic history into the mix and you've got a recipe for emotional disaster."

Damn! Was there a bean Jon hadn't spilled?

"Jon told me the guy who killed your parents was someone you were dating," he added, poking a finger in the wound.

I nodded, struggling to swallow, my mouth dry as a desert. Then I squared my shoulders and said, "The guilt of what my choices wrought will haunt me until the day I die." My voice sounded brittle but determined. "I'll never be able to forgive myself for bringing David Johnson into my parents' lives. I can only hope he'll eventually be caught and brought to justice."

"It must be hard for you, knowing he's still out there somewhere."

I nodded. "Here's the thing, though," I said as the saner part of my brain, which I was about to ignore, tried to shut me up. "I don't think David meant to kill my parents."

Wyatt arched a brow, prompting me to quickly elaborate.

"What I mean is, I don't think it was part of his original plan. I think he panicked when my father exposed him for the fraud he was and then something my father said or did must have made him feel cornered and he struck out impulsively." I saw worry on Wyatt's face, as if he'd only just realized he was sitting across the table from a homicidal Bonnie nattering on crazily about her Clyde.

"You're defending him?" he said, not bothering to hide his incredulity.

"God, no. I'd gladly administer a slow, painful death to the bastard if given the chance. But I've analyzed and rethought through the months preceding what happened thousands of times in the days since, and I have a hard time making sense of it all. I mean, apart from trying to avoid being exposed for his con, how did killing my parents benefit David?"

"Jon said your parents were wealthy, and with them gone, you inherited it all. And it sounds as if you were rather besotted with this David guy. Who's to say the two of you weren't in it together? The money could have been a motive for you as well as for David."

I probably should have been offended by this, but I'd heard it all before dozens of times, mostly from the cops investigating the murders. It no longer had the same effect on me. Besides, I was struck by the fact that Wyatt had used the word "besotted." I mean, what normal, modern-day man in his prime does that? Sometimes my brain takes the weirdest segues.

Was Wyatt testing me? Was this part of his job interview?

Maybe he wanted to determine if I was a total lunatic before sharing any more details about the case. Though if so, he could have done it before I had driven all the way to Elkhorn.

"It's true. I inherited a lot of money," I agreed. "But I'd happily give away every penny of it to have my parents back." The tears I'd managed to waylay earlier sprang forth. I swiped at them and went on. "I promise you, the only emotion I have for David at this point is hate. I want to see him caught and crucified. He haunts my dreams as well as my waking life."

"Jon mentioned you were having nightmares."

That set me back on my heels.

"It's nothing to be ashamed of," Wyatt said. "I have them, too, at times. I even had panic attacks back when I was still in uniform."

"Been there, done that," I said. I paused, licking my lips. "You know, I saw David not long ago."

"Really?" Wyatt regarded me with unabashed interest. "Jon didn't mention that."

Nice to know he kept something back.

"Yep, I even spoke to him, albeit very briefly and under, um, strained circumstances." This was an understatement of huge proportions given that it happened after I'd crashed my car and survived a hail of bullets.

"Hunh." Wyatt seemed to consider this revelation for a moment and then said, "Do you ever get panic attacks from hunting for cryptids?"

"Not really," I said with a smile. "But that might be because I tend to spend more time disproving cryptids than I do finding any."

"Good. That's exactly what I'm interested in having you do for me."

"No guarantees," I said, relieved we were off the topic of Jon and David. "Whatever I find is what I'll report."

"Of course."

"My process can be rather boring."

"That's okay," Wyatt said.

"Good. Now, tell me more about the Elkhorn werewolf. Any idea who it might be?"

CHAPTER 9

Wyatt Moorhead was nothing if not determined.

As I took out a pen and a notepad I had in my jacket pocket, he said, "I don't have an ID on the werewolf, and I'm happy to talk more about the case, but first I want to say one more thing about Jon Flanders. He cares a great deal for you. In fact, I'd venture to say he's in love with you."

I let out a weary sigh. "You determined this using your keen detecting skills?" I teased.

"Something like that," he said. "What's more, I can tell you have strong feelings for him, too. Surely there's a way to fix things?"

"You seem to have missed your calling as Cupid." The words came out snippier than I had intended but I didn't care. Wyatt's persistence on this topic felt off to me. There was more to it, something I wasn't seeing.

"I'm a romantic at heart, Morgan, more than you know. In fact, if I tell you a secret, will you promise not to tell anyone else?"

I glanced around dramatically and rolled my eyes. "Depends," I said, my voice low. "If you tell me you're a werewolf, I'll feel obligated to share it. And we're in a perfect place for me to do it." I wiggled my eyebrows to show him I was being comically theatric, but what he said next shocked me.

"I kill people on a regular basis."

Whoa!

I reared back in my seat. Wyatt's eyes sparkled with mischief; I felt certain he was baiting me but went there, anyway. "I'll bite."

"I write romantic suspense novels when I'm not policing, and I kill people on the page all the time."

He couldn't have surprised me more if he'd turned into a werewolf right there in the café. I stared at him wide-eyed, forgetting to blink until my eyes burned. "Seriously?" I managed, wondering if he was trying to put one over on me. "*Romantic* suspense?"

He nodded "I write under a pseudonym. I've always had a love of writing, and when I was young, I was told I had a knack for it. I used to write just for myself, suspense thrillers and secret agent stuff about situations I imagined myself in. I dabbled in fantasy for a while, but I quickly realized my imagination was too well-grounded in the real world. So, I switched to writing romantic thrillers. Eventually I reached a point where I wanted more validation, so I went looking for an agent. I found one who liked a novel I'd written, but she wanted to know if I'd be willing to rewrite it with a female protagonist and from a female point of view. The challenge appealed to me, I gave it a whirl, and it turns out, I have a knack for writing in a feminine voice. The book netted me a three-book contract with a New York City publisher and I'm still going. I'm working on my sixth book in the series now, and while I don't make enough at it to quit policing, it's a nice addition to my income. And I love it."

"Well, color me gobsmacked," I said, sitting back in my chair. "That's amazing. What's your pseudonym?"

"Jordan Sumner."

"Oh wow! We have your books on the shelves in my store. My employee Rita would have been fangirling all over you if she'd known who you were when you were there. She always gets giddy when she meets authors."

"I hope the books are selling."

"Oh, I think we've moved a few copies. Wait, is that why you're so determined to dissect my relationship with Jon? Are you using us as fodder for your next book?"

"No," he said, chuckling, "though I do consider myself something of an expert on romance based on my many failed relationships and my apparent ability to create it convincingly on the page."

I bit back a laugh, not sure if he was being self-deprecating or serious. "Not the best job qualifications," I teased.

"Probably not, but there's also my master's degree in psychology."

I stared at him, once again unsure if he was joking. He had a knack for unsettling me and I pitied any criminals he interrogated. His control of the conversation was masterful. "You're serious?"

"As a heart attack. I had plans to be a counselor at one point in my life, trying to compete with my overachieving brothers. But I enrolled in some criminal justice courses on a whim, and after finishing my master's degree, I found myself at the police academy. I haven't looked back since. My parents always considered me the black sheep of the family, the son who failed to make something of himself. And as I said before, my unwillingness to leave police work behind didn't exactly help my marriage." He smiled, but there was pain in it. "It wasn't wasted, though. The psychology degree comes in handy in my police work."

"Let me get this straight," I said, still in shock. "You're a shrink, a cop, *and* a published romantic suspense author?" I ticked the various jobs off on my fingers.

He shrugged. "Your classic overachiever, unless you'd ever talked to my parents."

I wasn't a trained counselor, but I didn't need to be to pick up on the undercurrent in his comment. A story for another day. "Okay, I admit I'm impressed," I said, meaning it.

"As you should be," he teased.

"Back to talking about werewolves," I said.

Our waitress sidled up to the table just then to ask if we wanted any dessert. Wyatt ordered a slice of carrot cake while I opted for coffee.

After taking our orders, the waitress leaned over our table and spoke in a hushed tone. "I heard you mention werewolves. Is that what killed that woman out on Bray Road?" It was hard to tell if she was concerned or intrigued by the possibility. Probably a little of both.

"What do you think?" I asked. "What are people saying?"

"Well, I heard the Beast of Bray Road might be back," she said, her eyes big. "Some of the older folks who come in here have been talking about how it was here back in the eighties. Someone else was in here asking about it earlier. A reporter, I think."

Never underestimate the power of gossip in a small town.

"There's no evidence to suggest there's a werewolf out there," Wyatt said. "Besides, they don't exist."

I shot him a look.

"Are you sure about that?" the waitress asked. "I mean, is it safe to go out at night? I walk home from here."

"You should be fine," Wyatt said.

The waitress went to fetch our coffee and cake, returning a minute later. I thought she might ask more questions, but she didn't.

"Okay, tell me more about Dylan Palmer," I said once the waitress was out of earshot. "I imagine the paralysis must have been hard for him, especially at such a young age. It's frightening how a moment in time can have such a devastating, life-altering effect."

Wyatt nodded, looking somber. "I was on duty the day it happened, though not directly involved with the investigation. I remember how distraught Lydia was. You could tell she was shattered."

I'm not a huge fan of carrot cake but the thick covering of cream cheese frosting on Wyatt's slice looked delicious. I wanted to snag a forkful of it for myself. Just the frosting.

"Did you know the Palmers before the accident?" I asked, caving and rudely diving in for a taste.

Wyatt nodded, swallowing a bite of his cake. "Help yourself," he said, sliding his plate closer to me. "And yeah, I grew up here, so I have a passing acquaintance with a lot of the locals. I went to school with Lydia, but we didn't run in the same social circles. I knew *of* her, but didn't really know her personally. Ervin I didn't know at all back then because he was a couple years ahead of us. Lydia got pregnant with Dylan near the end of her senior year and they married right after she graduated."

The frosting melted on my tongue, tasting so good, I almost moaned.

"Years later, when I was a patrol officer, I became familiar with most of the hell-raising kids in town and Dylan was one of them. He used to hang with a trio of boys who were into petty thefts and other mischief . . . knocking down mailboxes, stealing bikes, tagging, things like that. Dylan had a reputation for being an instigator.

"Then, when he was fifteen, he was arrested for stealing some items from a car parts store. He was restoring an older model Jeep and didn't have the money for what he needed, so he just took the stuff. He was caught on the store's security cameras but just laughed it off when he was confronted with the evidence. I think his pals dared him to do it and Dylan treated it as a badge of honor. He seemed disappointed when he didn't get jail time."

"Not even juvie?"

"Nah, first-time offense and a lenient judge. He had to do some community service and pay restitution for the items he took, but otherwise he got off scot-free, at least from a legal standpoint. I think Ervin might have inflicted punishments of his own because he tended to get mean when he drank, which was most of the time. We had several domestic calls to the Palmer house before Ervin died."

"How sad," I said.

"Yeah, Dylan had a great deal of anger after the accident, which I suppose is understandable. He went through a period of depression where he made comments about how he was the one who was supposed to die and how he wished he had. At one point, I thought maybe. . . ." Wyatt trailed off, shook his head, and shrugged before continuing.

"Anyway, I think he's finally come to terms with things, at least as good as anyone can under those circumstances. To be honest, I haven't seen much of him since he was discharged from the hospital and went to a rehab facility four years ago. He's been home nearly three years now and I think he's been living a reasonably well-adjusted life, all things considered and thanks in large part to the efforts of his mother. Her death has to be a huge shock for him and not just because she was his mother. From what I've heard, Lydia pulled out all the stops for Dylan after the accident and dedicated every spare moment she had to him. No sacrifice was too big."

Wyatt's phone let out an audible warble and he dug it out of his pocket and glanced at the screen. "That's the dispatcher letting me know the medical examiner's office has returned the personal effects Lydia had on her when she was found. Mind if we take a slight detour? I can grab the stuff and take it to Dylan when we go out there and give you a quick tour of our station in the meantime."

"Sure."

"You should bring Newt into the station. He'll be a good distraction."

The distraction comment puzzled me, though in time I'd come to understand what he meant and why it mattered.

CHAPTER 10

After paying our bill—Wyatt insisted on treating me—we drove out to the sprawling complex containing the county court, the jail, and the sheriff's office. It only took us a matter of minutes.

"Normally I'd enter the back way, down at that end of the building," Wyatt said, pointing left as I parked out in front. "But let's go in the main entrance so I can give you more of a guided tour."

We entered a large public lobby, where a man in a suit and tie carrying a briefcase was telling the woman behind a plexiglass window he was there to see his client.

"The jail is through there," Wyatt said, pointing to a door. "The court is at the other end of the building."

As the lawyer was buzzed through the jail door, Wyatt badged us through a different one into an area behind the plexiglass window where a half dozen people were seated at desks in cubicles. Introductions were made, Wyatt using first names only and telling the others I was a visiting friend. Newt was subjected to a host of oohs, aahs, and pettings, all of which he eagerly accepted. I saw two of the women I was introduced to giving each other sly winks when they thought I wasn't looking.

Eventually, after meandering through a maze of hallways and rooms and doing a handful of additional introductions, we ended up in a large space near the far side of the building filled with yet more cubicles.

"This is the detectives' area," Wyatt said. He nodded toward one of the desks. "That's my spot but let's go sit in the interview room for now. It will be more comfortable. Can I get you something to drink?"

I declined his offer and took a seat in the adjacent room he'd indicated, which looked more like a small conference room. I told Newt to lie down, and we waited. Wyatt returned a moment later, bag in hand, and shut the door.

"I don't want anyone to overhear us discussing the case," he said. "Closing the door will give us privacy but I should apologize ahead of time because it will also feed the rumor mill out there that now thinks you and I are in a relationship."

"What? Why would they think that?" I asked, askance.

"Because there are a couple of die-hard romantics working here who are determined to see me hitched up with someone sooner rather than later."

"I thought you said you were seeing someone."

"I am, but most of them don't know that. I tend to keep my personal life to myself, and between Hannah's work travel and my hours, we don't see a lot of each other, so it makes it easy to pretend I have no life." He flashed a smile that suggested there was more truth behind this statement than he liked. "You and Jon are the only people I've talked to about my relationship with Hannah in . . . well . . . ever and that's only because I see some similarities in your struggles and what I'm going through. I hope it hasn't made you uncomfortable."

"A little at times, but it's okay." Truth was, despite the occasionally painful moments, I rather liked talking this stuff through, though I would have preferred to do it with Jon. Still, an unlicensed quasi counselor with his own relationship problems would suffice. For now.

"My coworkers can be a little much," Wyatt went on. "They're determined to fix me up because they can't imagine I can write romance as well as I do if I'm not actively living it."

"They know about your alter ego?"

"Well, yeah," he said, giving me a *duh* look. "I work with people who are naturally nosy and suspicious. They're good at drilling down to the truth and you've seen the setup out there. After too many overheard phone calls with my agent and publisher, too many times closing my laptop when I was working on a manuscript during a slow spell, and too many times asking my coworkers about their love lives, they grew suspicious." He shrugged. "Though I've never really tried to hide it."

"Why do I get the feeling you're trying to hide the real reason I'm here?"

He gave me a guilty look. "You'd make a good detective."

"As a cryptozoologist, I already am one, in a sense. And you're avoiding my question."

"Busted," he said, grinning. "Let's just say I know my superiors won't be crazy about your involvement and I might have been a little coy in telling them."

"What do you mean by 'coy'?"

He winced, looking even guiltier. "I haven't mentioned it. At all."

I let out an exasperated sigh. "How are you going to explain spending all day with me today?"

"You're a friend. And today is my day off."

I wasn't happy with the deception, but I also wasn't surprised. Most of my recent cases had involved some degree of subterfuge and varying levels of embarrassment about hiring me.

"Sorry if I've put you in a bad spot," he said. "Jon assured me you could handle the pressure."

"Did he?" Not wanting to discuss Jon anymore, I sought a distraction. I focused on the clear plastic baggie Wyatt had carried in, which was currently resting on the table between us. It contained what I assumed were the personal effects of Lydia Palmer: a set of keys, some coins, a driver's license, and a small billfold. But I was keenly aware of Wyatt watching me.

"You care for Jon a lot, don't you?" he said.

"I do," I admitted. "But it's complicated."

"Isn't it always?"

"More so in our case. It's not just the emotional baggage we both bring to the table. There's also the simple matter of distance. We don't live far apart as the crow flies, but it might as well be ten times the distance when you consider we're separated by a treacherous channel of water known as Death's Door, which is filled with hundreds of shipwrecks. We can't just hop in the car and go visit one another. We're dependent on the ferry schedule. And in the wintertime, the term 'schedule' is sometimes used loosely."

Wyatt *tsk*ed and shook his head. "Excuses, excuses. If you want it enough, you'll find a way."

"Death's Door," I repeated with doomsday emphasis, eyes wide, more of a joke than anything because I didn't know what else to say.

"I've heard about this notorious body of water," Wyatt said. "And while I'd love to learn more about it, today isn't the time."

It wasn't the time for any of this if you asked me, but then nobody had.

"Both of you are wounded souls," he went on. "You've had your hearts broken in the cruelest of ways and it makes sense you'd be cautious and reluctant to commit."

"I think Jon's more ready than I am."

"I agree, though he's struggling with your. . . . How did he put it? Your headstrong disregard for your own safety."

"He said that?" I was back to wary annoyance, unhappy with Jon's willingness to share such personal thoughts about me. "Just how long did the two of you talk?"

"He invited me to spend a night at his house on Washington Island to talk things over before we came to see you. We shared a few beers and chatted about a lot of stuff, including your potential role in the case. Jon said he would put me in touch with you, but he didn't want to be directly involved. I, of course, was immediately intrigued as to why and started probing. We were well into our beers by then, and it didn't take much prodding from me before I got the full story about how the two of you keep dancing around your feelings."

"'Dancing'? Is that his description or yours?"

"Mine," Wyatt admitted.

"I can't live in a bubble," I said, again feeling a need to defend myself. "Life is risky."

"True, but it sounds like yours has been riskier than most because of decisions you've made in the past and continue to make to this day. It intrigues me because I feel a certain, um, kinship with you in that regard."

The truth of this hurt more than Wyatt knew. Or maybe he did know.

"It's who I am, Wyatt. It's how I roll. And technically, I could say the same thing about Jon. His job is risky."

Wyatt gave me a cynical look. "Yeah, I suppose," he said unconvincingly, "though it sounds like his job is much safer than what most police officers face. A purposeful choice, I think, after losing his wife and son the way he did. Many men in his situation would have been passively suicidal, choosing to police in areas where the danger levels are high. But instead, he chose a pacific job where the danger level is practically nonexistent. I think that makes it hard for him to understand why you keep doing the opposite."

Guilt had me squirming again. It was true both Jon and I were haunted by ghosts, but I'd always thought his were more of an interference in our lives than mine were. What Wyatt had just said made me question this. There'd been times when I'd felt jealous of Jon's dead wife, worried he was comparing me to her and finding me lacking in many ways. My logical mind knew I was being ridiculous, but my emotional brain ruled supreme all too often. It didn't help that I'd seen pictures of her: a stunningly beautiful woman who had passed on her looks to their son, an adorable, huggable little cherub.

Their happiness had been ripped away in an instant and I ached for Jon, knowing how much it had crushed him at the time. Too often I felt unable to compete with what had been, with what he'd once had. How could I ever bring a comparable level of happiness into his life? Plus, even though he'd assured me several times that he didn't judge me for my gullibility when it came to David Johnson, I had a hard time believing him. How could he have not? I'd been a naïve, foolish girl who was. . . . What was the word Wyatt had used? Besotted. I'd been besotted. Blinded by what I thought was love. My naivete and stubbornness had led to my parents' deaths. So, of course, Jon would have expected much of the same from me if he let me into his life. I hadn't shown myself capable of making solid, sensible decisions in the past, so why would Jon think things would be any different in the future?

"I'm curious," Wyatt said. "Did you take a lot of risks before your parents died?"

I scowled at him, not liking the question but unsure why. "I don't know," I said irritably. "Probably not. I had them around most of the time and they took the risks. In fact, I was often the sensible one among the three of us."

"That's interesting, don't you think?"

It was, and at the moment it irritated me.

"Maybe we should get back to the case," I said, tight-lipped. "Let's stick with the reason I'm here and drop this psychoanalytic crap. It's starting to grate on my nerves."

It didn't take a degree in psychology to read me at that point. My expression, body language, and tone said it all. I gestured toward the bag. "May I?"

Wyatt nodded. "Sure. My dispatcher just messaged me to say

the ME has officially determined Lydia's death was accidental and the result of an animal attack, so the case is now closed. I should have the final report later today or early tomorrow. That means this stuff is no longer considered evidence." He opened the bag and slid the contents out onto the table.

"Does that mean I should go home?"

"No way. I still want to know what animal it was."

"I'm not convinced it was an animal," I said. "Too many inconsistencies, but maybe I'll be able to resolve them."

There was also the mystery of what Lydia Palmer had been doing out there in the first place. I didn't like unanswered questions. I picked up Lydia's license and studied her photo. She'd been an attractive woman, with light blond hair, round blue eyes, a heart-shaped face, and pouty lips. I noticed her birthday was only a week away. She would have been thirty-nine, much too young to have seen so much sorrow in her life.

I shifted my attention to the loose change, a trio of coins dulled with age: a quarter, a dime, and a penny. The dime was a Mercury head, and I looked at the date: 1924. The quarter was dated 1920 and featured a standing image of Lady Liberty. The penny was from 1925 and had a wheat design on the side opposite Lincoln's head.

"Did you notice the dates on these coins?" I asked Wyatt.

He nodded. "Lydia was always looking for ways to make money. I'm guessing these old coins were part of that."

I considered this. "You found these on her body?"

Wyatt nodded. "They were in the front pockets of the pants she was wearing."

"These coins might be worth something. Maybe she had them

with her because she was meeting with someone to try to sell them."

"At three in the morning?" Wyatt said, looking skeptical. He had a point.

"Why else would she have had them with her? I mean, doesn't it strike you as odd she would bring these three old coins anywhere, much less at three in the morning? Keys, yes, driver's license, yes. But these?" I tapped the table next to the dime. "It feels off somehow."

"Maybe they were lucky coins?" Wyatt said in a tone of voice suggesting he found this idea as far-fetched as I did.

I didn't honor his theory with an answer, just a look.

"Yeah, okay," he conceded with a shrug.

"What about her laptop and phone? Are you going to return those to Dylan?"

"No reason not to."

"Any chance you'll let my guy take a look at them first?"

Wyatt frowned. "I'm not comfortable doing that. At least not without permission from Dylan."

"Did you look into her emails, online activity, and text messages to see if she had contact with anyone who might be interested in buying coins like these?"

"Of course," Wyatt said, sounding insulted. "This isn't my first investigation."

"Sorry. I wasn't trying to impugn your reputation. Just thinking out loud. Mind if I take a picture of the coins?"

Wyatt rubbed an earlobe as he debated his answer. "I don't see why not."

I opened the camera on my phone and snapped a couple of pictures, turning the coins over so I got both sides.

Wyatt's phone rang while I was doing this, and he turned around in his chair to take the call. While his back was to me, I sent the pictures of the coins to Devon with a brief message.

Wyatt responded to his call with a couple of "uh-huh"s and an "okay" before disconnecting and spinning back around. "Dylan is ready when we are. Shall we go?"

I had mixed feelings about visiting Dylan—about the whole case, if I was honest. But my curiosity had too firm a grip on me at this point. I couldn't walk away; I had to walk straight into it. And that, I realized, was why Jon and I were having trouble seeing eye to eye.

"Sure," I said. "But I have a request. Can you hold off on giving the phone, laptop, and other stuff to Dylan?" He looked hesitant. "Just a day. Maybe two?"

"I suppose. Can I ask why?"

"Those coins bother me, and I want to think on it some more."

He looked at me like I had a screw loose. Maybe I did.

"I don't see what the coins have to do with werewolves or the Beast of Bray Road," he said. "But I don't see the harm in waiting." He scraped the items off the table and back into the plastic bag. Then he opened the door, walked over to his desk, and tossed the bag onto it. "Your wish is my command," he said. "I'll give you two days."

CHAPTER 11

Elkhorn, like many Wisconsin towns, has a variety of home styles, everything from beautifully maintained Victorians to mid-century modern to futuristic-looking apartment buildings. The Palmer house was a ranch-style structure I estimated was at least sixty years old, maybe more. It had faded blue siding, dingy white fake shutters, some curling roof shingles, a scrubby yard, and chipped, peeling paint on the exterior trim. At the end of the gravel driveway, which boasted a healthy contingent of weeds down its length, was a single-car garage leaning at a precarious angle. A gray sedan was parked halfway down the driveway.

In contrast to the surrounding age and neglect, a sturdy wheel-chair ramp constructed of gleaming pressure-treated wood provided switchback access to the front entrance. It wasn't hard to see where Lydia Palmer's money and energies had been spent.

We parked in the street behind an older model Ford Escort, and after a moment's debate, I decided to bring Newt along at Wyatt's suggestion. "I heard Lydia was looking into getting Dylan a service dog," he said. "It might be good for him to meet Newt."

Though the sky above us was pebbled with gray clouds, a shelf of darker ones threatened off to the north, moving in fast. Thunder rumbled, still distant but ominous.

"I hope that storm makes its way here and drops a ton of rain," Wyatt said as we navigated our way to the small front porch. "We desperately need it."

The sky to the south and west cast a brilliant mix of gold, red, and pink light over the house and yard, and while the official sunset was still half an hour away, the fast-approaching storm would likely bring darkness early.

Wyatt was about to knock when the door opened. On the other side stood a man I guessed to be in his early to mid-thirties. He was dressed in green medical scrubs with white socks and no shoes. He was tall—well over six feet—with a lean, sinewy build, reddish blond hair cut close to his scalp, and a fresh-scrubbed complexion. His features were almost effeminate: long, albeit pale lashes rimming deep blue eyes, a pert nose, and full, well-defined lips.

"Hello, Detective Moorhead," he said with a smile. His eyes shifted to me, to Newt, and then back to Wyatt with a questioning tilt of his head.

Wyatt said, "Hi, Connor. This is Morgan Carter and her dog, Newt. She's helping me with the investigation into Lydia's death." Wyatt turned to me. "Connor is Dylan's live-in caregiver." He paused then, smiling awkwardly. "I'm sorry, Connor. I don't know your last name."

"It's O'Leary," he said. "Irish through and through."

"Nice to meet you, Connor O'Leary," I said with a smile.

Connor stepped back and Wyatt went inside, stopping a few feet in to remove his shoes. He gestured along the lower wall beside the door, where I saw two pairs of shoes neatly lined up: a pair of white athletic shoes easily twice the size of the casual oxfords beside them. The brown oxfords were a woman's shoe in an old-fashioned style and in what I guessed was a size six. Lydia's perhaps?

"Lydia was something of a neatnik and asked everyone to remove their shoes at the door," Wyatt explained.

"Happy to oblige," I said, slipping my shoes off and placing them in line with the others. "But what about Newt? His feet are mostly clean, but he's a dog so, you know. . . ." I shrugged.

Connor waved away my concern. "No worries. To be honest, I don't think Dylan cares. It was more Lydia's thing." He gestured toward the living room. "Go ahead and have a seat. Dylan is in his room. Let me go see if he needs any help."

I took a seat in one of two chairs straddling a brick fireplace in the small living room we were in, and Wyatt sat on a couch positioned perpendicular to the chairs. Connor disappeared into a hallway, and seconds later I heard a light knocking and the creak of a door opening. This was followed by the distant murmur of voices too low to make out any of the words. I expected Connor to return momentarily, but when he didn't, I spent some time taking in my surroundings, thinking it might help me better understand who Lydia Palmer had been.

All the furniture in the room appeared to be either old or secondhand, but the pieces were clean and someone—presumably

Lydia—had made an obvious attempt to tie it all together with a color scheme of dark greens and light browns. It gave the room a calm, woodsy feel, a sensation heightened by the overhead sounds of a light rain that had started to fall outside. A faint smell of smoke and burned wood emanated from the fireplace, where the grate bore ashes from a recent fire. Newt sniffed at it before dropping to the floor at my feet and resting his head on his front legs, waiting to see what new adventure was in store for him next.

After a few minutes, I heard a rhythmic squeak as the rubber on Dylan's chair wheels moved across the wooden floors of the hallway and into the living room, arriving with surprising speed and deftness. Newt was momentarily startled, and he raised his head, ears pricked forward, nostrils working overtime. Seconds later, he gave a tentative *thump, thump, thump* of his tail.

Dylan's broad shoulders and the tight fit of the crisp white dress shirt he had on showed off a well-toned upper body. He had hazel eyes bordered by thick, dark eyelashes and a messy mop of curly chestnut brown hair that hung down over his forehead but was cut short in a fade by his temples and above his ears. The rest of his features were even but unremarkable aside from a piercing in his left nostril with a small silver skull. He was a handsome young man, and I saw traces of Lydia in the shape of his face and his slightly pouty lips.

He greeted us with a smile, removing his hands from the wheels of his chair and settling them in his lap, fingers interlaced. Judging from the angled tilt of his legs, he had stood tall before his accident. With his white dress shirt, black dress slacks, and black socks, he looked ready to grab a briefcase and head for the office. All he lacked was a tie and some shoes.

"Well, well, what have we here?" Dylan asked, his gaze settling on my dog.

"This is Newt," I said. The tail thumps grew harder and faster once Newt heard his name. "Would you like to pet him?"

"Hell yeah," Dylan said with obvious delight. He unlaced his fingers and put his hands out.

"Go say hi, Newt."

Newt obligingly rose and trotted over to Dylan, settling his big, furry head in Dylan's lap. Dylan's face broke into a huge smile as he petted him.

Just then, a second person appeared in the door to the hallway, a petite young woman with long, wavy red hair, huge blue eyes, Cupid's bow lips, and alabaster skin. She had on a knee-length Bohemian-style floral dress with long sleeves and a denim vest. With her big eyes and waifish build, she reminded me of those Keane paintings that were popular back in the 1970s.

She glided to the side of Dylan's wheelchair, making no noise at all in her stocking feet, answering the question of whom the brown oxfords belonged to. When she saw Newt, she squealed with delight. "Oh, Dylan, a doggy!"

Dylan chuckled. "He's huge," he said as he stroked Newt's head. "Does he fetch things?"

I started to answer him, but before I could, the girl said, "How come he's not wearing one of those halters like the other service dogs I've seen? Do you have to provide that yourself, Dylan?"

I realized then there had been a misunderstanding. "Oh, no," I said. "Newt isn't a service dog. He's just *my* dog, my pet. Sorry if we confused you."

The girl glared at me with accusatory confusion, blinking those big eyes of hers.

I felt awful and snapped my fingers so Newt would come back to me. He did so immediately, once again settling into a furry comma at my feet. As if to emphasize the awkwardness of the moment, the wind outside howled, and rain began thrashing against the house.

"He's not your dog?" the girl said to Dylan in a tone of indignant disbelief.

"Of course not," Dylan grumbled, rolling his eyes. "Sit down and hush."

The girl pouted and made her way over to the chair across from me on the other side of the fireplace, collapsing into it like she had no bones. She folded her arms over her chest and glared at me with perturbed insolence.

"I'm sorry for the confusion," I said.

"Who *are* you?" the young woman asked, scowling at me.

"My name is Morgan Carter. I'm a . . . um. . . ." I shifted my focus to Dylan. "I'm here to help Detective Moorhead investigate your mother's death, Dylan." I looked back at the young woman then and smiled, though it didn't come easy. She was a prickly little thing. "And you are?"

"This is Brittany. She's a friend of mine I met when I was in rehab, and she recently moved here. This is Detective Wyatt Moorhead, Brittany. I told you about him."

"Nice to meet you, Brittany," Wyatt said. "And no need to use a title. Just Wyatt is fine."

"And I suppose you're also a detective?" Dylan said to me.

"Kind of," I replied.

"Morgan is a cryptozoologist," Wyatt said. "Do you know what that is?"

"Yes, I know what a cryptozoologist is," Dylan said. "I'm damaged below the waist, not above the neck."

Brittany snorted a laugh.

Wyatt, ignoring the sarcasm, continued to explain. "Morgan has worked with other law enforcement agencies investigating deaths where a cryptid might have been involved. I've asked her to look at what happened to your mother."

Brittany let out a grunt of disgust. "You shouldn't say things like that to Dylan," she said with an air of righteous indignation. "He's a paraplegic and he's differently abled. Calling him a crip is unacceptable."

I saw Wyatt suppress a smile. "No, *cryptid,* Brittany," he said, enunciating the word carefully. "It's a term for creatures thought to possibly exist even though there's no proof. Like Bigfoot, the Loch Ness Monster, or the Beast of Bray Road. Morgan is a cryptozoologist, meaning she hunts for cryptids."

"Whatever," Brittany muttered, sulking.

Dylan appeared amused, though I wasn't sure by what. "You're here to catch the Beast of Bray Road?" he said to me, his tone clearly skeptical. "I hope you're armed with silver bullets and plenty of wolfsbane."

My hand involuntarily felt for the pendant around my neck, and I was relieved it was securely hidden beneath my shirt. I felt a little silly wearing it. "No silver bullets," I said with a smile, hoping no one would notice I'd avoided mentioning the other item. "I'm here to try to find proof a beast exists and, if it does, to determine whether or not it might have been responsible for your mother's death."

Brittany uncrossed her arms and dropped them to her sides. "Of course, the werewolf killed her," she scoffed. "It happened during a full moon, and everyone knows that's when werewolves come out."

"Brittany, hush, please," Dylan said. He stared at me for an uncomfortable beat of time before turning to Wyatt and saying, "Is she taking over the case now?"

"No, she's simply here to help me. I'm still in charge."

Brittany shifted to the edge of her seat. "Is this the best you can do investigating her death?" she challenged, gesturing toward me. "What about the guy down at the library . . . Percy or Chester or whatever his name is. Dylan said the guy was obsessed with his mom. Have you investigated him?"

"His name is Lester," Wyatt said patiently. "And I—"

"Have you even talked to him?" Brittany demanded. Apparently it hadn't taken her long to abandon the werewolf theory. "Does he have an alibi?"

Wyatt sighed. "Yes, I spoke to him, and no, he doesn't technically have an alibi because he lives alone. Not many people who live alone have alibis for three in the morning."

"Can't you check the GPS data on his phone? They do that all the time on those cop shows on TV," Brittany said.

"Brit, please. Enough," Dylan said, tight-lipped.

Sensing things were heading in the wrong direction, I tried to turn the conversation back to my role in things. "Dylan, if you're okay with it, I'd like to have a look at your mother's things in her bedroom or any other place in the house she used a lot. Did she have a desk?"

Brittany opened her mouth as if to object but a look from Dylan made her shut it again.

Instead of answering me, Dylan looked at Wyatt and asked, "When can I get my mom's car back?"

"Soon. We're almost done with it. Another day, maybe two."

"I need the car, dude."

"Why? You can't drive it," Wyatt said.

I bit my lip and Wyatt winced when he realized what he'd said.

"Thanks for reminding me," Dylan said. "Brittany can drive. She's been driving me around in her car, but my wheelchair doesn't fit well in it."

"Give me another day or two," Wyatt said.

"For what?" Dylan asked, clearly exasperated. "What could you possibly need it for at this point?"

"I'm sorry, Dylan. We have a process, and I'm obligated to follow it. Once all the evidence is in and a final determination has been made by the ME as to the cause of death, we can release it."

"What's the holdup? You said it was an animal attack of some kind. What difference does it make if it's a werewolf or a regular wolf?"

"I have to wait for the report," Wyatt said with impressive patience.

I decided to help Wyatt out by changing the subject. "Dylan, there's something nagging me about what happened to your mom. I'm puzzled by what she was doing out there on Bray Road at three o'clock in the morning. Any ideas?"

"You tell me," he said with a shrug. He looked away and then said, "One thing my mother got very good at when my father was alive was learning when and how to keep things secret. It was a survival tactic because it didn't take much to set my father off, especially when he was drinking. If my mother went out there at that hour without telling anyone, it's because she didn't want anyone to know. As for what her secret was. . . ." He cocked his head to one side and gave me a critical look. "Do you really believe in any of these cryptids you chase around?"

"Let me guess," Brittany said with a flip of her red hair. "She probably thinks Bigfoot is real."

I opened my mouth to answer with my standard plausible-existability line but there was a bright flash of light followed by a loud *pop* as the lamps in the living room went out. Wind howled, rainfall drummed on the roof, and thunder shook the walls and rattled the windows. Newt jumped up and put his head in my lap. He's never been keen on thunderstorms.

"Great," Dylan said, rolling his eyes. "There goes the power again. Connor!"

I'd forgotten about Connor, and he appeared so quickly in the doorway to the hall, I felt certain he'd been lurking just around the corner, eavesdropping on our conversation. Despite his size, he moved across the room with little to no noise in his stocking feet—the only giveaway the occasional creak of a floorboard. "No worries. I've got it," he said. He disappeared into what I could see was the kitchen and seconds later I heard a door open, followed by the rhythmic creaks of someone descending a flight of stairs.

"The circuit breaker panel is in the basement," Dylan explained. "Just one of the many things in life that are unreachable for me. Mom wanted to have an electrician move it to this level, but she never had the money to get it done. That and a lot of other things," he added with a doleful shake of his head, "though not for a lack of trying. My mother thought everything could be fixed if she only had enough money. She was constantly trying get-rich-quick schemes and looking for any way to make an extra buck." He rolled his head back, staring up at the ceiling for a moment. "My God, the things she tried," he said with a derisive chuckle. He raked his teeth over his bottom lip and then lowered his head with a sigh.

"We didn't have any health or car insurance when this happened," he went on, circling his hand over his lap. "And the medical bills before I was approved for Medicaid were brutal. Mom tried to earn extra money doing this work-at-home thing where she did mass mailings of invoices to big companies. The names of the companies, the addresses, and the name of the person to mail the invoice to were provided for her by some guy who said he was a third-party bill handler. All Mom had to do was mail the invoices. They even provided the postage."

It wasn't hard to see where this was going.

"Turned out, it was a scam," Dylan said, confirming my suspicion. "The guy she was working for knew a certain percentage of large companies would simply pay an invoice without ever questioning or verifying the bill. He would research what department and employee paid the bills and then he'd have Mom mail them random invoices using fake company names for stuff they used regularly, like office supplies, toilet paper, and paper towels. Apparently enough of the invoices were paid to make it worth the guy's trouble, but Mom had only been doing it for a few months when the guy was busted. Mom was afraid she might go to jail over it."

There was a click and a hum as the lights came back on. "Thank you, Connor," Dylan muttered.

"I heard about that," Wyatt said. "The local guy was part of a national ring. It's scary how much the thieves were able to swindle before they were caught."

Brittany said, "Tell her about the Bitcoin thing."

"Yeah, that one ended up costing Mom nearly a grand," Dylan said sadly. "And then there was this pyramid scheme involving the online sales of cleaning products. That fell apart in a matter of months. This past winter, she was making plans to sell the house and move us somewhere warmer so I wouldn't have to navigate my wheelchair through snow anymore."

"Did she change her mind?" I asked.

"No," Dylan said with a sad little smile. "She already had a second mortgage on the house, and she owed more than she could get for it." He paused and sighed. "She meant well, and her heart was in the right place, but nothing ever seemed to work for her."

"At least she tried," Wyatt said.

Dylan nodded and swallowed hard as tears welled in his eyes. "Don't get me wrong. I loved my mother and I'm going to miss the hell out of her, but between her frantic need for cleanliness and her cockamamie moneymaking schemes, the woman drove me crazy at times."

"It sounds like she did it all out of love for you," I said.

"There's nothing like a mother's love," Brittany said wistfully.

Dylan visibly deflated, his erect posture sagging. Brittany got up and went over to him, standing behind his wheelchair and massaging his shoulders. She leaned forward and kissed the top of his head.

"Sometimes your mom's ideas worked," she said. "She managed to pay for the wheelchair ramp out front."

“True,” Dylan said, “though the guy who built it donated his labor. That’s also how she adapted the bathroom for me. The contractor only had us pay for supplies.”

“She also worked two jobs most of the time,” Brittany said, continuing her defense of Lydia.

“Where was she working most recently?” I asked.

“She had a part-time position answering phones and doing basic office management stuff for an insurance broker,” Dylan said. “And she did some night shifts at the hospital working as a unit clerk. Neither position was full-time and there were no benefits attached. She kept looking for something full-time with bennies but there wasn’t much she was qualified for. If I had a dollar for every time she said she wished she’d gone to college instead of marrying right after high school, well . . . I’d be better off than I am.” He smiled grimly and then looked at Wyatt.

“Speaking of money, I can’t file a claim for the life insurance until I have a death certificate.”

“I know. I’m hoping the medical examiner’s office will issue it tomorrow.”

“I really need the money. Connor gets free room and board in exchange for helping me and he said he can contribute to some household expenses in the interim, but my disability check barely pays to keep the lights on and food on the table. I’m going to have two mortgages to pay on this place, and my part-time job is temporary. There aren’t a lot of employers out there looking to hire a paraplegic.”

“What does Connor do?” I asked.

“He works night shift in the metal shop of a company that makes prosthetics for people. You know, artificial arms and legs for amputees, that kind of thing. They're all custom and Connor helps mold the metal parts, the joints and sockets, so they fit each person. I met him while doing my therapy at the hospital here—he used to be a physical therapy aide—and we kind of hit it off. Mom was eager to find someone who could help me with some of the, um, more personal aspects of my care and Connor happened to mention he was looking for a new place to live because his lease had run out and he didn't like the landlord or the neighborhood. So, Mom offered him free room and board if he moved in with us and could be here to help me out from time to time. He's been here . . . what, close to two years now?"

"Smart move on her part," I said. "It sounds like she was successful with that scheme at least."

"True," Dylan conceded. "Connor has been a big help to me and it's nice to have a friend to talk to."

"You have me," Brittany whined, pouting and smoothing his hair with her hand.

"Where do you work, Dylan?" I asked, hoping to derail Brittany's pity train.

"I'm doing data entry for the same insurance company my mom worked for. She got me the job. They're changing over to new software, and the owner offered me a job transferring data. It's nice because I can do it from home and the guy is paying me under the table, so it doesn't impact my disability payments." He shot Wyatt a guilty look and Wyatt responded with a shrug of indifference. "But it's only temporary and I'm almost done with it now," Dylan went on. "I've got maybe another month of work left."

"That job is probably the only reason his mom even had a life insurance policy," Brittany said. "Dylan's boss talked her into it after explaining why it was important, particularly with his situation."

I felt sorry for Dylan, though I tried not to show it, sensing he wouldn't appreciate the sentiment. Even so, I felt a certain kinship to him. His life had been turned upside down in the blink of an eye much as mine had been, his future irreparably altered just as mine had been. The big difference was that my life-altering event had left me well off financially with nothing to worry about moneywise, whereas Dylan had been, and likely would continue to be, worrying about money. It gave me some perspective while also serving as yet another reminder of how unfair life can be.

CHAPTER 12

Outside, lightning, thunder, and a howling wind continued to rage as rain beat against the house.

"Would it be okay if I had a look around your mother's bedroom?" I asked Dylan, raising the issue again.

He shrugged. "Whatev. It's the second room on the left down the hall." He nodded toward the door both he and Brittany had come through.

I got up and thought about telling Newt to stay but then decided to have him come with me. Wyatt followed, too, and while I would have preferred to look around on my own, I couldn't very well tell him to go fly a kite. It was his case, after all, and I imagined he could use a break from Dylan. And Dylan from him. Fortunately, no one else followed.

As we walked down the hall, we passed a room on the right that

I gathered was Dylan's. Clothes were strewn about and a gaming console and TV were on a dresser at the foot of the bed. A bifold door to a closet hung open on the other side of the room and I saw a row of shirts hanging low on one side and a dresser on the other. There was a shelf higher up containing stacked boxes. In front of one of two windows looking out onto the driveway was a desk with a laptop on it and a kneehole big enough to fit a wheelchair into. I gathered Dylan was largely independent and wondered what exactly Connor did for him. Or Brittany for that matter.

Across from Dylan's room was a bathroom with a nice wide doorway, a low open sink that a wheelchair could roll under, and a walk-in—or rather roll-in—shower. At the end of the hall were two smaller bedrooms. The one on the right had a made-up double bed, a dresser, and a nightstand. The furniture was mismatched stuff, but the room was neat, clean, and devoid of dust and clutter. A pair of large men's slippers beside the bed suggested this room was Connor's.

A door at the end of the hallway hid a stackable washer-dryer unit and overhead shelves filled with linens and an assortment of laundry products.

Lydia's room was on the left and I realized that in keeping with her storied history of self-sacrifice, she had given the larger bedroom space over to her son, no doubt making it easier for him to get around in his wheelchair and giving him access to the modified bathroom. Her bedroom had attached to it a small bathroom with a toilet, sink, and stall shower, but it was barely big enough to turn around in, much less maneuver a wheelchair.

The room had a few obviously feminine touches: lacy curtains on the window, a white spread and pink throw pillows on the simple twin bed, and a mirrored vanity with a stool, the seat of which was covered in a pink-and-green floral material. The top of the vanity displayed a hairbrush; a container with some mascara, lipstick, and face powder; some hand cream; and a second container with four colors of nail polish and a set of manicuring tools—everything neatly lined up and meticulously clean. There were no hairs in the brush, no drips on the nail polish bottles, no dark smears on the outside of the mascara tube.

In addition to the vanity, Lydia's bedroom had a tall five-drawer dresser painted glossy white, though a closer look revealed a few marks and chips. There was a closet next to the bathroom, and upon opening the door, I was surprised to discover it was a deep space with shelving and plenty of room to hang things. Closet space had apparently come at the expense of bathroom size, though it didn't appear as if Lydia needed it. There were two pairs of shoes on the floor—basic black pumps and a pair of brown loafers—and a half dozen blouses, two pairs of dress slacks, and a mere three dresses hung above them. To the left, at the far end of the closet, was a second, smaller dresser.

I took a quick look through the drawers of the dresser outside the closet, finding nothing but the expected items of clothing, all of them basic, simple, and well-worn, every piece neatly folded and placed in its respective drawer. It was obvious Lydia Palmer hadn't been a clotheshorse—one more piece of evidence demonstrating how she'd prioritized her minimal budget for her son's needs over her own.

I looked through cardboard boxes on the closet shelves, finding in the first one old photos organized in rows by what I assumed was the date they had been taken. One of the pictures was of Dylan, his mother, and a man I assumed was Ervin from about ten years earlier. It was a happy family moment captured as the trio posed in front of the Chicago art piece officially named *Cloud Gate,* though most folks knew it by its nickname of the Bean. Dylan's father had been a handsome man who had passed on his dark curly hair and overall height to his son. All three of them had big smiles and I wondered about the moments in their lives that hadn't been captured in a pose, the ones that had led to all those domestic calls Wyatt had mentioned.

Another of the boxes held bills and dunning notices, while a third box was filled with letters. I thought about setting the box of letters aside to go through them but realized it would take too much time. Then I considered trying to sneak them out of the house but there were too many of them and I didn't want to invade Lydia's privacy more than I had to. Finally, I settled on a quick thumb through of the contents, looking at the addresses and dates on the envelopes. The bulk of them went back a decade or more and the recent ones were mostly holiday cards from acquaintances.

I returned the boxes to the shelf and moved on to the drawers of the closet dresser, finding more clothing that had been washed, carefully folded, and neatly stored according to color. What I found didn't strike me as much as what I didn't. There was no sexy lingerie, not even a nice set of matching bra and panties, something I would think any woman would have on hand if she was in a romantic relationship.

I poked my head out of the closet and saw Wyatt sitting on the bed doing something on his phone. "What kind of underwear was Lydia wearing?" I asked him.

It took him a second to register the fact that I was speaking to him, and then he looked perplexed. "Underwear?" he repeated.

"Yes, you know, bra and panties."

Wyatt blushed. "I know what underwear is. I just wasn't expecting the question. It wasn't anything special. Plain white cotton undies, if I remember right. I think the bra might have been pink. Why?"

"If we try to ascribe Lydia's presence out there on Bray Road at three in the morning to some type of romantic assignation, I'd expect her to have had on sexy lingerie or, at the very least, something new and matching. I don't see anything of the sort among her clothing."

"I know the ME said there was no evidence of sexual assault."

I ducked back into the closet and focused on a large, elaborately carved wooden jewelry box with colored inlays located at the far end of the upper shelf. It looked oddly out of place amid the simple plainness of the other items Lydia owned, and that alone piqued my curiosity. I eased it down from the shelf—it was surprisingly heavy—and set it on the dresser. Inside were a few pieces of costume jewelry—organized by type and color—a gold wedding band, and one pair of nice pearl earrings with a matching necklace.

Disappointed, I was trying to put the box back on the shelf when Newt goosed me from behind with his nose. I juggled the box, barely managing to hang on to it after several clumsy grabs. I set it back on the dresser and was about to turn around and chastise Newt when I noticed something irregular on the bottom-left side of the box. Somehow, in my awkward attempts to keep from dropping the thing, I'd managed to open a hidden drawer. I looked back at Newt, who was grinning and wagging his tail.

"Did you do that on purpose?"

From outside the closet, Wyatt said, "Did you say something?"

"Just talking to my dog."

I took a closer look at the box, taking in the fine craftsmanship and the way the carved wooden design and inlays neatly obscured the outline of the drawer. I kept a stock of similar puzzle boxes in my store, though none as big or lovely as this one. Upon closer inspection, I spotted the piece of wood I'd unknowingly managed to slide to release the drawer mechanism.

I pulled the drawer fully open and found a tiny booklet inside about the same size as one of those pocket notepads Jon carried around all the time. The cover appeared to be made of reddish brown leather that was cracked around the edges and darkened in spots. As I opened it, a peculiar odor emanated from the pages, which were yellowed with age and brittle along the edges. Written on the inside-front endsheet in faded blue ink was *F.N. March 1930–September 1930.* I carefully sifted through the inside pages, finding rows containing handwritten dates, initials, and dollar amounts. About halfway through, I came across a folded piece of yellowed paper tucked snugly between the pages.

I glanced over my shoulder to make sure Wyatt was still outside the closet. Then, after a split second of indecision, I closed the ledger with the paper still inside, slid it into the pocket of my pants, shut the hidden drawer, and put the box back on the shelf.

CHAPTER 13

"Any great insights?" Dylan asked hopefully as we prepared to leave.

Brittany sat on the couch intently picking at a cuticle, her long red hair obscuring her face.

"Not yet," I told him. "There are still a lot of questions."

"Such as?"

"Well, as I mentioned before, the question of why your mother was out there on Bray Road at three in the morning."

Dylan nodded, staring out a nearby window as heavy rain continued to pelt the outside world. His hands on the wheels of his chair rocked it back and forth. "I wish I knew," he said.

"We both do," Brittany said, inserting herself into the conversation again. She sat back and flipped her hair over her shoulder. "Do you think the werewolf put some kind of spell on her? Because they can do that, you know. They're like vampires. They hypnotize their victims."

I studied her for several seconds, trying to determine if she was serious or just messing with me. I half expected her to crack a grin, but she stared back at me perfectly straight-faced.

"While it appears certain aspects of Lydia's injuries are suggestive of an animal attack," I said, "the idea of a werewolf being the culprit strikes me as highly improbable, bordering on ludicrous. There's no evidence to support it."

"Of course there is," Brittany argued. It seemed impossible but her eyes appeared to grow even bigger. "What about those scratches on Lydia's car? Dylan said they're big gashes with the paint scraped right off."

"There are things about those scratches that don't make sense."

"Oh, really? Like what?" Brittany challenged, jutting her chin at me.

I decided to ignore her question because I had a feeling this was a debate I'd never win. I was wedded to using logic and facts. Brittany, on the other hand, appeared to live in a fantasy world.

"I'm not ready to discuss any of my findings yet," I hedged. "I don't mean to be obtuse. It's just that I've found I do better interpreting things when I have all the evidence in front of me."

Brittany opened her mouth to say something more, but Dylan beat her to it. "Give her a chance, Brit," he said. Then he smiled at me. "I appreciate you looking into it at all, even if you are a somewhat, um, unorthodox investigator." He shifted his attention to Wyatt. "And, dude, sorry if I was snippy with you before. I'm just frustrated and I . . . um . . . I miss my mom, and I want some answers." His eyes welled with tears, and he blinked hard, looking away. My heart went out to him.

Wyatt said, "I know this is hard, Dylan, and I promise I'll get things settled for you as soon as I can. I'll see if I can get the car back to you tomorrow."

Dylan nodded, whipped his chair around, and wheeled out of the room, disappearing down the hall. Brittany watched him go before turning back and giving us a sad look. "It's been so hard on him losing his mom like this, you know? He really misses her. And he doesn't do well with emo stuff."

"I can relate," I said. "I lost both of my parents a few years ago unexpectedly. It's quite a shock to one's system."

"Yeah, but I'm betting your parents weren't killed by a werewolf," Brittany said with classic one-upmanship.

Not knowing how to respond to this, I ignored it and turned to Wyatt instead. "We should get going." After putting our shoes on, we said goodbye to Brittany and left.

The heavy downpour had eased into a steady, pattering rainfall and the air outside was redolent with the scents of wet lumber, rain-drenched grass, mud, and the early-spring flowers budding in front of the house. Once we were settled in my car, the overwhelming aroma switched to that of wet dog—decidedly less pleasant.

"Sorry the search of Lydia's bedroom was a bust," Wyatt said as I drove us back to my motel. "I could have told you as much since we'd already been through it, but I figured you'd want to look for yourself."

Guilt washed over me, and I couldn't look at him. "Thanks for tolerating my whims," I said. "I know I can be stubborn about doing things my own way." This was as much of an admission as I was willing to offer for the time being.

"Yeah, Jon mentioned something along those lines," Wyatt said. I was relieved to see him punctuate the remark with a smile and a wink.

"Brittany is a bit of an odd one, isn't she?" I said, hoping to change the subject. "Does she truly believe there's a werewolf running around out on Bray Road?"

"Are you sure there isn't one?" Wyatt challenged. There was a twinkle in his eye, making me think he wasn't serious. At least I hoped he wasn't. When I didn't rise to his provocation, he said, "If you want to come by the station tomorrow to chat some more, I'll be there by eight in the morning. Or just call me."

I told him I wanted to play things by ear and see how the day progressed but promised to call him if I needed anything. After watching him walk through the rain to his car, I took Newt for a quick walk, getting soaked in the process. When I slipped a hand into my pocket to get the key card for the outside motel door, I felt the small ledger I'd stashed in there earlier. Was it related somehow to the coins Lydia had had in her pocket? The two were connected by dates if nothing else, though I couldn't quite put the puzzle together yet.

Back in my room, I dried my hands and then carefully slid the ledger from my pocket and set it on the desk before shrugging out of my coat and toweling off my hair. Once I was relatively dry, I gingerly opened the small book so I could take a closer look at the pages. Some of the entries were faded; others were illegible due to bleeding ink. The money amounts weren't large, at least by current standards, but they would have been significant in 1930.

When I got to the folded page tucked inside, I removed it and gently undid it, spreading it out flat on the desk. At the top of the page, there was the date of September 17, 1930, and scrawled handwriting followed. It was a letter from someone named Frank N., though I struggled to make out some of the words because the ink had smeared in places. It appeared to be newsy stuff, something about a taxman and then a recitation of daily minutiae that seemed random and oddly worded. The contents weren't particularly exciting, but my heart did a little leap when I saw whom the letter was addressed to. A quick internet search verified my suspicions.

I used my phone to snap pictures of the letter as well as of the outside and the inside of the small ledger. Then I sent it all to Rita in a text with some instructions. When I was done, I delicately folded the letter again and stuck it back in the booklet where I'd found it.

I had a text from Devon asking me to give him a call, but before I did, I checked my email to make sure I hadn't missed anything from Jon. I thought, hoped, he might inquire as to how things were going, but there was nothing. Newt sensed my disappointment and came over to rest his big head in my lap and look up at me with those soulful eyes of his. It didn't make everything better, but it helped.

I missed Jon, not just romantically but also as a friend. Calling him while in the middle of these investigations, and occasionally having him by my side during them, had been fun, exciting, and at times comforting. We'd made a good team, or so I'd thought, and his absence and recent silence left me feeling oddly incomplete. I desperately wanted to call him to share what I'd found and bounce ideas off him.

I sat there mentally debating the idea for a few minutes until I managed to talk myself out of it and then wondered if this was an example of the stubbornness Jon had mentioned to Wyatt. I felt that I was merely being practical, that it made sense to wait until I'd talked with Rita and Devon first. Then I could decide what to do about Jon.

I called the landline at my store back home, knowing Rita would be there and hoping Devon might be, too. Rita answered before the first ring had finished.

"It's about time," she said with a hint of irritation after I greeted her. "You should have checked in hours ago."

"Sorry about that. I spent the day with Detective Moorhead, and he kept me busy."

"Any progress?"

"Not really. I have a lot of questions, though."

"Anything I can help with?"

"As a matter of fact, yes. I sent you a text message and some pictures a few minutes ago with some instructions."

"Oh. Sorry. You know how I am with this newfangled technology," she said. "You're the only person who ever sends me text messages and it happens so rarely, I forget to check."

"Well, check it now and put on your historian's hat. Dig up anything you can for me on the history of this area, particularly around the 1920s and thirties."

This request was met with a long silence before Rita said, "Oh, my goodness. Are these for real?"

"I gather you're looking at the pictures I sent you?"

"I am."

"Then I need *you* to answer that question."

"I'm confused. Aren't you supposed to be looking for werewolves?"

"I am, but there's something bugging me about the victim, and I think it might be related to the ledger and letter I found. She had them stashed inside a hidden drawer in a jewelry box."

"I can dig into the history, but in order to know if the items are legitimate, I'd need to see them in person."

"The pictures will have to suffice for now."

"I know someone in the area who might be able to look at them for you and give you a better idea. Bill . . . Bill. . . . Crap, I can't recall his last name off the top of my head—it's Thompson or Thornton . . . something with a T. He lives in Lake Geneva, if I remember right. George used him a lot to verify the authenticity of some of the older books we had. I have his contact information written down somewhere."

"Send it to me as soon as you can," I said.

"Will do. I'll try to find it when I get home this evening."

"Thanks. Is Devon there by chance? I need to speak to him, too."

"He is. I figured you two must have something to discuss when I saw him waving frantically and pointing at the phone once he realized who I was talking to. Hold on."

Rita put me on hold briefly and then Devon picked up and greeted me with a cheery "Hey, boss!"

"Hey, Devon. Whatcha got for me?"

"Some interesting stuff. Let's talk about your coins first. The 1920 Standing Liberty quarter is probably the most valuable of the three. If it had an S mint mark and was uncirculated, it would be worth a pretty penny, if you'll excuse the pun. There's one listed on eBay right now with an asking price just over six grand. But the one you have is probably worth between fifteen and a hundred dollars, give or take. Since your coins have some wear and they're tarnished, I'd expect the lower end of the range. The 1925 wheat penny is interesting because some were minted that year with the L in 'Liberty' offset so it appears on the rim of the coin. If yours was one of those it would value out somewhere between five hundred bucks and a grand. If it was uncirculated and bore a D for the Denver mint, the prices get quite impressive, fetching anywhere from two grand to seventy-five thou."

"Wow," I said.

"Yeah, I need to start paying more attention to cash in the till. Your coin, however, is worth about a dollar. And finally, the Mercury head dime dated 1924. Honestly, before I got into researching these, I thought it was going to be the most valuable of the three but it's not. It's worth around three dollars, maybe three and a half."

"Interesting." I pondered their presence in Lydia Palmer's pocket and made a mental note to ask Wyatt about Lydia's recent finances, assuming he'd looked into them. He might not have, given that her death didn't appear to be a homicide. "What else?"

"I couldn't find a lot on Lydia Palmer or her son, though I came across one thing that might be of interest to you. Lydia sued the sheriff's department there in Walworth County."

"What?" I couldn't hide my shock, not over the suit, but over the fact Wyatt had hidden this detail from me. "What is the basis of the suit?"

"It claimed Dylan's paralysis resulted from the actions of the first deputy on the scene. According to the police report, the deputy didn't think Dylan was breathing and couldn't find a pulse, so he rendered CPR as first aid. But in turning Dylan over from where he landed after being ejected from the car and then positioning his neck to assist his breathing, he caused spinal cord bruising so severe, it resulted in Dylan's paralysis."

"Wouldn't the officer have been protected by the Good Samaritan law?"

"There is some vague terminology in the law, like the first responder must be providing reasonable care within the standards of practice, that sort of thing. But defining what's reasonable and standard is where things got murky. The deputy swore he followed proper neck precautions in moving Dylan and administering first aid and there was no one who could contradict him because he was the only one on scene for a spell and the medical experts couldn't say for sure that the spinal cord injury wasn't due to Dylan being ejected from the car. The case has dragged on for, well, for nearly three years now."

"I'd be surprised if it goes anywhere."

"Perhaps, but juries can do funny things when confronted with a fatherless teenager in a wheelchair. Might make them inclined to settle."

"Hm, good point. Do you know the name of the lawyer for the Palmers?"

"Yeah. The primary one is a woman out of Lake Geneva named Gillian Ashcroft. She's in a firm with two other lawyers."

I jotted down the name. "This is great. Now see if you can find anything on Lydia Palmer's finances for me."

"I'll try. I'm combing through her social media, too."

"Good. Look for any mention of coin collectors or an interest in old coins."

"Got it."

"And see if she followed any history sites or historical societies, specifically for this area between 1920 and 1935. Extra points for finding anything on Prohibition Era stuff."

"It would help if I could get access to her computer or phone."

"Yeah, not sure I'll be able to swing that one, but I'll keep trying."

"Okay. Moving on. As for Dylan, it looks like he had quite the little crime spree before his accident. Mostly petty stuff like shoplifting, tagging, and the like. He was quite proud of his antics and posted about them on TikTok and Instagram."

"Yeah, the detective I'm working with mentioned the juvie stuff. Not sure it's relevant, though. How about the other name I sent you earlier: Paul McNamara, the guy who swears he saw a werewolf on Bray Road a couple nights before Lydia Palmer was killed?"

"Nothing much to report there. The guy's clean as can be. No red flags. Not even a parking ticket."

"Good to know. Thanks. Excellent work as usual, Devon."

"Anything else I can do for you, boss?"

"Not right now. Wait. There is something. See what you can find on a romantic suspense novelist by the name of Jordan Sumner."

"Looking for new inventory?" I heard the gentle tap of Devon's fingers on a keyboard and the answer came seconds later. "Actually, you already have her books on the shelves."

I debated telling him Jordan was a man but decided against it. It would be more fun to let him dig around in the online rumor mills.

"Isn't this author stuff more Rita's territory?" he asked.

"I have her doing something else and don't want her getting distracted."

"Got it. On it."

"Thanks, Dev." After a brief discussion about how busy the store had been—a good sign so early in the season—I ended the call.

While I still had a lot of questions, I felt as if I'd made a bit of progress, and I wanted to talk it out with someone. A specific someone.

After several minutes of annoying internal debate, I gave in and placed a call to Jon. When it went to voicemail, I disconnected without leaving a message.

CHAPTER 14

In need of busywork, I spent a few hours on my laptop researching what I could find about Elkhorn, its history, werewolves in general, and the Beast of Bray Road in particular. I learned that in stark contrast to Elkhorn's dark, beastly reputation, the city was also known as the Christmas Card Town. It had earned this moniker after an artist named Cecile Johnson was commissioned by the Ford Motor Company to produce images of small-town life. Johnson recalled how Elkhorn had been the subject of a 1952 show called *The March of Time,* which highlighted the town's elaborate preparations for the holidays. Most of the decorations and events were centered around the large town square park I'd driven by earlier, though the majestic remnant of the entrance to the old bank building got some attention as well. These scenes provided the inspiration Johnson used to create six wintertime watercolors later chosen by a major greeting card company to be featured as Christmas cards.

The city of Elkhorn had embraced its newfound fame then and still did by continuing to go all out with their decorations and activities every year, including a Christmas Card Town parade. This homey holiday heritage contrasted sharply with the chaotic mayhem of werewolf lore.

While my trip to the lighter side of the city's history was fun, I was eager to explore the darker stuff. I dug out the articles I'd brought with me from my parents' files.

Most of them were centered on werewolf ideology, which I found fascinating, though I thought it might have been why my parents had shown less interest in the Beast of Bray Road than they had in other cryptids. The possibility of a man turning into a wolf was more "out there" than the plausible existability of many of the other cryptids they had pursued.

Unlike my parents, I found the symbolism and mythology surrounding werewolves intriguing. Werewolf lore dated back thousands of years. In fact, werewolves are one of the oldest monsters we human beings have managed to dream up. Symbolically, they are thought to represent a basic duality of human nature: the inability to overcome our base desires and primal instincts in much the same way a werewolf is unable to control its conversion into a savage beast.

While the terms "werewolf" and "lycanthrope" are often used interchangeably, they are distinctly different. Werewolves are thought to be powerless against the forces making them change from human to wolf form, subject to the pull of the full moon and, sometimes, extremes of emotion. On the other hand, lycanthropes—

a term derived from Greek words that, loosely translated, means "wolfman"—are thought to have more control over the change from their human form and to utilize a type of magic or simple will-power. Whereas werewolves are considered aggressive, animal-istic, and filled with out-of-control bloodlust, lycanthropes are thought to retain more of their human characteristics and may be associated with traits like enhanced wisdom.

Wolf-human hybrids appear in several cultures throughout history. The ancient Egyptians had Anubis, the god of the dead depicted in ancient hieroglyphs as having a man's body and a jackal's head. Anubis dictated the fate of souls by weighing their hearts against an ostrich feather. The hearts of people who had led a decent life would balance with the feather, and their souls would then be allowed to ascend to the heavens and live in paradise with Osiris. This is often credited as being the origin of phrases like "light of heart" or "heavy of heart."

In Greek mythology there was the legend of Lycaon, the king of Arcadia and an irascible fellow who wanted to challenge the omnipotence of the gods. To test Zeus, the king invited the god to dinner and fed him a meal containing the remains of Lycaon's own son. Zeus, realizing what Lycaon had done, became enraged and punished Lycaon by turning him into a wolf, a form he felt was more appropriate for eating human flesh.

There are also mentions of werewolves in Nordic legends, most notably in the *Saga of the Volsungs,* in which a father and son find some wolf pelts possessing the power to turn one into a wolf for ten days. After donning the pelts, the duo embarks on a killing spree that ultimately results in the father attacking his own son.

One of the oldest mentions of a werewolf can be found in *The*

Epic of Gilgamesh, a heroic story from ancient Mesopotamia in which Gilgamesh, a Sumerian warrior, rejects the advances of Ishtar, the goddess of fertility and love, because he's afraid she'll turn him into a wolf the way she did her previous lover.

I did some online digging and found two articles that speculated on how people afflicted with rabies might have helped create and advance werewolf lore. Late-stage symptoms of rabies include excess saliva production, agitation, unusual vocalizations that can sound like a bark or a howl, and severe muscle spasms that can be quite painful. There was no treatment for rabies prior to 1885, and people who were bitten might not have shown symptoms for weeks or even months after the bite occurred, making it hard to correlate the two.

In medieval times, werewolves were feared as much as, if not more than, witches and treated much the same. I found horrific drawings online of people being beheaded or burned at the stake because they were believed to have been werewolves.

Some online sources believed silver bullets first became attached to werewolves in the 1700s when a man killed a large, supposedly man-eating wolf known as the Beast of Gévaudan by shooting it with bullets forged from a melted-down, previously blessed silver chalice. Other sources claimed the idea of silver bullets originated with storytellers in the twentieth century.

The connection between werewolves and a full moon was a thoroughly modern contrivance brought about by twentieth-century movies. While the ancient Greeks and Romans believed wolves tended to hunt or howl more during a full moon, the simple truth is they howl at night regardless of the moon's phase. Despite this, even in modern times, there are those who believe the phases of the moon play a role in human behavior, triggering reckless or chaotic actions in some. Chat with any EMT, paramedic, police officer, or ER staffer and they'll swear the full-moon shifts are always the busiest and most bizarre.

It was after midnight when I finally decided to call it quits, my mind filled with images of barbaric sacrifices, tortured deaths, and big, bloody, sharp teeth that would have scared the bejesus out of Little Red Riding Hood. Plus, the storm had revved up again outside, with howling winds and rain flinging against my window. I put my laptop and papers aside and was about to take Newt out for one last walk, planning to stick close to the overhang in front of the hotel, when my phone rang with a call from an unknown number. I could have—and probably should have—ignored it, because answering that call took me into a realm darker than any I'd spent the past few hours reading about.

CHAPTER 15

"Hello, Morgan."

I gasped, unable to help myself. The voice of David Johnson, or rather the man I knew by that name—an identity he'd stolen—was instantly recognizable.

"Please, don't hang up. I need to talk to you."

Gooseflesh rose along my arms and raced down my back. It didn't help that my reading material for the past few hours had at times been gruesome and terrifying. I was already close to the edge. This had me teetering.

"I don't want to talk to you," I managed to say, my throat dry as dust.

"Then don't. Just listen. And take some notes. Do you have pen and paper handy?"

Ridiculously, I nodded before coming to my senses. I pulled the phone away from my ear, my finger poised over the disconnect icon. For what seemed like an eternity, I sat there frozen, unsure of what to do. And then I put the phone in speaker mode and set it down. I picked up the pen and notepad I'd left on the bedside stand. "What do you want?"

Perhaps sensing my willingness to tap the little red phone icon at any second, he talked fast. "I know you think I killed your parents. I didn't but I know who did. Or at least I know now. It was the other couple in the Barrens. They killed someone else, and your parents witnessed it. I'm guilty of not doing anything to try to save your parents but I'm not guilty of killing them. Had I not stormed off into the woods to cool down after your father confronted me, I'd probably be dead now, too."

Fine by me. "Why'd you run off, then?"

"Because I knew how it would look once the police got involved and started checking into my background. I wasn't honest with you about who I was, and I understand you feeling betrayed because of it. But despite my deception, I genuinely came to care for you, Morgan. I ran because I feared for my own safety and because I knew I'd be the primary suspect in your parents' deaths."

"*I* was the primary suspect, you ass!"

"I know, I know. And I'm sorry, but it all worked out in the end, didn't it?"

"For you maybe. My parents are still dead. And I haven't been fully ruled out as a suspect, thanks to you. I live every day with suspicion hanging over my head."

"But you weren't arrested. I knew you'd be able to afford a decent lawyer whereas I would have been on my own with some public defender. Had you been arrested, I would have come forth with what I saw."

"Right. Easy to say now. I don't believe you. You're a psycho."

Newt, sensing my rising pique, came over and nudged my free hand. I stroked his head not only to reassure him but to calm myself.

"I don't blame you for hating me, Morgan, but whatever you think of me, I'm not a killer. I saved your life back in January, remember?"

"Did you? Because all I remember is you being there while a lot of shooting was going on. For all I know, most of those bullets coming at me could have been fired by you. It seems like death and mayhem follow you wherever you go."

I heard him let out an exasperated sigh. "Okay, do me and yourself a favor and put that brilliant mind of yours to work. Research a couple of people by the names of Francesca Allbright—that's Allbright with two Ls—and Nicholas Vincento, both in New Jersey. Search for both names together."

Against my better judgment and wondering if I was being pulled down some absurd rabbit hole by David's latest ruse, I scribbled down the names.

"Spell both names fully," I said, wanting to be sure I got things right. My request was met with silence. "David? Are you there?" I realized the line had gone dead, and punched the mattress in frustration. "Oof!"

Newt let out a concerned whine.

"I'm okay, buddy," I said, patting him on the head. But was I? My hands shook and my thoughts were whirling like the spin cycle on my washing machine. Was David outside my motel right now watching me? He'd done it before. Was this some kind of disturbed mental game he was playing? What I knew about him, or at least thought I knew, led me to believe his intentions were anything but kind. Yet my gut didn't buy it. It felt—I don't know—wrong somehow.

Good God, Jon is right about me.

I grabbed Newt's leash, put on my coat, and headed outside armed with false bravado and my half-blind dog. I stared into the surrounding darkness as soon as I set foot out the door but saw nothing. More important, Newt didn't react at all. I walked the entire perimeter of the motel, getting soaked in the process. I even scanned the parking lot of the shopping mall next door. By the time I came back inside, I was convinced I'd overreacted. My nerves were calmer, my mind steadier, and after toweling off both myself and Newt, I settled in with my laptop and the names David had given me.

The most recent hit I found was a couple of months old. It was a news article detailing a double homicide in Elizabeth, New Jersey, the victims of which were Nicholas Vincento and Francesca Allbright, an unmarried couple living together. They had been found dead inside their home, shot execution-style, and items found at the scene suggested it might have been a drug deal gone wrong or a turf war killing. Grainy pictures of the two victims were included, though they looked much younger in the photos—high school or college age—than the late forties they reportedly were when they died. And as I studied the pictures, I had a niggling sense I'd seen them before.

The second link I found was for one of those crime-based blogs where the writer shared theories about unexplained or unsolved murders. When I read his theory about the Vincento–Allbright murder, my world began to slip sideways. Tiny lights danced along the periphery of my vision, and I felt an all-too-familiar tightness in my chest. A feeling of impending doom washed over me, my breathing grew labored, and my heart sped up from a casual walk to a full-throttled gallop. I knew I was having a panic attack and so did Newt. He climbed up onto the bed and stretched his body alongside mine, resting his head on my heaving chest. I squeezed my eyes closed, buried my hands in the soft ruff around his neck, and focused on controlling my breathing, exhaling slowly through pursed lips while mentally reciting a chant.

You're okay. You're okay. You're okay.

Gradually, my heart slowed, my breathing eased, and the feeling of dread dissipated. I picked up my phone and called Jon. No hesitation or second-guessing myself this time. It rang and rang while I mentally pleaded with him to answer. On the sixth ring, he did.

"Morgan?" His voice had the slur of sleepiness to it, and only then did I realize it was nearly two in the morning.

"Oh, Jon! Thank goodness you answered. I was afraid you wouldn't."

"I was asleep. Are you okay?"

"Yes. Well, no, but yes. Oh, hell. I'm not making any sense. I'm fine, at least physically. I'm sorry; I didn't realize how late it was. I got a call from David just a bit ago."

A pause. "David? *The* David?"

"Yes."

"Is he following you again?"

"No. At least I don't think so. His call was short and succinct.

He gave me two names to look up on the internet and hung up before I could ask him any questions. He told me to type both names together and what I found has me kind of stunned."

"Why? Do you think he killed someone else?"

"No. Quite the opposite. The two people whose names he gave me were found dead in their home in Elizabeth, New Jersey, a couple of months ago, both shot execution-style. There was a newspaper article about the killing, and it said the police were investigating rumors the couple had been dealing drugs, and their deaths were related to that. But then I read a crime blog, and the author, a retired detective, said he'd talked to an anonymous source at the Elizabeth Police Department who thought the killings might be mob related."

"A crime blog," Jon said tiredly.

"I know. It sounds far-fetched. Even the guy who has the blog thought so at first. But now he thinks these two were contract killers for some Mafia group or gang, and they were either killed by their own people or by a rival gang. The blogger guy did some digging around and discovered the two victims were suspects in several other killings in recent years, including—get this—the disappearance three years ago, right around the time of my parents' murders, of a New Jersey criminal with Mafia ties by the name of Joey Mangino. Joey's cell phone last pinged in northeastern Cumberland County before the signal was lost, and subsequent searches there didn't find him, or a body, or any trail to follow. But guess what lies in eastern Cumberland County, just a few miles away? Part of the Pine Barrens. The part where my parents were killed."

"Okay," Jon said with a heavy sigh. "What does this have to do with David?"

"Both the newspaper article and the blog site had pictures of the murder victims, and while they're about twenty years out-of-date, I recognize them. Do you remember me telling you there was a couple camping near us in the Pine Barrens when my parents were murdered? And that this couple supposedly told the police they saw me arguing with my father?"

"You admitted you argued with your father."

"Yes, but there was also a couple who said they witnessed the argument."

"Are you saying it was this couple?"

"Yes! Did your uncle have any idea these two had Mafia connections or might have been involved in the disappearance of this Joey Mangino guy when he interviewed them?"

"I don't know, Morgan. Besides, David could be making this up, taking advantage of a couple of deaths and a rumor to try to convince you he's innocent. Heck, he might have killed this couple and started the rumors himself. I wouldn't put it past him."

"Seems a bit of a stretch," I said, frowning because it really wasn't *that* much of a stretch. David was smart and all too clever. "David said if he hadn't stormed off into the woods after my father confronted him, he might have been killed, too. I think my parents might have seen these two people kill Joey Mangino, forcing the killers to then eliminate them."

Several seconds of contemplative silence ticked by before Jon said, "I don't know, Morgan. I think you—"

"I saw them, Jon. I saw them there in the Barrens. I'm certain of it."

"Absolutely, positively certain? No doubt at all?"

Crap. "Ninety percent certain."

Jon let out an exasperated sigh. "Okay. What are the names?"

I gave them to him, making sure I told him to spell Allbright with two Ls. "Type both names into Google together."

"Okay, hold on." I heard the screech of a chair being pulled across the floor, followed by the tapping of keys on a keyboard. "Are you sure you're okay, Morgan?"

"I'm fine."

"No panic attack?"

"I had the start of one a bit ago, but I was able to stop it in its tracks."

"Good. Okay, I've got the article and the blog. Let me read them and call you back."

"Okay."

I disconnected the call and spent the waiting time conducting additional internet searches for the two names, only to be thoroughly frustrated. Other than their recent deaths and the one news article, the lives of Nicholas and Francesca were something of an enigma, at least where the internet was concerned. Was that intentional? Had they purposely lived off the grid given what they might have done for a living?

When Jon finally called back an hour later, I bypassed a normal greeting and answered with "Well? What do you think?"

He laughed and the sound of it rang pleasurably in my ears. "Slow down. I agree there might be something to it, but we shouldn't jump to conclusions. The speculation of one imaginative, unnamed source at the police department is hardly a reliable indictment."

"But the blog guy is a retired detective," I insisted. While I appreciated Jon's ability to be the voice of reason, at moments like this it frustrated me. I forgave him quickly, however, after what he said next.

"I called Uncle Karl, who didn't appreciate being awakened at three in the morning, and asked him if he'd looked into the backgrounds of these two when he used them as witnesses."

In an ugly twist of fate, Karl Swenson, the New Jersey detective who had investigated my parents' murders and pegged me as the primary suspect, happened to be Jon's uncle. Because, you know, my history with Jon wasn't complicated enough already.

"Uncle Karl said the names from the newspaper article didn't sound familiar and he doesn't think those were the names they gave him," Jon went on. "He couldn't be sure the people pictured in the story you found were the ones he interviewed three years ago but he was certain he'd checked their IDs. It's routine."

"If they were professional killers, they probably had multiple IDs under a host of different names."

"Okay, let's say your theory is right. Why did they leave your parents there for the police to find but not this Joey what's-his-name?"

"Maybe they had connections to this Mangino guy and didn't want his body found. They knew I was there, and they saw me and my father arguing. They must have killed Mangino after I'd stormed off in the car. When they realized my parents saw what they did, they knew they had to silence them. They killed them the way they did to set me up as the suspect and cover their own tracks, a ruse that worked, at least in the short term."

"It's a bit of a stretch but not totally improbable," Jon said. "Uncle Karl said he'll look into it. I'll let you know what he finds."

Relief washed over me. “Thank you. I appreciate you hearing me out on this.” After a moment’s hesitation, I added, “I’ve really missed talking with you.”

“I’ve missed you, too,” he said, giving me a glimmer of hope. “More than I like. Other than your crazy ex stalking you, how’s the investigation going? Is Wyatt keeping an eye on you?”

I bristled at the idea of anyone needing to keep an eye on me but kept it to myself. “He is,” I said. “I’m being careful.” So, okay, maybe not the whole truth. But I was trying.

“Find any weird creatures?”

“Not yet, though there is an eyewitness account worth looking into. And some things about the victim are bugging me, little details that don’t seem to fit.”

“Such as?”

I couldn’t help but smile, knowing I’d piqued his interest. “Well, for one thing, she had these 1920s coins in her pocket when she was killed. And in her bedroom closet I found a wooden box with a hidden drawer that held a letter tucked inside a small ledger book . . . pocket-sized, old-looking.”

“So, she liked collecting old stuff.”

“Maybe. But since we’re already talking about Mafia types and gangsters, there may be a connection to the stuff I found and Al Capone. The letter was addressed to someone named Alphonse and signed Frank N. Frank Nitti was one of Capone’s lieutenants, a right-hand man.”

“Your victim had a letter addressed to Capone, written by one of his henchmen?” Jon’s skepticism rang clear.

“Maybe. I’m not sure if the items are legit, but I’m looking into it. The point is, why did my victim have these items hidden away?

Why did she have those coins on her person when she was killed? And what was she doing out there in the middle of nowhere at three in the morning?"

"You think she found some kind of hidden cache belonging to Capone," Jon said, and I could tell from his tone he thought the idea bordered on the absurd.

"Until I can find a better explanation, I'm leaving all options open. Besides, what seems more far-fetched: a secret Capone treasure or a werewolf on the loose?"

Jon avoided answering by changing the subject. "Wyatt told me there was some weird damage to the victim's car, scratch marks. Have you looked at them?"

"I have. And speaking of Wyatt, there's something about him you might not know."

"He thinks werewolves are real?"

"No . . . well, maybe. I don't know yet."

Jon chuckled.

"The surprising thing is he writes romance novels on the side."

"No way."

"Way. I even have his books in my store. He writes under the pseudonym of Jordan Sumner. Technically his books are thrillers, but they're heavy on the romance side."

"Hunh. I wouldn't have guessed." With my mind's eye I could see Jon sitting in his home office, pulling on his chin as if he had a beard there as opposed to baby-faced skin. It was something I'd seen him do dozens of times. "I wonder if his coworkers know."

"They do. He said they tease him about it though he also said some of the guys have come to him for relationship advice. Did you know he also has a master's degree in psychology?"

"He mentioned it when we talked. I wonder if his coworkers make him sign an NDA before they confide in him."

I laughed. "They probably should, but Wyatt says he refrains from giving them romantic advice in case it gets him into trouble."

"Smart man."

"Though it didn't stop him from offering me advice about you."

As soon as I heard myself utter those words, I wished I could snatch them back. In my excitement over what had felt like a return to the good old days, I'd let my mouth get ahead of my brain. Jon's silence was deafening. "I think he was trying to help," I added, hoping to mitigate the damage.

After a few more seconds of weighted silence, Jon said, "I'm going to dig into this business regarding the couple David called you about. I'll be in touch."

And with that impersonal non sequitur, he ended the call.

CHAPTER 16

I woke earlier than my tired brain wanted to the next morning when my phone dinged a little before ten with a notification. Because I'd dreamed about Jon during the night—nothing overtly romantic or salacious—I hoped it meant a text from him. It wasn't. It was from Devon, letting me know he had sent me some information via email.

I swallowed down my disappointment, did my morning routine, threw on some clothes, and took Newt for a walk. It was no longer raining but the world was thoroughly drenched with mini rivers running along curbs; leaves plastered on walls, windows, and cars; soggy grass that drenched my shoes as soon as I stepped on it; and lots of downed branches. My phone rang while I was out, and once again, I found myself excitedly anticipating a call from Jon.

"Morning, sunshine!"

"Oh, hi, Wyatt. What's up?" My voice must have communicated my emotional state.

"Are you okay? You sound upset or disappointed."

"You figured this out from me speaking"—I thought back to how I'd answered, counting on my fingers—"five words to you?"

"Part of the job," he said. "Question enough suspects and you learn to pick up on the tiniest of nuances, though in your case it could simply be the hour and a lack of caffeine. I recommend an immediate trip to Starbucks, which just happens to be next door to your hotel. They have this sour cream and cinnamon coffee cake that's to die for. And I should know; I'm a homicide detective."

I admit his joke made me smile despite it being cornier than the surrounding fields would be in a few more weeks.

"It's like crack, it's so addictive," he went on. "The way it melts in your mouth with a burst of cinnamon and just a hint of tartness. Seriously, the stuff should be outlawed."

I was nearly salivating in anticipation, not only from his description of the coffee cake, but the way he said it, as if he were making love to the thing. Nuances indeed! Still, I didn't want him tailing around with me all day long. Plus, I had a bone to pick.

"I want to spend the day doing research."

"Okay. Need help?"

"Not really, though there is one question you can answer for me."

"Happy to, if I can. Fire away."

"Why didn't you tell me the Palmer family filed a lawsuit with the sheriff's department?"

This shut him up for a few beats. Then he said, "Oh, that," dismissively as if he thought it would be enough to get me to move on.

"Yes, that. You didn't think it was an important thing to share?"

"Not especially. How did you find out?"

"Does it matter? Why didn't you tell me?"

"I didn't want it to interfere with your judgment and it's not relevant to the current investigation. Besides, I'm pretty sure they're about to settle."

"I'm not happy you withheld this from me."

"Look, I wasn't trying to mislead you, I promise. Let me make it up to you. I've got the medical examiner's final report, and if you swear not to tell anyone I showed it to you, I'll spring for the coffee cake. You can look it over while you enjoy a breakfast treat and then I'll leave and let you get on with your day and your research. Okay?"

I knew he was dangling the ME's report—not to mention the coffee cake—before me on purpose, but he had correctly surmised one or both would be too much of a temptation for me to pass up. *Damn detectives, anyway.*

"Okay," I said with a sigh. "I'd also like a vanilla latte with a double shot."

"Done. See you in twenty."

While waiting for Wyatt, I checked Devon's email, which coincidentally included a copy of the police report for the accident involving Dylan and his father. It included several interesting tidbits, including a statement from a witness who saw Dylan and Ervin at a filling station minutes before the accident. He said the two had been arguing and he swore it was Dylan behind the wheel once they drove away. Except Dylan didn't have a license yet and he later told police it was his father who had been driving. There was enough of a resemblance between Dylan and Ervin to explain away this witness's statement as simple mistaken identity.

As to the cause of the accident, there was an estimate the car had been traveling at least twenty-five miles an hour over the fifty-five-mile-an-hour limit, but it had occurred on a relatively straight stretch of county road. Investigators hadn't found any skid marks, making them think Ervin had either passed out or fallen asleep and then overcorrected upon awakening, making the car leave the road and roll several times. And given the observation at the gas station that father and son had been arguing, there was also speculation that a struggle had occurred between Dylan and his father and perhaps Dylan had grabbed for the wheel.

Regardless of how it happened, both men had been flung from the car as it rolled because neither one had a seat belt on. The result was one sixteen-year-old boy paralyzed and his thirty-six-year-old father dead at the scene, his head crushed by the rolling car. It was all mysterious and tragic, but since it bore no relevance to Lydia's death, I pushed it out of my mind.

Wyatt arrived, and while his morning eagerness made me feel even more tired, the coffee and cake provided a much-needed pick-me-up. We spent a few minutes indulging before Wyatt removed a curled manila folder from the inside pocket of his coat and set it on the table between us.

"I have to warn you, the details are graphic," he said, sliding the folder toward me but leaving his hand on top of it. "There are photos in there of the wounds, and if you have a weak stomach, you might want to pass."

"I'll be fine. I have a cast-iron stomach."

"And remember, don't tell anyone I let you look at it. Basic demographics are public records, but the rest is supposed to be for next of kin and law enforcement only."

"My lips are sealed." I mimed a locking motion at my mouth. Then, after finishing off the last bite of my cake, I took a deep breath and opened the folder.

I hadn't lied about my tolerance for such things, at least gastronomically. Blood and gore had never bothered me. I'd been exposed to death and even mutilation while traveling with my parents—animal carcasses and pictures of dead bodies purportedly killed by some sort of cryptid—but seeing my parents' bodies had been a visceral gut punch, heart-wrenching and devastating. When I'd found them it was as if the world stopped for some immeasurable amount of time while the image of them lying there, their throats cut, their lifeblood spread out around them, branded itself into my brain, searing so deep, it scarred my soul. Later, there had been times when the scab on this wound came off unexpectedly because I'd picked at it with a memory or viewed a similar scene, or sometimes I remembered their bodies for no identifiable reason at all. Then anxiety would build inside me, erupting in a paralyzing miasma of emotional and physical responses.

I was keenly aware of Wyatt watching me as I studied the photographs, and it gave me the focus I needed to concentrate on the here and now. The first picture was of Lydia's body where it had been found in the woods. She was on her back, her pale blond hair fanned out above her head, one foot covered with only a sock, the other encased in a red sneaker. The color of her skin contrasted sharply with the dark ground around her, and the wound on her throat appeared jagged, the edges crusted with dried blood and dirt. Part of her shirt was torn over her belly. Her arms were extended to the sides and bent at the elbows, hands palms up, fingers curled. What I could see of her fingernails revealed them to be broken and dirty, almost as if she'd clawed her way to her final resting place. This seemed out of character to me if Lydia was as fastidious as everyone had indicated, particularly given the manicuring setup I'd noticed on the vanity in her bedroom.

The second picture was of the body turned onto its right side. There were smears of blood, dried leaves, and other plant debris visible in Lydia's hair, and smears of dirt and blood on the back of her shirt and the butt of her jeans. The hem of her shirt was rolled up, exposing the skin. For some reason, the sight of her bare lower back—that soft, vulnerable, yet seemingly insignificant part of her body—bothered me more than her ripped-open neck.

"She was wearing only one sneaker when you found her?"

Wyatt nodded. "We found the other one close by. There's a separate picture of it in there."

"Do you know what the temperature was that night around the time of her death?"

"It was chilly, high thirties."

"So why isn't she wearing a jacket?"

Wyatt shrugged. "Don't know. We didn't find one."

"Not even in her car?" Wyatt shook his head.

I sifted through the remaining photos, including shots of Lydia's naked body laid out on a morgue table—one with her on her back, one with her on her stomach—prior to being cut open. Her back was smeared with dirt, the skin dark and mottled. In contrast, the front of her was ghostly in its whiteness except for faint bruising over her sternum and a strip of four scratches, like a claw mark, down her belly where the tear in her shirt had been.

More autopsy photos followed, and I skimmed through most of

them, focusing on the close-ups of her neck wound. Eventually I came to the picture of the missing sneaker lying on its side beneath a tree, its sole clotted with dirt. On closer examination, I could see the upper edge by the laces looked as if it had been scraped hard with something because bits of the material had been pulled up and torn. Inside the shoe was some kind of debris. I looked up at Wyatt, who was still watching me with a disturbing level of scrutiny. He read my mind and answered my question before I could ask it.

"Pieces of bark from the tree."

I set the photos aside and picked up the written summary, skimming over the vital statistics. Lydia Palmer had been a small woman, only five feet four and a hundred twenty pounds. From there, I skipped to the summary.

A couple of things stood out to me as I read, including an odd linear bruise on the bottom of one of Lydia's feet—the one that still had a sneaker on it—blisters on both of her palms, and a wood splinter along the inside of the index finger on her right hand. Her hair had been combed to remove clumps of soil and leaf debris clinging to the strands, and samples of the dirt had been sent out for analysis. The fresh bruise on her chest was noted along with a second, irregularly shaped impact mark near the base of her skull, indicative of blunt force trauma. The medical examiner speculated the injury to the base of the skull might have been caused by Lydia hitting her head on a rock or a fallen tree branch. Plenty of both could be found near the site, and it made determining the exact location of the initial attack difficult. The ME also concluded, as Wyatt and I had, that Lydia had been dragged on her back for some unknown distance as evidenced by mild abrasions to the exposed part of her back. Yet because the ground had been so hard and dry, no discernible drag marks had been found at the site.

The cause of death was listed as a fracture of cervical vertebrae C2 and C3 severe enough to sever the spinal cord. In layman's terms, Lydia had died from a broken neck and had been instantly paralyzed in every muscle other than those in her face, including those needed to breathe. The manner of death was listed as accidental from an animal attack—possibly a bear—and the cause was asphyxiation secondary to paralysis from the cervical fractures with a contributing cause of exsanguination.

The description of the surface- and deep-tissue damage to the neck was brutal—ragged tearing through the musculature—though I hoped the paralysis and severed spinal cord meant there hadn't been any pain.

I recalled Paul McNamara's description of the way the creature he'd seen had viciously shaken whatever animal it had had in its mouth. Such behavior was a common means of incapacitating prey employed by many predators in the wild. Could the wound on Lydia's neck have been from a bite? If so, there should have been punctures in two places, marking the upper and lower teeth of the biting animal's jaw, but no such injury had been found. The injuries she had suggested the neck wound had been the result of a claw swipe rather than a bite.

I closed the folder and slid it back across the table to Wyatt.

"Thoughts?" he said. "Think I should just close the case and move on? Am I wasting your time?"

I took a deep breath and blew it out slowly. "To be honest, I'm inclined to agree with the medical examiner."

Wyatt nodded slowly.

"Except . . ."

Wyatt perked up. "Yes?"

"The report says her body was moved from wherever the attack initially occurred."

"Yeah. So?"

"So, how?"

Wyatt looked confused. "What do you mean?"

"How was she moved? The only obvious external injuries are a scratch across her belly and the gash in the throat area. The ME speculates it was a bear attack, but black bears aren't usually this aggressive. And how could an animal have moved the body? Lydia wasn't a big woman, but it would still take some effort to carry a hundred twenty pounds of dead flesh. You'd think there would have been other injuries if an animal had dragged her. Like puncture marks."

Wyatt shrugged. "Maybe it dragged her by her clothing."

I shook my head. "According to the ME the only damage to her clothing, which is odd in and of itself when you think about it, was a tear in the front of her shirt corresponding to the abdominal injury."

"If it was a werewolf, it might have carried her in its arms," Wyatt said, a wicked gleam in his eyes.

I shot him an incredulous look, and he came back at me with a goofy grin.

I said, "It looks like she was dragged on her back, feetfirst."

"I agree." He eyed me warily, clearly sensing there was more to come.

"Did the scratch marks on the car show any evidence of blood?"

"No, but my working theory is they were made before Lydia was attacked."

"Were there any traces of the car's paint in her wounds?"

Wyatt shook his head.

"And doesn't it strike you as odd those driver's-door scratches were on the panel below the window? Our creature is supposedly five to seven feet tall and bipedal. If it's standing on two legs next to the car, why are the scratches down so low? I suppose you could explain the ones on the hood and the trunk easily enough, but the ones on the door seem wrong."

"Just because it sometimes walks on two feet doesn't mean it always does," Wyatt countered.

"Then there's the jacket or rather the lack thereof. It bothers me. I find it hard to believe she went out there at three in the morning in thirty-something-degree weather wearing only a long-sleeved shirt."

Wyatt scowled at me, and I sensed he felt I was criticizing his work. I suppose I was in a way. But little details like the ones I'd mentioned couldn't be ignored.

The two of us sat in thoughtful silence for a minute, a wall of tension building between us. Wyatt tapped his fingers on the table with one hand and pulled at his lip with the other. I caught myself dabbing at cake crumbs with my finger and then licking them off. The easy camaraderie we'd shared earlier had evaporated.

"I'm going to be honest with you, Wyatt," I said finally. "I have enough questions about Lydia's death to keep me here for another day or two, but I doubt I'll be able to rule some kind of werewolf in or out simply based on the evidence so far."

"I understand. I appreciate you looking into it at all because things are bothering me, too."

"Fair enough. Give me a little more time. I'll get more done if I work at it on my own for now, but if I need anything from you, I'll give you a call."

This must have been a snub too far because Wyatt's lips drew into a thin line just before he said, "Whatever." Then he shoved back his chair, got up, and left.

CHAPTER 17

Shortly after Wyatt left, I got a phone call from Rita. I answered with "Everything okay?"

"Everything is fine," she said. "And is it so hard to answer a phone call with a friendly greeting of some type? I realize caller ID makes it easy to tell who's calling but it doesn't mean it's okay to forsake the common niceties of society. Honestly, you young people are going to be the death of decency."

"Sorry. Good morning, Rita. How are you doing today? Feeling contumacious, are we?"

"*Pfft.* I'll admit that's a good word but I'm not sure you used it properly. I am neither stubbornly perverse nor obstinate. And 'contumacious' tends to be used more in legal settings. 'Querulous' would have been a better choice."

"I rest my case."

"Okay, I see what you did there," Rita said grudgingly, making me laugh. "I'm calling to follow up on the assignment you gave me."

"Good. What can you tell me?"

"You need to visit Bill Townsend and let him look at the letter and small ledger you found. I want to know if they're the real deal or fakes."

"Bill Townsend is the antiquities guy you mentioned yesterday?"

"Yes, the one who used to help George. He's in Lake Geneva."

"Tell me what you're thinking, Rita. Could this really be a letter from Frank Nitti to Al Capone?"

"I'm hesitant to say anything until Bill can have a look but I think it's possible. The little booklet looks like a record of monies Nitti might have collected from area bootleggers. The cover on it appears coriaceous but without seeing it personally—"

"Hold on. Cory who?"

"Ooh, I got you for once! Coriaceous. It means 'resembling or having the texture of leather.'"

I couldn't help but smile over Rita's obvious joy in besting me. It did my heart good to hear happiness in her voice, whatever the source. On the mental board I maintained for our little obscure word game, I chalked a tally mark in her column. With her extensive knowledge of history and old texts, there was no way I'd catch up with her, though I never stopped trying. She was always at least one point ahead of me.

"You win this one," I conceded. "And I can tell you're excited by whatever it is you think I've found here, Rita. So, come on. Spill."

"I shouldn't."

There was a hint of naughty delight in those two simple words, and I think she was secretly happy to be holding something over me. I also knew her well enough to know she'd cave before our call ended.

"Elkhorn isn't far from Burlington and that's where most of the tunnels were."

"Tunnels? What tunnels? You're losing me, Rita."

"Oh, dear. I'm getting ahead of myself. Let me backtrack a little. There's an intriguing bit of history related to the Prohibition Era in that part of the state, mostly in Burlington but also in Elkhorn. There's this network of tunnels beneath Burlington thought by some to be remnants of the Underground Railroad because rumor has it they connect all the way north to the Canadian border and beyond. Whatever their source and wherever they go, it's a known fact the tunnels were heavily used by bootleggers during the Prohibition Era."

"Bootleggers and Al Capone. Exciting!" I said.

"It can be. It's an intriguing chapter in American history. I'm sure you've already looked up Francesco Nitto, more commonly known as Frank Nitti. He was one of Capone's most trusted lieutenants and he ran Capone's liquor smuggling and distribution operations, selling stuff they imported from Canada through a network of speakeasies in and around Chicago. Back in the early thirties, when Capone went to prison for tax evasion, Nitti did, too, though his sentence was only for eighteen months whereas Capone got eleven years. When Nitti was released, he inherited Capone's criminal empire."

"Those initials on the inside cover of the booklet were F.N."

"Exactly. And the dates would have been right before both men were arrested, tried, and sent to prison."

"But what does that have to do with Elkhorn? Didn't Capone operate primarily in Chicago?"

"Mostly, yes, but Nitti's bootlegging empire grew to include areas as far west of Chicago as Elkhorn and other neighboring towns. There was a vast assemblage of speakeasies in the area operating during Prohibition, and Nitti might well have traveled to collect money from them, particularly if he did so to hide it from the taxmen."

"So, you think the ledger belonged to him?"

"It's possible. And there's another reason to think Nitti might have been in the area. There's a place called Camp Wandawega about fifteen minutes from Elkhorn. It's hidden away in the woods, nice and isolated, with a lake on the property for boating and fishing. It was considered a welcome escape from the hustle and bustle of Chicago, and it became a favorite vacationing spot and hideout for mobsters. Both Capone and Nitti owned places in the Northwoods, but a regular parade of Chicago mobsters stayed at Wandawega back in the day, including Capone."

"Okay, but how does the letter inside the notebook tie in? Do you think it was really written by Nitti?"

"Well, the timing is right. The letter mentions trouble with the taxmen, and the date of the letter is around the time Nitti was indicted. But again, without authentication. . . ."

"Okay, I'll reach out to this Townsend guy to see what he says."

"Already done. He's in Lake Geneva, about twenty minutes from where you are. He's home right now and waiting to see you."

"You called him already?"

"I did. He'll be there until two, so you best get a move on."

I glanced at my watch and saw it was pushing noon. Clearly

Rita was more excited over this than I realized. "Consider me gone," I said.

"Good. Call me as soon as you leave his place. I want to know what he tells you."

"I will."

When I arrived in Lake Geneva, it was in the mid-fifties and overcast, though it didn't feel like more rain was coming. Since it's a toss-up as to which thing Newt does more, drooling or shedding, I typically leave him outside when visiting someone's home for the first time unless they specifically invite him in. While I didn't know Bill Townsend or his home, the simple fact that he was an antiquities expert had me envisioning a house filled with precious and potentially fragile antiques just waiting for one swish of a dog's tail to knock them to the floor. It made my decision easy, and when I cracked the windows and told Newt to wait in the car, he flopped down on the seat and sighed like a sullen teenager.

Townsend's place was a large brick colonial in an upscale neighborhood of similar homes, though his stood out because of its exquisite landscaping and lush green lawn. The man himself perfectly fit my mental description of dapper. I gauged him to be in his seventies, though I might have erred on the high side because of his white hair and bushy white mustache. He was dressed in a pair of beige slacks with a sharp front crease, a pale peach-colored dress shirt, a button-down vest in a peach-and-beige plaid, argyle socks, and shiny black loafers. Add a top hat and he could have passed for the Monopoly man.

"You must be Morgan," he said with a pleasant smile. "Rita said you'd be coming straightaway. Please, come in."

The interior of the home was as formal and old-fashioned in appearance as its owner, with wide wood trim painted white around the windows and doors, and golden oak floors that gleamed. (It would have been a crime to sully their finish with the inevitable collection of drool and dog hairs Newt would have brought in.) Most of the furnishings were early-twentieth-century antiques, and each room we passed was a different color—colonial blue, hunter green, ripe plum, and brick red. As I'd suspected, there were plenty of vases and other delicate-looking tchotchkes on display. We ended up in a lovely library with shelves built on three walls and a bank of tall windows on the fourth overlooking a backyard even more stunningly landscaped than the front. A heavy, ornately carved desk stood in front of the windows and Townsend stepped behind it, gesturing toward an upholstered wingback chair with nailhead trim.

"Show me what you have and take a seat while I look at it," he said.

"It's actually two items, though one was found tucked inside the other."

I took the booklet and letter from the bag I was carrying and went to hand them to him. "Please, just set them here," he said, waving a hand over the blotter on his desk.

I did as he'd instructed and then settled into the chair, which was surprisingly hard and uncomfortable.

Townsend eyed the objects while opening a drawer in his desk and removing a pair of white cloth gloves that triggered a wash of guilt in me as I recalled how I'd handled the items with my bare hands. He donned the gloves and positioned the booklet directly in front of him, removed a magnifying glass from a different drawer, and gingerly opened the booklet's cover, carefully inspecting the writing on the flyleaf before closing it again. Next, he examined the cover, surprising me by putting his nose down close to the booklet and taking a couple of big sniffs.

Setting the magnifying glass aside, he picked the booklet up and cracked it open with much less finesse than he'd used initially. Then he set it down and looked at me with an empathetic smile. "It's a fake. Rita will be disappointed."

"Really? You can tell that quickly?"

"I can. For one thing, it doesn't pass the sniff test."

"I take it you mean that literally."

"Indeed, I do. Have you smelled it?"

"Can't say I have."

He slid it across the desk toward me. "Take a whiff. A long one."

I picked it up, held it under my nose, and inhaled long and hard through my nostrils. "I'm not sure what I'm supposed to be smelling here," I said after repeating the action.

"It's as much what you don't smell as what you do, though not completely. If this booklet were nearly one hundred years old as the dates seem to imply, it would have a musty odor, particularly given how the ink is smeared in places, indicating it was exposed to moisture at some point. And old leather has a smell all its own. This leather smells new and the other thing you may not detect but my trained nose can is a hint of tannins."

A glimmer from one of the classes I took in college came back to me. "You mean like what's in tea?"

"Exactly that, yes!" He looked pleased with my answer. "And there is another odor I detect: rubbing alcohol. It's often used to make leather look aged. Spray it on, use a light touch with some sandpaper or a bristle brush, rub in a bit of dirt, maybe even light the alcohol on fire for a second or two. If you do it right, you end up with leather that looks decades older than it is. The tea is used to age the paper pages inside and it might also have been used to add staining to the leather. The whole process takes a bit of time and effort, but all in all, it's not hard to do. If it's done well and properly, it can produce a reasonable facsimile of age." He sighed and shook his head in dismay. "This booklet, however, while apparently making use of the right tools, appears to have been rushed. Clearly the work of an amateur."

"And the letter?"

"Ah, yes, the letter."

Townsend set the booklet aside and put the folded letter in front of him on the blotter. Gently, he unfolded it before studying it for a long minute with his naked eye. Then he did the same thing with the magnifying glass. After several tense minutes, he picked up the letter and sniffed it. I tapped my foot impatiently, eager for Townsend to render his second opinion.

Finally, he leaned back in his chair and smiled. "This handwriting closely resembles the style popular at that time but there is no way to verify if it's Frank Nitti's. As far as I know there are no verifiable samples to use for comparison. But I find the syntax to be odd. It has a more modern tone overall. Plus, I question whether Frank Nitti would have addressed Capone by his proper first name of Alphonse. Given all that, I doubt the letter was written by Nitti.

"In addition, it's a simple matter to artificially age paper using many of the same techniques used to age leather. I've even seen some fakes who went so far as to make their own paper. But I suspect if we analyze it and the ink used to write both the letter and the entries in the notebook, they will test out as modern."

"Okay," I said, more puzzled than ever.

"I'm sorry if you're disappointed."

"Not disappointed so much as confused. The person who possessed these items had hidden them. And she ended up dead with coins from the same era in her pocket. I thought her death might have had something to do with these being valuable and someone knowing she had them. Now I don't know. Why the forgeries? To what end?"

"Well, to fool someone, of course, though I can't speak to anyone's state of mind. However, any expert in the field would spot these as fakes right away, though if there was an unsuspecting buyer who thinks he or she is getting a bit of valuable history . . . who's to say what someone might be willing to pay?"

I couldn't imagine Lydia Palmer paying serious money for the booklet or the letter since she didn't have any to spare. Nor did she seem the type to try to defraud someone with faked artifacts despite the many "schemes" Dylan had said she was a part of. How had she come by the items? And had she tried to sell them? But if so, why hadn't she had them with her on the night she was killed?

So many questions with no answers. I kept coming back to the same old problem. Why would Lydia have been out there at that time in that location? It made no sense.

"Anything else I can do for you, Ms. Carter?"

"Rita mentioned some tunnels in Burlington. What can you tell me about them?"

Townsend smiled. "Ah, yes, the Capone connection to the tunnels." He leaned forward, elbows on his desk, hands held in a prayer position. "You should understand, all the rumors about Capone in this part of Wisconsin are just that—rumors. Anecdotal evidence at best. Don't get me wrong—the area was rife with mob activity during the Prohibition Era and Capone's tanker trucks were reportedly seen in these parts."

"Tanker trucks?"

"Oh, yes. That's how he moved his illegal booze. The trucks were disguised, of course, made to look like milk tankers, even oil tankers. And there are tunnels under the town of Burlington rumored to connect all the way to Moose Jaw, Saskatchewan." He paused, wrinkling his forehead.

"I can't say for sure they go that far, and the tunnels are supposedly sealed off now. But Capone, his cronies, and the rival gangs all used them to move about undetected, transport their hooch, and evade the FBI agents. Most of the tunnel entrances remaining today are in the basements of buildings that were once speakeasies. They popped up all over Burlington and Elkhorn during Prohibition, and while the local police were paid to look the other way, not all did. There were some notorious arrests made in the area."

"Anything specific regarding the speakeasies or the tunnels related to this Nitti guy?"

"Not that I'm aware of, but anecdotal evidence says Capone had men who collected from some of the speakeasies, so it's possible. Rumors have surfaced from time to time about money Capone buried in the area to hide it from the tax agents, but nothing has ever been found." He shrugged and leaned back in his chair, hands still in prayer formation. "Despite the possibilities, which are admittedly fascinating, the items you have there are fakes, so I'm not sure it matters. There is plenty of Capone history in Wisconsin, but most of it is in the Milwaukee area and the Northwoods. Less so here. Anything else?"

"No, thank you. I appreciate your time. What do I owe you?"

"Nothing. Consider it a favor for Rita."

"Thanks. That's very generous of you."

Mr. Townsend escorted me to the door, and once I was back in my car, I called Rita to give her the bad news.

"Well, drat," she said. "I was hoping they'd be real."

"I kind of was, too. I'm not sure if they're relevant to Lydia Palmer's death, but I feel like I need to know where they came from even if they are fake. She had some old coins from the same era in her pocket when she died. Maybe it's a coincidence but it doesn't feel like one. I need to figure out how these things tie together."

"Sounds like a tall task," Rita said.

"I know, but I'm determined to try. The enigma of Lydia Palmer's death has me far more intrigued than the possibility of a werewolf on the loose. I need some answers."

"Don't ignore the werewolf. I can overnight your father's silver bullets to you if you want."

I'd forgotten about those. The silver bullets, three of them, were something my father had collected years ago when we were in Poland investigating rumors of a werewolf-type creature. My father hadn't given much credence to the rumors, but he'd bought the bullets because he thought they'd be a great item for the store. We never sold them, and I wasn't even sure where they were.

"They're in the back of the drawer below the cash register," Rita said, apparently reading my mind.

"I should have brought them along to sell," I said. "Pretty sure I'd have a few takers down here."

"I can drive to the UPS store in Sturgeon Bay and have them to you tomorrow. Better safe than sorry."

"I wouldn't have a way to use them even if I had them, Rita. I don't have a gun."

"And why not?" she chastised me. "You should take your father's pistol with you when you go cryptid hunting. Heaven knows it would have come in handy on past trips."

She had a point. Still. . . . "You know how I feel about guns, Rita."

"I'll bet that hunky detective you're working with has one."

"He does, but I'm going it alone for now. Besides, I don't believe in werewolves."

"Foolish girl. Don't say I didn't warn you."

"No worries. I'm wearing my wolfsbane charm." To get her off the subject, I told her about Wyatt's alter ego, Jordan Sumner. Her reaction was as expected.

"Oh, my goodness! I wish I'd known when he was here. I could have had him sign inventory. I could have had him sign one of *my* books. You need to bring him back. Invite him to come up and do a signing. Promise me you'll bring him back."

"I'll see what I can do," I said. "But first I have a puzzle to solve."

CHAPTER 18

I needed to do more research. The tunnels intrigued me, as did the tie-in with bootleggers and Prohibition. While the leather booklet and letter Lydia had hidden away were fakes, they had been created by someone with knowledge of the area and this particular bit of history. I thought a local historian might be able to help, but after looking up an address for Elkhorn's historical society, I was dismayed to see they were only open for a few hours on Thursday afternoons, two days away.

Disappointed, I remembered the local library I'd passed while driving through downtown Elkhorn and decided to go there instead. Hadn't Wyatt said something about someone there being "sweet" on Lydia according to Dylan? Maybe I could kill two birds with one stone.

I parked on the street in front of the Matheson Memorial Library and gave Newt an apologetic look as I once again relegated him to the confines of the car. I promised to make it up to him later with a long walk and a cheeseburger, one of his favorite food treats.

The inside of the library was cool and quiet and had a wonderful book smell that made me flash back to memories of helping my mother open boxes of tomes she'd bought for the store. She had always acted like the contents were a big surprise even though she was the one who had ordered them. She would ooh and aah over each book as she took it out, making it feel like we had dozens of Christmases or birthdays each year.

How I missed her.

I started out at the library by simply wandering the floor, checking out the employees and patrons. Of those who appeared to be employees, only one was a man. He sat behind a desk clicking away on a mouse while he stared at a computer monitor. I looked for a nameplate on his desk and didn't see one, but judging from the papers spread out before him, several of which had *Matheson Memorial Library* written across the top in a large colorful font, I felt certain he worked there.

I walked up to his desk and cleared my throat. He blinked, turned, and stared up at me with dark brown eyes behind tortoise-shell framed glasses. A ring of hair circled an otherwise bald scalp from ear to ear and his skin was ghostly pale, making me think he spent too much time indoors with his nose buried in books. Or a computer screen. I took a guess at his age and settled on somewhere in his forties, though I might have been off by a decade to either side. He was wearing a basic pale blue dress shirt with a red-and-white-checked bow tie that might have been cut from a picnic tablecloth. A pin on his shirt bore the name *Lester H* and I tried to remember what Wyatt had said his last name was—something like Hoffman but more unusual than that. Lester's face broke into a rudimentary smile.

"Can I be of assistance?" he asked.

"Maybe. I'm wondering if you could help me find something?"

"Of course." He shifted in his seat and poised his fingers over his wireless keyboard. "What is it you're looking for?"

In contrast to the milquetoast appearance, there was an eagerness to Lester's response, as if he lived to help people navigate the library. Maybe he did.

"Well, I'd like to view any materials you might have on the Beast of Bray Road. I'm interested in local stuff."

Lester's smile faltered slightly, and he dropped his hands into his lap. Disappointment or something else? After a moment's hesitation, he pushed back his chair and stood. "Follow me."

I followed him up some stairs to a metal filing cabinet standing against a wall. He opened the top drawer, reached in, and pulled out a manila folder. "This cabinet is where we keep much of our local history. All items on the Beast of Bray Road are in here."

"Right up front?" I said. "It must be a popular topic."

"Yes, well, someone else recently requested the information, so I knew exactly where it was." He handed me the folder. "You can just slip it back into the drawer when you're done with it."

"Can I ask who else wanted this information?"

"It was someone doing a documentary on the topic. I'm not sure why. It's been done before."

Perhaps so, but now the stakes were higher. Someone had died.

"Do you know much about the history of the beast," I asked as Lester started to turn away, "or the woman who died recently out on Bray Road?"

Lester froze for a long moment before turning back to me with a sad expression. "I heard about what happened, of course. The whole town did. Such a horrible thing." He pushed his glasses up on his nose. "She was a nice lady. It's very tragic." His voice warbled on these last words. He took a hankie from his pocket and dabbed his forehead with it.

"You knew her?"

Lester swallowed hard and his neck flushed a bright red. "I did. Lydia came into the library often to find new books to read. We shared some interests." He paused, repocketed his hankie, and sighed wistfully. "She was easy to talk to."

"What kinds of things did she read?"

"Oh, she liked romance novels, not the ones she called bodice rippers but the more highbrow ones with a bit of suspense in them. Some of her favorite authors were Sandra Brown, Nora Roberts, and Jordan Sumner."

This last name made me smile and I wondered if Lester knew who Jordan Sumner was and that he lived and worked locally.

"Did Lydia ever do any research you know of?" I asked.

"Oh, sure. She was a curious person, always eager to learn something new. She also liked history and read a lot of those fictionalized stories based on real people, like the novels by Philippa Gregory. Are you familiar with those at all?"

I was and said so.

"They're wonderful books. Lydia loved historical fiction, and her favorite eras were those of the Plantagenets and the Tudors, though lately, she was more focused on twentieth-century American history."

"Did she ever show any interest in or do any research on the Beast of Bray Road or werewolves that you know of?"

"Not to my knowledge. I've heard the current gossip, and I know folks are saying she was killed by a werewolf, but I think they're letting their imaginations run wild. Lydia enjoyed the occasional bit of romantasy, but she wasn't into fantasy or the occult. People who say the beast is some kind of werewolf are . . . well. . . . Let's just say I don't think they have a good grasp on reality." His tone was faintly questioning, as if he was looking to me to validate his theory. I turned the tables on him instead.

"Does that mean you don't believe in werewolves?"

"Gosh, no," he said a little too quickly. He shook his head emphatically. Then he leaned in closer, dropping his voice to a more conspiratorial level. "I grew up around here, and if there was anything out there to see, I would have seen it. I'd know about it. It can't be possible."

Was there a hint of desperation in his voice? "Plenty of people claim to have seen one," I said.

Pfft. He dismissed the idea with a wave of his hand. "Anything anyone thinks they've seen is either the product of a vivid imagination or some other animal." He clucked his disapproval, shaking his head. "That movie they made years ago? That's the real monstrosity regarding Bray Road."

No argument from me. "If it wasn't the beast that attacked and killed Lydia, what do you think it was?"

Up until now, I wasn't sure if Dylan's characterization of Lester as someone with a romantic interest in his mom was accurate. But Lester's reaction to this question eliminated any doubts.

His lower lip trembled. Both hands balled into tight fists. His eyes welled, and when he spoke, his voice was tremulous. "It must have been an animal attack of some kind. A wolf—a regular wolf, not a werewolf—or a wildcat. Maybe a bear. So tragic. So unexpected."

"You cared a lot for Lydia, didn't you?"

Even though we'd been speaking in hushed library tones the whole time, Lester looked around before answering me, his voice even lower than before. "We were friends. She was a very nice person."

"Did you ever meet outside of the library?" The rapid flush racing up Lester's neck gave me my answer.

"We met over coffee once. But it wasn't anything romantic," he was quick to add. "We were just friends."

"You would have liked it to be something more?"

For a second he looked relieved, as if admitting his true feelings might lift a huge burden from his soul. But then his expression turned angry, and I changed the subject.

"Do you know her son, Dylan?"

Lester's hunched shoulders relaxed. "Not really. He's been here with her a time or two, but it's been a year or more, I think. Lydia told me he doesn't read much. He's more into computers and gaming."

"Did she talk about him a lot?"

He smiled. "Oh, yes. She doted on the boy and would have done anything for him. *Did* do anything for him. Last year, she mentioned she'd been able to buy him a gaming system and Dylan liked the shoot-'em-up role-playing games. She asked if the library had any she could check out for him because they were so expensive to buy. We didn't, but I know a little bit about them and suggested an online site where she could buy used ones at a discount." He sighed. "In hindsight, I kind of wish I hadn't because it broke her heart to watch him pretend to be these characters who were mobile and physically fit. She thought playing those games was his way of compensating for his limitations, but I could tell it was hard for her."

The beatific expression on Lester's face as he talked about Lydia convinced me he had been quite enamored of her. I wondered if it had been reciprocated at all, though I doubted it, as Lester had an air of unrequitedness about him when he spoke of her.

"You mentioned you met Lydia for coffee once. Did you ever go on a date with her?"

Lester's pale face flashed a brilliant red. "Gosh, um, no. I liked her, but like I said, we were just friends." He hung his head.

"Do you know if she was dating anyone else?"

Lester's head jerked up. "No," he said definitively. Then, looking as if I'd just struck him, he added, "I mean, I don't know but I don't think so. She never mentioned anyone."

"Would she have mentioned someone to you? Did you have that kind of friendship with her? Were you confidants?"

Lester jutted his chin toward me. "Yes, I believe we were."

"Then help me understand something. I can't figure out what she was doing in the woods along Bray Road at three in the morning. Any ideas?"

It was like a switch had been flipped. Lester's entire demeanor changed. "No," he said, his lips tight. He glanced at his watch. "If you'll excuse me, I'm late for a meeting I need to get to." He gave me a perfunctory smile, turned, and hurried off down the stairs.

I watched, stunned, as he disappeared around a corner of bookshelves. Was Lester hiding something? I made a mental note to come back another time and try to talk to him some more, maybe even invite him out for a coffee. I'd also get Devon to work on finding out what he could about the guy, though I'd need to find out his last name. I decided I'd work on that later because first I wanted to look through the Beast of Bray Road folder Lester had found for me. I settled in at a nearby table and dug into the file, which was only about half an inch thick.

Some of the articles were printouts of ones I'd already read online but others, mostly accounts in local weeklies and some online sites like Weird Wisconsin, were new to me. Linda Godfrey's original write-up for the weekly paper was in there, as were reports of sightings similar to the Bray Road ones but in different locations around the state. The werewolf theme remained a constant as did general descriptions of the creature. I used my phone to take pictures of the articles I found the most interesting, and then tucked them all back inside the folder. I went to the top of the stairs and peered down at Lester's desk, but he wasn't there. His chair was tucked neatly in place and his computer screen was dark, suggesting he was gone for the day. I glanced at my watch, surprised to see it was nearly five already.

I returned the folder to the filing cabinet drawer, making sure to put it right up front again. I really didn't want to have to contact

Wyatt to get Lester's last name, so on my way out, I took a closer look at Lester's desk and the trash can next to it. In the garbage I found an envelope with his full name on it: Lester Hofheyzer. I used my phone to snap a quick pic and then sent it to Devon with instructions to find out what he could about the man.

CHAPTER 19

When I returned to my hotel, I saw three saddled horses across the parking lot outside of Starbucks. A young woman held their reins, and I assumed the other riders were inside the store. Newt's curiosity was obvious as he stared in their general direction, his nose busily sniffing the air. After assurances from the young woman that the horses were okay with dogs, Newt and I approached the nearest one, a lovely reddish-brown bay. Newt raised his snout up toward the horse, his tail wagging eagerly. The horse in turn lowered his head until their two noses touched. Nostrils and whiskers mingled for a few seconds, and then the horse pulled back, and Newt did an abrupt about-face toward the motel. So much for touching moments.

When I got back to my room, the interaction between Newt and the horse had me thinking about the scene Paul McNamara had witnessed the night his drinking buddies had abandoned him out on Bray Road. Had the animal the beast carried in its mouth been a dog? More specifically, the local farmer's missing dog? If so, how had the beast caught the animal? Had the dog approached it, thinking, as Newt might have with the horse, that it was just another, bigger version of dog? Technically, wasn't a werewolf exactly that, just a larger, stranger, wilder species of dog?

I dismissed the idea. Animals tend to sense instinctively when another animal means them harm. There weren't many predators in the animal kingdom capable of luring another creature to its death by faking friendliness—that behavior lies solely in the human basket of talents. However, there were animals capable of using aggressive mimicry to lure in or fool a victim. The tree ocelot or margay imitates the call of a baby pied tamarin monkey to entice adult monkeys to within striking distance.

There were also examples of mimicry among some insects and birds, though in the case of the latter it could be a form of self-sacrifice, as the birds would fake an injury to lure a predator away from the nest. Sometimes they did too good a job of it and lost their lives in the process. Had the creature Paul witnessed used some type of mimicry to lure its prey? Could a werewolf bark, howl, or yip like a real wolf or a dog? Paul had mentioned hearing a howl before he heard something thrashing in the bushes. And then there was the smell he'd noticed. Could that have been enough to lure a dog? Newt had taught me many a time how much dogs love things that reek.

So many questions and so few answers. It seemed to be the hallmark of this case.

I thought about what to do next and realized the key was Lydia

Palmer and learning as much about her life, activities, and interests as I could. I decided to pay another visit to Dylan and have a chat with him about his mother without Wyatt around. Since I didn't have Dylan's phone number, I opted to try my luck, drive to the house, and drop in unannounced. Rude perhaps but I find it's always better to talk to people when they don't have time to prepare. And it really is easier to ask for forgiveness than it is to get permission.

Mind made up, I loaded Newt into the car and took off. When we arrived at the house, I was disappointed to see Connor's car wasn't in the driveway. Did that mean Dylan was gone, too? I hoped not and parked out in the street, not wanting to block the driveway in case Connor returned.

I knocked at the front door, and after waiting several minutes to give Dylan plenty of time if he was home alone, I knocked a second time, a little harder and a little louder. Still no answer. There was no doorbell, only a hole in the siding where one had presumably been sometime in the past.

Disappointed, I started to go back to my car, but Newt trotted off down the driveway toward the leaning tower of a garage. There were double doors on the front of it that had, at one time, provided access for a car to drive inside, and the door on the left was ajar. I was certain that on my previous visit, both doors had been closed tight, and I wondered if Lydia's car had been returned and was now parked inside. If so, I wouldn't mind another look at those scratch marks.

As I approached the double doors, I saw the one on the left was only open about a foot and there was a large hump in the driveway that prevented it from opening any wider. I could see an arc in the dirt where it had scraped over the ground, and the wood along the bottom edge of the door was splintered and broken in places. I gave it a couple yanks, anyway, to see if I could widen the gap but was afraid to pull too hard lest I pull the whole structure down.

The door on the right was stuck tight in the closed position, with the lower-middle corner where the two doors met firmly embedded in the ground. Its hinges were rusted, and if there had ever been a handle, it was gone now. After telling Newt to stay, I turned sideways and slipped in through the narrow opening on the left.

There were windows on both sides of the garage, and beams of early-evening sunlight shone through one of them, highlighting tiny motes of dust dancing in the air. Despite this, the interior was dark, and I had to stand a moment to let my eyes adjust. The air smelled of dirt, oil, gasoline, and a cedarlike scent I thought might have been mulch. Off to my left something small—a mouse or a chipmunk perhaps—scurried behind some stacked cans of paint. Outside, Newt whined.

"I'm okay, Newt," I said. "You stay and I'll be out in a sec."

I saw a light fixture in the ceiling and felt along the wall to the left of the door for a switch. I found one, managing to knock something over in the process, but flipping the switch did nothing. Gradually my eyes adjusted to the interior darkness. The car wasn't there—no surprise given the situation with the doors—and anyway, it would have been hard to fit one inside given the small size of the structure and the fact it housed a lawn mower, a seed spreader, a snowblower, a wheelbarrow, and a bicycle. I looked to see what I'd knocked over when groping for the switch and saw a hoe, a leaf rake, a snow shovel, and a garden rake on the floor. I bent down, grabbed them, and propped them back up against the wall.

There were two sets of wooden shelves running down the length of the garage to my left. On them were cans of paint, brushes, pans, and rollers, a variety of flowerpots, some seed packets, two pairs of small heavy-duty gardening gloves, a couple of empty buckets and a third one filled with garden implements, and some miscellaneous tools including a jigsaw, a Skilsaw, a power drill, a vise, a hammer, three screwdrivers, a staple gun, and a hatchet. There was also a plastic container with drawers containing an assortment of nails, screws, washers, nuts, and drill bits, including some grinding tools. Had this been Ervin's area or had Lydia had a handywoman streak? I guessed the former when I spotted a small stack of cut-wood pieces and a partially constructed birdhouse farther down the shelf, all of them knitted to the wall with cobwebs.

Newt whined again, so I slipped back outside and let him follow me into the backyard, where there was a raised flower bed along the rear wall of the house. I imagined the garden would be lovely come summertime, but for now it was a dirt bed covered with the rotting brown remnants of last year's plants and gray clumps of old mulch. I spotted an area at the far end where some dead growth had been scraped away and a dozen daffodils had broken through to the surface. There were signs of someone's—presumably Lydia's—recent efforts to till the dirt but the long drought had left much of it hard as brick and an overhanging eave had apparently kept a lot of last night's rain off the bed. I imagined this flower bed had been a labor of love for Lydia, one that would now, sadly, likely go to seed. It added one more visual to the overarching tragedy of the woman's death.

Newt found a small hole in the yard—a chipmunk or vole, no doubt—and he started digging madly until I told him to stop. I headed back to the car but hesitated when I noticed light coming from a basement window. Curious, I walked over and bent down to peer inside. To my surprise, I saw a small office area set up with a desk, a chair, and a tall four-drawer filing cabinet. Sitting on top of the desk was a laptop.

How curious. Whose laptop was this? It was a question I had to log away for later because there was a car pulling into the driveway.

CHAPTER 20

Connor and Dylan stared at me through the windshield of Connor's car while I smiled, waved at them, and tried to look like I hadn't just been snooping around the property.

"Hi, guys," I said cheerily. Newt went up to the passenger side of the car, wagging his tail furiously. Dylan opened his door and leaned over to pet him.

Connor got out and went around to remove Dylan's wheelchair from the trunk of the car. He set it on the ground, opened it up, and then wheeled it over to the passenger door, making Newt move as he positioned the chair close to the side of the car before applying the brakes.

"I wasn't expecting company," Dylan said. Using his hands, he lifted first his right leg, then the left, letting them dangle over the side of the seat and out the open door. In one swift move, Connor bent down, grabbed Dylan under his arms, hoisted him out of the car, and pivoted to place him in the wheelchair. He then lowered the footrests as Dylan lifted his legs with his hands and positioned his feet on them.

"Sorry," I said. "I would have called but I don't have a number for you, and I didn't want to bother Wyatt."

"Really?" Dylan said, his eyebrows shooting up in amusement. "I figured you two were joined at the hip."

"Oh, gosh, no," I said in my best aw-shucks voice. "He gave me an introduction but I'm pursuing things on my own now."

"I see."

Connor pushed the wheelchair over to the ramp and I followed along as they switchbacked their way to the front door. I stepped inside quickly before anyone had a chance to object or stop me. Connor and I both removed our shoes—I did so not just out of politeness but because I felt it indicated I meant to stay for a spell—while Dylan wheeled himself into the middle of the room. Newt went over to Dylan, tail still wagging.

Dylan's demeanor lightened briefly as he scrubbed Newt's ears and talked to him in classic aren't-you-a-good-boy doggy talk.

"Would it be okay if I asked you some more questions about your mom?" I said, hoping to get the request in while he seemed to be in a good mood.

Dylan shrugged as Connor disappeared down the hallway to the bedrooms. "What else do you want to know?"

"Do you have any idea why she would have gone out that night in thirty- or forty-degree weather without a jacket?"

Dylan's face screwed up in puzzlement. "She wasn't wearing one?"

I shook my head. "One wasn't found out there in the woods, either. Is there a jacket of hers you've noticed missing?"

He shook his head. "Sorry. I don't pay much attention to my mom's clothes. But I'll look around and see if anything jumps out at me."

"That would be great. Was your mother a collector of old coins?" Dylan gave a tiny jerk of his head over the abrupt change of subject. "Look at these," I said, taking out my phone and pulling up my pictures of the coins.

I watched as Dylan scrolled through them. "Where did these come from?" he asked.

"They were in the pocket of the pants your mother was wearing the night she was killed. They're worth a little money, though you won't get rich off them. Older coins like these need to be in pristine condition to fetch a high dollar. These look like something your mom dug up."

Dylan stared at me, an inscrutable expression on his face. "You think she was out there digging in the woods for old coins?

"Maybe. Was your mother a collector?"

Dylan shook his head. "If she had any interest in old coins, she never told me about it. And I never saw any around the house."

"Well, they'll be yours now," I said. "Wyatt will return them to you at some point. I did wonder if your mother might have had others she gave or sold to someone that night. Or maybe someone took them from her."

Dylan gave me a surprised look. "Are you suggesting my mother's death wasn't caused by an animal attack?"

I debated my answer. This was his mother, after all. But I wanted to shake him up a little, get him thinking about the bigger picture and the full chain of events because he knew his mother better than anyone else I could talk to. Maybe there was an angle to this he knew about without realizing it.

"I'm leaning that way," I said. "The evidence so far does point to an animal, but as I told you before, some things don't make sense."

"We may never know why she was out there at that crazy hour."

"It's not just that. It's the scratch marks."

"What about them?"

"They're in an odd location, too low down on the car. And there are four lines in them. The scratch mark on your mom's body also showed four lines. The popular theory seems to be she was attacked by a bear, but a bear has five toes on each paw, not four."

Dylan tilted his head to one side and narrowed his eyes at me. "It wasn't the Beast of Bray Road," he said as if trying to convince himself. "I mean, come on, do you actually think it could have been a werewolf?"

I raised my eyebrows and gave a half-hearted shrug. I wasn't inclined to believe this though I hadn't fully ruled it out. But I wanted to get Dylan thinking outside the box. "There's a witness who swears he saw a werewolf out on Bray Road two nights before your mom was killed. And a wolf has four toes if you don't count the dewclaws they have on the front. A scratch mark made by a wolf would typically show four lines."

"Get real," Dylan said with a dismissive wave. "You're putting me on. Couldn't it just as easily have been your garden-variety wild animal like a regular wolf? An animal on four legs"—he paused, gesturing toward Newt—"like your dog here might make scratch marks lower on the car, right?"

I wagged my head from side to side. "Maybe. But why would *any* creature leave those marks? What was it trying to achieve? There wasn't anyone in the car at the time."

Dylan looked thoughtful. "How can you be sure? Maybe she was in the car when the creature approached, and she stayed inside while it tried to get to her. She could have waited until it got bored and left before she got out of the car."

I gave him a doubtful look. "Why wouldn't she just drive away and come back another time? Do you think your mother was that brave? Or that stupid?"

I suspected this last question might anger him and I was right. His face contorted into an angry scowl.

"I don't for a minute believe she was stupid," I added quickly. "In fact, that's precisely my point. Your mother was a smart woman . . . clever, adaptable, and creative. There's no way she'd simply sit in her car and do nothing while some crazed animal tried to break into it."

"Maybe she did try to get away," Dylan suggested. "That car isn't the most reliable thing. Maybe she panicked and flooded the engine."

"All possibilities," I conceded. "But would she have then left the relative safety of the car and wandered into the dark woods once the creature disappeared? You knew her better than anybody, Dylan. Does it sound like something she would have done?"

Dylan sighed, gripped his wheels, and began rocking the chair back and forth. "I don't know," he said. "There are homes and farms out there. Maybe she got out to try to get to one of those for help."

"Except she wasn't found on the road. She was deep into those woods."

"Wyatt said it looked like she died somewhere other than where they found her. Maybe she was attacked on the road and dragged into the trees."

I considered pointing out that the distance from the road to where Lydia's body had been found would have been a stretch for most animals to drag that much weight, especially through the trees with all the roots and vines there. Then again, werewolves weren't most animals.

"But then I keep coming back to the same old question of what she was doing out there in the first place," I said with a sigh.

Dylan continued rocking his wheelchair, appearing deep in thought. "I know," he said eventually. "It's nagged at me, too. I mean, Mom was always doing crazy stuff, always looking for a new way to make money, or trying to find some new alternative therapy for me. She was never satisfied and some of her actions. . . ." His voice trailed off and he shook his head. He took his hands from the wheels of his chair and settled them in his lap, staring down at them for a moment before he began picking at a cuticle. "Honestly, I think she had a mental health problem. Connor said some of her behaviors pointed toward it."

"Like what?"

Dylan looked out one of the windows, though he continued to pick at his finger. "Well, she was a fanatic when it came to having a clean, neat house. She was constantly washing and wiping things... scrubbing and mopping and dusting and vacuuming. She probably cleaned the kitchen counters hundreds of times a day and the windows every week. Everyone had to take their shoes off as soon as they came in the door, and I swear she scrubbed the toilets every few hours. Honestly, it was exhausting just watching her." He paused, smiling grimly. "After my accident I used to feel guilty because I couldn't help her much even though I had never really helped her much before the accident. But eventually I realized the cleaning was therapeutic for her."

Now we were getting down to some nitty-gritty on Lydia. At the risk of stepping into Wyatt's psych territory, I wondered if Lydia's OCD tendencies had evolved as a reaction to the car accident, a way of exerting control over her environment after feeling so helpless in the face of her husband's death and her son's paralysis. "Was she always that way?" I asked.

"Oh, yeah," Dylan said, chuckling and shooting down my theory. "Sometimes my dad, who was an asshole by the way, would purposely do stuff to trigger her."

"Like what?"

"Oh, he'd spill something on purpose and leave it, or he'd track cut grass or mud into the house. Mom was always lining things up just so on the kitchen counters or in the bathrooms and Dad would come along and move it all around, knowing she'd get upset and put everything back the way it had been. One time he emptied out the canister in the vacuum cleaner and stored the contents in some baggies. For weeks afterward he'd wait for her to dust and vacuum and then he'd get out one of the baggies and spread the contents around."

Dylan looked over at me and must have seen the horror on my face. He smiled grimly. "Yeah, like I said, my father was an asshole. He and my mom fought all the time."

"Did he get physical?"

Dylan nodded and looked away, lips pursed. "Anyway," he said after a few seconds, "Connor said he's pretty sure Mom had an obsessive-compulsive disorder."

I wasn't sure Connor should have been diagnosing Lydia, but in this instance I was inclined to agree. The symptoms Dylan described were classic.

"OCD isn't necessarily a bad thing," I said.

"Oh, I know," Dylan said. "Mom's attention to detail was amazing and it worked for her in a lot of ways. There was nobody better if I needed help with my homework. She kept a strict budget and tracked expenses like an IRS accountant. And her need to make lists all the time meant we never ran out of things. She was obsessed with finding ways to make my life easier or digging up the latest research and experimental treatments for spinal injuries. She spent a lot of time at the library, especially lately. I asked her recently what she was onto and she was kind of cagey, saying she was looking into something that might finally turn things around for us. Another one of her crazy schemes, no doubt."

I felt like we were finally getting somewhere, though there were still a lot of questions. Was research or Lester the reason Lydia had been visiting the library so often lately?

"Despite her need for tight control, it always felt like Mom was walking the edge, you know?" Dylan said. He was gazing out the window again, a wistful expression on his face. "Like it was a struggle for her to maintain the balance." He shrugged. "Maybe she finally lost it. Maybe she was so out of her mind the night she was killed, she didn't know where she was or what she was doing."

This assessment of his mom's behavior seemed harsh to me,

but who was I to judge? Clearly Dylan knew his mother better than I did.

"Was there anything else with the coins?" Dylan asked.

My thoughts were elsewhere, and his question threw me momentarily. "What?"

"Those old coins my mother had. Was there anything else she had with her?"

"Nothing of value. Just her car keys and her license." I felt it was time to change the subject to something less morose and said, "I noticed there's some kind of office in your basement. I assume it was your mom's and the last time I was here I didn't get a chance to look at it because I didn't know it was there. Would it be okay if I looked at it now?"

Dylan gave me a quizzical look. "How. . . ."

"Oh, when I got here and knocked on the door, I happened to look down the side of the house while I was waiting and saw a light coming from the basement window. I thought maybe Connor was down there and hadn't heard me knock, so I went around and peeked in the window."

"But Connor's car wasn't here," Dylan said.

Gulp. I'd been hoping he wouldn't pick up on that hole in my explanation.

"Right. Of course, I realized that after I'd looked in there. I even slapped myself on the side of my head for being such a ditz." I rolled my eyes, smiled crookedly, and did my best crazy-lady look. "But once I saw the desk and computer, I realized it must have belonged to your mom. Maybe there are some clues there to explain what she was doing out on Bray Road that night."

"Sorry," Dylan said, shaking his head. "I gave my mom's laptop to the police. That basement computer is Connor's. The desk was already there but my mother never used it, and when Connor agreed to move in here, he asked if he could use it."

"Oh, I see. Bummer." As if on cue, Connor appeared, smiling briefly at us as he crossed the living room into the kitchen. Seconds later I heard a door open and then footsteps descending stairs.

Dylan glanced at his watch. "Listen, I appreciate you stopping by, but I've got some work to do."

"Of course. Would it be okay if I use the restroom before I go?"

Dylan nodded. He was still petting Newt, so I showed my dog my palm, a hand command for stay. "Keep an eye on my dog for me, would you?" I said.

I didn't wait for an answer before disappearing down the hall, bypassing the bathroom Dylan used and heading for Lydia's instead. The door to Dylan's bedroom was open and I glanced inside as I passed, noticing the bed was again unmade and several items of clothing had been strewn about on a chair, a dresser, and the far side of the bed. On a bedside stand next to the door was a pill bottle, and I glanced at the label. It was for something called cyclobenzaprine.

At the end of the hall, the guest bedroom door was also open. It was still neat as a pin with the bed made, the accent pillows in place, and not a stray item to be seen. Connor was a very tidy guy. I wondered if he had military training in his background.

As I entered Lydia's bedroom, I paused and gave the room a quick once-over, wondering if I'd missed anything the first time around. I stepped quietly, listening for the approach of anyone coming down the hall, and quickly searched under the bed's mattress. I started to open and feel under the drawers of the dresser, but the third one I tried to open made too much noise and I quit and went into the bathroom, shutting the door behind me.

Following a gut feeling that Lydia had something more to tell me, I opened the medicine cabinet and looked over the contents. There were no new hiding places or unexpected finds, though I did note Lydia had prescriptions for an antidepressant and alprazolam, which I recognized as a powerful antianxiety drug and sedative.

There was a small built-in linen closet that offered nothing but towels and washcloths, all neatly folded and stacked. A quick search between each one proved fruitless and I next turned to the cabinet beneath the sink. All it held was a hair dryer, a box of tampons, and a couple of rolls of toilet paper. Disappointed, I flushed the toilet in case anyone was listening and was about to shut the cabinet door when, on a whim, I picked up the box of tampons and opened it. Inside, rolled up and nestled amid the other contents, was a yellowed piece of paper.

I swear my heart skipped a beat when I carefully unrolled it and saw a crudely drawn map. A quick look revealed one readily identifiable landmark, but it was a key one: Bray Road. I flipped on the water in the sink and let it run while I carefully rolled the map back up and gently slid it into a pocket. The paper looked fragile, much like the paper from the fake Nitti letter. I closed the cabinet door, briefly wet my hands before turning off the water, and dried off on the towel hanging next to the sink.

Back in the living room, Newt and Dylan appeared to have bonded. My dog had his head resting in Dylan's lap, his eyes closed, while Dylan massaged around his ears. There was a smile on Dylan's face, and he looked content for the first time since I'd known him. One more example of the Newt effect.

"Wyatt told me you might be getting a service dog," I said.

Dylan shrugged. "Mom was looking into it through some charity group. I think I'm on a waiting list, but the last time she mentioned it, she said it could be a while."

"I'm sorry," I said. "Sometimes life isn't fair."

"Yeah." Dylan stroked Newt's big head a few more times and I noticed all the fur clinging to Dylan's black slacks—the price we humans pay for dog love.

I went to put my shoes on, and it was with some reluctance I called Newt to come as I headed for the door, wincing at tiny clumps of mud he left on the floor beside Dylan's chair. Judging from the state of Dylan's bedroom, he clearly hadn't inherited his mother's hang-ups about neatness and cleanliness. I guessed it didn't matter so much now that Lydia was gone. Yet it still felt disrespectful somehow.

Dylan's eyes followed Newt's departure with such a saddened expression, my heart went out to him. I wondered if there was anything I could do to expedite his receipt of a service dog and made a mental note to look into it.

Once I was outside by the driveway, I subtly steered Newt along the side of the house until I was by the basement window. Newt paused to pee, as I'd hoped he would, and I used the moment to glance through the window, trying to look as casual as I could. Inside, I saw Connor seated at the basement desk, looking at something on the laptop, his head blocking most of the screen. Not that it mattered. It seemed Dylan was right, and the computer belonged to Connor, not Lydia.

I needed to make another attempt to get Wyatt to give me, or rather Devon, access to Lydia's laptop and phone. But first I had to decide what to do with the map I'd found in the tampon box.

CHAPTER 21

I drove back to my motel and settled in at the table with the rolled-up map I'd found inside the tampon box. It looked old—stiff, yellowed, and frayed along the edges—but thanks to my visit with Townsend, I knew better than to assume. I sniffed at the paper and picked up the same hints of tannin I'd smelled in the fake Nitti and Capone letter and a quick online search showed me how easy it was to create a frayed edge like the one on the map.

Still, while the aging of the paper might have been faked, I couldn't shake the feeling the map itself was somehow important. It was hand drawn and showed the entire length of Bray Road and the surrounding area, including some key landmarks like woods, fields, and farms. There were letters written down the left margin of the page, beginning with A and ending with H, and numbers written across the top margin, starting with a one on the far left and going to ten on the far right. It would have been nice and probably a bit too easy if there had been a big old X drawn somewhere on the page but no such luck.

There was a date inked in the lower-right corner—1930—and this placed it squarely within the time frame of the notebook Lydia had hidden in her carved box, the letter contained within its pages, and the coins Lydia had had on her when she was killed. I felt certain they were all connected. I just had to figure out how. Bill Townsend had mentioned rumors of Capone having buried treasure in the area. Could it be this was what Lydia had been up to? Could the rumors possibly be true? Or would they prove to be as much of a bust as the infamous Geraldo Rivera reveal of Capone's vault in Chicago? And how had Lydia come by the faked artifacts and the map?

My stomach growled so loudly, it startled Newt, and I realized I hadn't eaten anything since breakfast. No wonder my brain was having trouble sorting through it all. A glance at my watch told me it was after six thirty and the angle of the light out my window told me the sun was making its descent. I wanted to drive out to Bray Road and take another look with the map in hand, but I wanted to do it by daylight and not wait until tomorrow. A quick online check told me sunset would be at seven forty-three. I calculated that if I left right away, I'd have a little less than an hour. My stomach growled again in protest.

It took me ten minutes to drive to the same spot I'd parked at when Wyatt had been with me. This time, however, the area off the shoulder was boggy and muddy from the rainstorm last night and my tires left rutted tracks in the grass. I walked to the path between the two wooded areas, dismayed to see the first half of it was a giant mud puddle big enough that it forced me into the trees to avoid getting my feet wet. When I finally emerged in the cornfield, my stomach protested again and Newt let out a whimper.

"It's okay. Just a little hungry," I told him. He looked at me, wagged his tail, and raised his nose to the air, sniffing. After a few seconds, he whined again but his tail was still wagging. "It's okay," I said, patting him on the head. "We're going to explore a little and then we'll head back and get something to eat."

I was about to take the map out and study it when I heard the distinct sound of something large moving through the trees off to my right. I froze, as did Newt, the hackles on the back of his neck raised. Newt emitted a low growl, and the sounds of movement stopped.

I cursed under my breath, realizing I didn't have anything with me to use as a weapon except Newt. Jon was right. I took foolish chances, didn't think things through well enough, and put myself at risk unnecessarily.

After Newt and I stood still as statues for some interminable amount of time, the sounds started again. Something was moving through those trees quickly, making no effort at stealth. Panic rose in my chest, and I was unsure of what to do—stand my ground or run. Then I realized the sounds were moving away from us, back toward the road.

At that moment I had no idea what the wise decision would have been. I didn't think; I simply acted on instinct and impulse as I turned back toward the road. When I got close to the giant puddle, I slipped in the mud and nearly went down but managed to right myself at the last second. I paused to catch my breath and listened for the sound of retreating footsteps but all I could hear at that point was my own ragged breathing. Was something still lurking in the woods or had whatever it was exited the trees and crossed the road, disappearing into the shrubs on the other side?

I gave up jogging and walked the rest of the way to my car, checking behind me several times to make sure nothing had emerged from the woods. Newt seemed wary but not on edge, which reassured me. When I got to my car, I unlocked it and took out my headlamp and a flashlight I kept in the glove box. Then I went around to the back and dug out my tire iron. As weapons go it wasn't the best, but it was better than nothing.

It wasn't until I'd locked up and prepared to head down the trail again that I noticed the tracks. In the grass behind my car were ruts made from another car's tires crossing over part of mine. I could see where someone had pulled in right behind my car and then backed up and headed down the road, trailing fresh mud onto the blacktop.

Had someone followed me out to Bray Road? Had they gone through the trees after me, doing a quick turnabout when they realized I was onto them? But why the stealth? Why go through the trees where the terrain was harder to navigate? And why hadn't I heard a car engine?

Darkness was rapidly descending, and I cursed my stealthy guest because they'd cost me valuable daylight time. I needed to get back out to the field, back to where Lydia's body had been found. I followed the rutted trail once again, carefully sidestepping the big puddle, this time with my headlamp on. It was already hard to see because the woods on either side heavily shaded the path, shutting out the last few remnants of sunlight. When I rounded the curve and saw the cornfield beckoning up ahead like a lit doorway, I sped up. Then Newt stopped and whined. Something was stressing him.

My nerves were already strung tight, and I was about to call it quits and turn back when Newt barked and took off, running ahead of me.

"Newt! Wait! Come back here!" Newt was an obedient dog most of the time, but every once in a while, he seemed to go deaf. This was one of those times. He kept on running, tearing out into the cornfield and then disappearing off to the right. I hurried after him, calling constantly until a yelp brought me to a terrified stop. I froze and held my breath to hear better, gripping the tire iron in my hand. Another yelp, the sound of a dog in pain.

Oh, God, Newt!

Frantic, I hollered for him again and then cursed my stupidity. Why hadn't I thought to bring my night vision binoculars with me? The answer, of course, was that I hadn't intended to be out here in the dark, much less hunting for my dog. If something happened to Newt. . . . I couldn't begin to contemplate it.

I tore across the cornfield still yelling for Newt, intending to run along the back edge of the woods to where the fence separated the trees from the plowed-up field. But after only a few feet, I heard frantic barking, followed by a whine, and knew it was coming from somewhere farther back in the cornfield. I ran in that general direction, still calling for Newt until I heard another bark. This one sounded like it was from inside the fenced area off to my right. I looked over there but the light from my headlamp didn't extend far enough. I took out my flashlight, aiming it out over the field and along the fence line.

"Newt? Where are you? Newt, buddy? Come! Please!"

I expected to see my dog come bounding toward me. Instead, all I saw was the detritus of last year's corn crop on this side of the split-rail fence and the clots of dirt in the field beyond casting eerie shadows along the ground. Tears burned in my eyes, making it harder to see anything. I heard another bark, and then another. I homed in on the sound, following the fence on the cornfield side because the ground was flatter there. I waved my flashlight back and forth between the fence rails, looking for Newt, afraid of what I would find.

And then I saw him.

He stood in the plowed field a few feet on the other side of the fence looking back at me. I nearly cried with relief.

"Newt! Are you okay?" He wagged his tail, whining as I narrowed the distance between us. My feet slid in the mud of the cornfield, and I made the foolish decision to duck between the rails of the fence into the plowed field, thinking it might be easier to navigate. It wasn't. I had to step carefully over damp, slippery clumps of dirt that would sometimes dissolve beneath my feet, and my shoes quickly became caked with mud. Newt appeared to be okay and every few feet I'd turn the flashlight on him and call him, confused as to why he wasn't coming to me.

When I finally reached him, I dropped the tire iron and nearly cried with relief, running my free hand over his fur, shining the light on him, searching for blood, wounds, or any other injury. There was nothing. Newt whined again looking straight ahead.

"What's the matter, boy?"

I aimed my flashlight in front of him, and at first all I saw were more clumps of dirt. But after taking a couple of steps forward, I realized there was a hole in the ground beyond the clumps. It was roughly three feet square, but I couldn't tell how deep it was until I came right up on it. Then I saw it was deeper than it was wide. And it wasn't empty.

Two glowing eyes looked up at me.

"Oh, my!" I said, looking back at Newt. "I thought you were hurt and the whole time you were trying to get me to this little guy."

A dog lay on its side at the bottom of the hole, its back right leg clearly broken. With the depth and the steep, muddy sides, it would have been a challenge to get out of the hole for a normal dog, much less one with a broken back leg.

I had a pretty good idea whom this dog belonged to. "Your owners are looking for you," I said in a soft voice. "I'm going to help you, okay?"

His tail thumped tentatively, and I wondered if he'd broken the leg falling into the hole or if he'd broken it elsewhere and then fallen in.

"It's okay, little guy. You're such a good boy, such a good boy." The dog whimpered and staggered to its feet, the injured leg hanging uselessly. "No, no. You stay. Don't hurt yourself more." I shone my flashlight up and down his body, looking for other injuries. There were a few burdocks stuck in his fur, mud was caked on his front paws, and he looked hungry, but other than the leg he seemed okay.

I fished my cell phone out of my pocket and looked to see if I had a signal. One bar flickered on and off and I tried calling Wyatt. Thankfully, the call went through.

"Hey, Morg . . . what's new?"

"I found the farmer's missing dog. The Beast of Bray Road didn't eat it, after all."

Several seconds of what I assumed was stunned silence ticked by before Wyatt said, "You . . . kid . . . me."

He was breaking up and I feared I'd lose him. I held the phone out farther and tried different positions to improve the signal. One bar was the best I could do but I found a spot where it at least stayed steady. "I'm standing here looking at him and I need your help. I'm out on Bray Road beyond where Lydia was found and on the other side of the fence in the plowed field. The dog is in a hole about four feet deep, and it has a broken leg. I need help to get him out and to a vet."

"Um, right. Okay. I'll, um, ask you what you're doing out there at night when I see you."

"I'll keep my headlamp and flashlight on to help you find me."

"Okay. Be there shortly."

I spent my waiting time trying to reassure the poor dog, grateful it didn't try to climb out of the hole. I didn't neglect Newt, either.

"You're such a good boy, Newt. You probably saved this little guy's life."

It was full dark by then and a waning, barely gibbous moon had risen over the horizon, shedding just enough light over the surrounding landscape to calm my nerves. Just then a howl emanated from the direction of the cornfield, and when I looked, I saw something moving some distance away, heading toward the trees. It stopped before entering the woods, and with the moon behind it silhouetting its shape, it stood on two legs.

Gooseflesh prickled down my arms and spine. Newt wasn't reacting, but he was busy sniffing around the edges of the hole. I couldn't tell if the creature in the cornfield was facing me because it was too far away and backlit, but I felt watched. It looked tall and appeared to have a lean, muscular outline and pointed ears. I stared at it as it stood there, still as a statue and perfectly silhouetted against the moon.

Newt was on the other side of the hole digging in a small pile of dirt. I glanced over at him, worried he might be too close to the edge. He wasn't, but by the time I looked out at the cornfield again, the creature was gone.

"Morgan! Where are you?"

The sound of Wyatt's voice coming out of the woods between me and the road made me breathe a sigh of relief. I turned on my flashlight and waved it. "Over here."

"There she is." Wyatt had someone with him. I aimed my flashlight in their direction to help guide them, while also looking out across the field to where the creature had been.

There was nothing there now and I had to wonder if anything ever had been.

CHAPTER 22

The man Wyatt had with him introduced himself as Dr. Newsome, a local veterinarian. I stepped back out of the way, taking Newt with me, and Dr. Newsome eased down into the hole. While he examined the injured dog, whose name I learned was Augie, I watched, pondering the presence of the hole. Why was it there? It was clearly man-made. What purpose did it serve?

I shone my flashlight around the general area—looking for what exactly, I didn't know. The hole was significant—I felt certain of it, though I didn't yet know how. Then the beam from my flashlight caught something on one of the fence rails that looked silvery in the moonlight. A closer look revealed several light-colored strands of hair about eight inches long trapped beneath a large splinter of wood. I started to touch the hair but then thought better of it.

I bent down to peer more closely at it and then looked over at Wyatt. He was distracted, busy helping Dr. Newsome splint Augie's broken leg.

"Wyatt, did the two of you drive out here together?" I asked.

"No. Why?"

"Not important. I'll explain later."

The two men secured Augie to a small stretcher they'd brought along, and with some minimal help from me, we managed to lift him out of the hole and over the fence into the cornfield. Augie was a sweet boy, and he remained docile through it all, licking any hands near him even when it was obvious from his yelps that our movements caused him pain.

I retrieved my tire iron from where I'd dropped it, earning a questioning look from Wyatt, and then Newt and I followed the men as they carried the litter along the fence line—me checking the cornfield every few seconds to see if my moonlit beast had returned. I stuck close to the men as we walked the path between the woods—once again skirting the big mud puddle—and when we reached the road and were back in moonlight, I breathed a sigh of relief. I watched as the men slid the litter into the back seat of the king cab pickup Dr. Newsome had driven, where it was then secured with a seat belt.

I thanked Dr. Newsome profusely. So did Newt, who went over and licked his hand. Once we saw the vet drive off, I turned to Wyatt and said, "Do you have an evidence bag of some type on you by any chance?"

"I do. I carry a few basics around all the time. Why?" I opened my mouth to answer but before I could he said, "And what the hell are you doing out here in the dark, anyway?"

"I'm doing the job you hired me to do."

"Why didn't you call me so I could come out here with you?"

"I didn't need anyone else."

"Walking around out here in the dark with a lug wrench for protection is a fool's errand."

"It wasn't dark when I got here, and if it hadn't been for someone else lurking in the woods, I would have been long gone before it was dark."

"You could have—" He stopped, eyes narrowed, head tilted to the side. "What do you mean, there was someone else out here?"

"I heard someone walking through those woods over there." I pointed to the trees in question.

"Someone or something?"

"Pretty sure it was a someone unless the local beasts know how to drive a car. I tried to see who it was, but they hightailed it back to the road and drove off before I saw them or their vehicle, though they did leave some tracks in the mud. Unfortunately, you and the good doctor have since driven over them, so I don't think they'll be much help. Best I can deduce, the car was either electric or a hybrid given how quiet it was. Whoever it was, they were sneaking around and then ran, making it clear they didn't want to be caught. I can't help but wonder why."

Wyatt frowned, hands on his hips. "You haven't told me what you're doing out here."

"I wanted another look at the site."

"This is private property. Technically, I could arrest you for trespassing."

"Technically, I'm under no obligation to tell you I saw the beast right before you got here."

Wyatt reared back in surprise. "You what?"

"I saw it. Saw something, anyway. It was large and it had pointed ears, and it stood on two legs. It saw it silhouetted by the moon along the edge of the cornfield by the woods."

"Was it hairy? Furry?"

I threw my hands up in exasperation. "I couldn't tell. It was backlit and too far away."

Wyatt raked a hand through his hair and stared at the woods. "What about sound? Did it make any noise?"

I hesitated to answer honestly, knowing what it might make him think, but I went all in, anyway. "I heard a howl."

"Really? It howled?"

"I didn't say that. I said I heard a howl. It seemed to come from the same general direction as the creature, but it sounded farther away. The howl is what made me look in the first place. It could have been a wolf or even another local dog. All I know for sure is, it wasn't Newt or Augie." I paused, scowling. "To be honest, I'd decided earlier today that Lydia's death had most likely come at the hands of a human monster rather than any beastly one. Now I'm not so sure."

"What you're describing sounds a lot like the same thing Paul McNamara saw."

I shrugged, unwilling to commit. Yet. "We'll see. Now, how about the evidence bag?"

"Oh. Right. How big?"

"Small."

"You know we don't use evidence bags for casts of tire imprints, right?"

I chuckled. "I know. The tire marks are all messed up now, anyway."

Wyatt scratched at his sideburn, went around to the back of his car, opened the hatch, and rummaged through a large canvas tote. A few moments later he held up a small plastic bag. "Will this do?"

"It will," I said, tossing the tire iron back into my car. "Now we need to go back out to the hole. I saw something there I think might be important."

We made quick work of the passage between the trees and stuck to the cornfield until we were adjacent to the hole poor Augie had fallen into. I stopped, pointing to the hairs trapped in the wooden fence rail.

"Well, I'll be damned," Wyatt said, eyeing them closely.

"Think they could be Lydia's?"

Wyatt didn't answer, but his actions told me all I needed to know. He handed me the plastic bag and said, "Hold this open for me, will you?" I obliged while he donned a pair of nitrile gloves he had in his pocket and I watched as he worked to release the hairs from beneath the split in the wood rail. They were wedged in tightly, which was probably how they had survived the storm. Once he got them loose, he dropped them into the evidence bag and took it from me, sealing it closed. He took out a Sharpie pen and wrote on the bag before putting both items back into his pocket.

I pointed at the fence. "Look at the sharp angle of the wood rail where the hair came from. If Lydia hit the back of her neck hard on it, might it not have been what caused the fracture?"

Wyatt nodded slowly, scratching his sideburn again. He stared back at the woods toward the spot where Lydia's body had been found.

Reading his thoughts, I said, "Whatever or whoever killed her must have dragged her body into those woods." My use of the word "whoever" earned me a quick sidelong glance. I shrugged. "It's not typical animal behavior to drag a dead body that far unless there was a burrow of some sort near where the body was found. And if the animal simply wanted to hide the body from other predators, those woods back there beyond the far edge of the cornfield are closer. All of this makes me wonder two things: Why was Lydia's body dragged into those particular woods, and why is this hole here?"

Wyatt's lips had pursed into a thin white line as he stared at the fence for a few seconds, then looked toward the woods, then over at the hole. "None of this makes much sense to me. Does it to you?"

While it made more sense to me than it probably did to Wyatt given the items Lydia had hidden away, I was still struggling to make the pieces of this puzzle fit into a logical and rational explanation. "Not yet," I said, a half-truth.

"The thing you saw tonight. . . ." Wyatt said, staring out over the cornfield. He hesitated before turning to look at me. "Don't laugh or mock me, please. This is a serious question. Could it have been a werewolf?"

I started to shake my head but stopped. "I don't know, Wyatt. I spent some time researching the history of the Beast of Bray Road sightings and I'll admit what I saw tonight matched the descriptions others provided, including Paul McNamara and those from back in the eighties and nineties. It didn't look like any normal animal I know, but I'm having a hard time buying into this werewolf stuff."

"Maybe the hair on the fence is a coincidence," Wyatt suggested. "Or maybe it was from Augie."

My expression told him what I thought of the idea, but just to be sure, I said, "The hair on the fence looked a little long to have come from Augie."

Wyatt cocked his head to one side and scrunched his face. "You don't really think there's a werewolf running around out here, do you?" It was more a statement than a question, but I answered anyway, the rational side of my brain kicking in.

"No, I don't."

"How sure are you?" he challenged me.

"I'm not ruling it out completely yet. I need more answers."

"Damn it." He raked a hand through his hair while I laughed. "What are you doing for the rest of the evening?"

"Getting some dinner, going back to my motel room, and then crashing."

"Can I take you out to eat? Maybe all of this will make better sense under the harsh lights of some fluorescents and with a little food in our bellies."

"Thanks, but I want to do some research and think all this through on my own tonight. I have some other ideas I want to explore."

And some evidence I haven't told you about.

"Besides, I wouldn't want to provide any fodder for the matchmakers' gossip mill," I added. This earned me a laugh. "How about I call you tomorrow morning?"

"Sure." He looked and sounded disappointed. "I'll be at work. Call anytime."

We hiked back to the road and got into our respective cars,

though not until Wyatt had a good look at all the tire tracks in the mud and took a couple of pictures. He then tailed me to my motel parking lot before breaking off and going his own way. Part of me was annoyed at him for following me but another part of me was grateful. It had been a highly unnerving day.

CHAPTER 23

By the time I arrived back at the motel it was after ten and I had to apologize to Newt because there was nowhere to get him the cheeseburger I'd promised him earlier. I made it up to him, however, by walking over to the Domino's located in the shopping center next to my motel. After cheeseburgers, pizza crust was his next-favorite snack.

I hooked Newt's leash around a metal bench outside the store and went in to order the pizza, grabbing a bunch of napkins and a bottle of water before returning to the bench. Newt, already sensing what was to come based on the smells emanating from the pizza store, was drooling, and his feet were a muddy mess. My shoes didn't look much better, and I set about using the napkins and the water to clean us both.

I was washing off Newt's front paw and hadn't been at it very long when I became aware of someone standing close by.

"Oh, sorry. I didn't mean to stare," said a woman with long dark hair. I gauged her to be about my age and thought she looked vaguely familiar. "It's just that I love your dog. What a handsome beast he is. You're staying at the Hampton Inn, aren't you." It was a statement, not a question. "I am, too, and I saw you and your dog the other morning in the hallway. May I pet him?"

I nodded, remembering her. She was the person I'd almost collided with in the hallway the other day. "If you don't mind a little drool," I said, using a napkin to wipe a string of it hanging from Newt's jaw.

"Naw, nobody ever died from a little dog drool," she said, and then she began stroking Newt from head to tail. Newt dutifully subjected himself to the woman's ministrations, sighing contentedly. "Are you waiting on a pizza?" the woman asked.

"I am."

"Me, too. I didn't expect anyone else to be eating this late. Mind if I sit?" She gestured toward the space beside me on the bench.

"Of course not." She sat down and continued applying lavish attention to Newt. "My name's Donna Diamond. My friends call me DeeDee, which is better than the nickname I had in high school of Double Dee. What's this guy's name?"

"That's Newt. And I'm Morgan."

"Hello, Newt." DeeDee got right down by Newt's nose and added, "You are a handsome boy, aren't you?"

Newt clearly agreed and wagged his tail in acknowledgment. "I'm here for a family wedding," DeeDee said. "My cousin is getting married, and she's planned this whole weeklong thing. We kind of grew up together but I hardly know her now. She's being quite the bridezilla and my whole family is a dysfunctional mess. *So* much drama! And that's why I'm here buying pizza so late. Well, that and because my cousin has been on a strict diet so she can lose weight for the wedding and all she served us today was so-called health food—dried-up fruit and veggie chips, some kind of tofu dip and pretzel thing. . . . Honestly it was like eating sticks and cardboard. My cells are screaming for a good old greasy slice of pepperoni."

I laughed. "Families can be challenging," I said.

"Sorry. I overshared, didn't I? I always do that. What brings you to Elkhorn?"

"I'm helping a friend with something," I said vaguely.

"Are you going to be here long?"

"Hopefully only another day. Maybe two."

"I'm here until the end of the week," DeeDee said. "I shouldn't have come but I got guilted into it. To be honest, little towns like this give me the willies. Especially this one. Did you hear about the woman who was killed recently? My cousin said there's some kind of werewolf out there in the woods."

I looked over at her, gauging her expression to try to determine if she was seriously considering this idea. "There's no such thing as werewolves."

"Yeah, it does sound kind of far-fetched, but my cousin and her family swear it's a real thing. I mean, couldn't it be real? How do we know for sure werewolves don't exist?"

The conspiracy theorist's favorite tool—you can't prove a negative. "Science and logic," I said.

"I suppose. What do you think killed her, then? Something like a regular wolf maybe but a rogue one? Or maybe a bear?"

"I haven't the foggiest." I went back to cleaning Newt's feet, hoping the pizza would be ready soon.

"Wow, you guys got into something muddy."

"It's one of Newt's favorite things. I'm lucky he didn't roll in it."

"Did you go hiking? Because werewolf or not, I don't think it's safe to be out in the boonies around here. You need to be careful."

Fortunately, a guy came out with my pizza then and I excused myself with some comment about wanting to eat it while it was hot, eager to escape. Newt was reluctant to leave DeeDee, who had been petting him the whole time, and I had to tug on his leash and say, "Pizza, Newt," to get him to move. He left a trail of drool behind us.

Back in my room, I was about to dig into some sausage and mushrooms with extra cheese when I got a call from Jon. I debated not answering for about a millisecond because I was desperately hungry at this point and the smell of the pizza had me drooling nearly as much as Newt. Jon won, and Newt, who usually gets my end crust after I've eaten the rest of the slice, shot me a look of utter betrayal when I went for the phone. This prompted me to tear off some crust and toss it to him after I put the call on speaker and set the phone down.

"How's it going down there in the thriving metropolis of Elkhorn?" Jon asked.

"Definitely not boring. I found and saved a creature today."

"Details, please," Jon demanded.

"It was a dog, nothing exotic." I debated telling him I might have seen the actual Beast of Bray Road but decided adding to my list of foolish ventures—in Jon's mind at least—might not be wise.

Instead, I told him about finding Augie and how we rescued him, leaving out the parts about me traipsing around in the dark and trespassing on private property.

"Listen," Jon said when I was done telling my doggy tale, "Uncle Karl and I have been looking into this thing with David and the New Jersey couple. It's possible there may be some truth to his story."

"Oh. Wow." I took a second to digest this. "Are you saying you don't think David killed my parents?"

"No. I'm not willing to make that leap yet. David has proven himself too slick, too clever by far. And as I've said before, I wouldn't put it past him to try to retrofit facts into something other than the truth. But"—he exhaled heavily—"I will go so far as to say I think it's possible he didn't do it. This New Jersey couple gets more and more mysterious the deeper we dig into them, and it does look like they might have been operating as a kill team for someone. The Feds have tied them to a couple of murders over the years with circumstantial evidence but nothing strong enough to indict. And their apparent MO often involved slashed throats."

"Oh, wow. This changes everything," I said, feeling as if a two-ton weight had been lifted off my shoulders.

"Whoa, not too fast," Jon said. "David might not be a murderer, but he most certainly is a con man and thief. Don't go putting your trust in him just because he might not have killed your folks."

"Of course," I said. "Believe you me, I harbor no kind feelings toward David. But, Jon, if he didn't do it, it means I'm not responsible for my parents' deaths. It wasn't my fault. I didn't bring the killer to them."

"Of course. Sorry. I wasn't looking at it from your perspective."

"And if David didn't kill my parents, I no longer need to be afraid of him." I let out a huge sigh of relief. "You have no idea how much this has been weighing on me over the past few months. It's like someone just opened all the blinds and let light into the room."

"Slow down, Morgan. He *was* stalking you, remember? And apparently doing so before he knew about this Jersey couple."

"Well, yeah, okay. There is that."

Jon chuckled. "We're still hoping to find and arrest him, if for nothing else than identity theft."

I envisioned David behind bars. It was a far kinder image than what I used to conjure up about him. When this case was over, I'd need to sit down and rethink everything I'd once believed of him. I still hated him for duping me the way he had, making such a fool out of me. But deep down inside, I knew I was as guilty as he was in that regard, and on some level, I also hated myself. I'd gone headlong into my relationship with him, not only heedless of the warnings my parents had given me, but rubbing their noses in it because I was angry over the way they'd been monitoring and controlling my life at the time. I'd even ignored my own gut instincts, all in the name of what I thought was love.

"We need to sit down and talk when you get home," Jon said. These were words I'd been desperate to hear, and my heart leapt. "I'm thinking of making some changes and I want to talk to you about them. Because they will impact our relationship."

Okay, hold on.

On the one hand, this sounded encouraging, but on the other, it had an ominous ring to it. I decided to be optimistic.

Optimism or avoidance, Morgan?

"Absolutely. I look forward to getting together and talking."

I started to say something more, but before I could, he said, "Hold up, Morgan. I have another call coming in and I really need to take it. Let's talk more later."

And just like that, the call ended.

I spent the better part of the next hour eating pizza, feeding Newt my crusts, and dissecting my conversation and history with Jon to a degree that annoyed even me. Then I started psychoanalyzing myself. Eventually, I picked up my phone and called Wyatt.

He answered with "Uh-oh. What's happened?"

"Nothing. Am I interrupting anything important?"

"Nope. I was just about to go to bed."

I looked at my watch and saw it was pushing midnight. "Sorry. I didn't realize how late it was."

"It's okay. What's up?"

"Are you really a shrink?"

"No, I'm not a shrink. I'm a cop. Do I have a master's degree in psychology? Yes, I do. But I've never practiced."

"Well, I think I've had a revelation of sorts, and I want to bounce it off someone who knows about these kinds of things."

"Okay. What kinds of things would that be?" Wyatt asked, sounding wary.

"Psych things. For instance, I diagnosed myself with PTSD after the death of my parents. I've had nightmares and panic attacks ever since and I never had them before."

"It's never a good idea to self-diagnose, but in this case I'd say you're right. Have you seen a counselor since your parents were murdered?"

"No, I haven't. Thought about it but never followed through. I thought I was coping well enough on my own. But tonight, I realized something. I've been blaming myself for my parents' deaths, for bringing David into their lives and creating the situation that led to him killing them. The piece I hadn't realized is how much I loathe myself for it."

"'Loathe' is a strong word," Wyatt said. "It's understandable you feel guilt over it, but you didn't kill your parents. This David guy did."

"Except now I've learned he might not have."

"Are you serious?"

"It's not for sure yet, but until I considered the possibility, I didn't realize just how much I hated myself for my part in it."

"Look, Morgan, I'm not comfortable doing this, especially over the phone. Let me come over there so we can talk in person."

"There's no need. I'm fine. I promise."

"Are you having any thoughts of hurting yourself?"

"Gosh, no, nothing like that. Although in a way, that's kind of why I called you. You said you spent some time talking to Jon about his past and my relationship with him. You know he's uncomfortable with some of the risks I've taken."

"O-o-o-kay," Wyatt said, back in wary mode.

"Is it possible the decisions I make and the risks I take are a subtle way of punishing myself, of literally risking death because on some level I don't believe I have a right to be alive?"

"Okay. Wow. We're really going to do this. Um . . . you don't need a shrink. You seem to be rather adept at shrinking yourself."

I laughed. "I haven't done any deep psychoanalysis on myself. But when I learned I might not have been responsible for my folks' deaths, it was like a huge weight was suddenly lifted off me. I was struck by a flash of clarity of how numb and uncaring I've felt toward my own safety. Honestly, if it wasn't for Newt, I'm not sure I would have survived the past three years."

Newt pricked his ears up at hearing his name and thumped his tail on the floor a few times. I threw him another bit of pizza crust.

"Um, yes, I suppose you could be onto something there," Wyatt said. "Does this mean no more trips out to Bray Road at night by yourself?"

Baby steps, Wyatt. Baby steps.

Eventually, I'd get there but I had some things I still wanted to do out on Bray Road, most likely at night. But as a compromise, I'd be sure I was better prepared next time.

I was saved from having to answer Wyatt by the beep of my phone letting me know I had a call coming in from Devon. "Wyatt, Devon is calling, so I need to go. But thanks for helping me out."

"I'm not sure I did anything, but okay."

"I'll call you tomorrow sometime."

"Please do."

I switched over to Devon. I couldn't wait to share the news about David with him and Rita.

"Hey, Dev."

"I hope I didn't wake you."

"Nope. I'm still up. Have you got something good for me?"

"Possibly," he said. "But first, I have a question for you. Any idea why Jon has his house up for sale and his position as chief is listed as open?"

CHAPTER 24

It was as if I'd been pushed off a cliff. My high spirits plummeted, and my previous thoughts scattered like shards of broken glass. This was not at all what I had been expecting when Jon said he planned to make some changes in his life. Before I could respond to Devon, the arrival of the email he'd sent me with links to both items dinged on my laptop. I clicked on them and stared at the screen, my thoughts spinning.

"I had no idea," I managed to say. "I just spoke to him a little while ago and he said he was going to make some changes in his life, but I wasn't expecting something this drastic. He didn't say anything about leaving."

"I'm sorry, boss," Devon said.

Heavy of heart, I fought back tears. "Me, too, Dev. Me, too."

Disappointment and sadness settled over me like a weighted blanket. "Maybe it just wasn't meant to be."

"Let me see if I can cheer you up. I've been delving into Mr. Lester Hofheyzer and found some interesting things. First, he belongs to a group for numismatists on Facebook."

Thanks to the word game I played with Rita, I knew what a numismatist was. "He's a coin collector?"

"You got it. He's also a member of the American Numismatic Association."

"Hard to believe that's a coincidence," I said, my brain struggling to focus.

"He also belongs to several groups on Facebook related to history. Judging from his posts, he's something of a scholar on twentieth-century American history."

"That *is* interesting, Devon. Excellent work."

"And I'm not done. It turns out your victim, Lydia Palmer, was also involved in the Facebook history groups."

"Excellent," I said, a picture beginning to form in my mind.

"Any luck getting me access to Lydia's phone or laptop?"

"No, and unless Wyatt gives them back to Dylan and he lets me have a crack at them, I'm not sure it's going to happen. In the meantime, I have something new for you to work on. See what you can find for me on a guy by the name of Connor O'Leary, thirty-something. He lives with Dylan and works for a company that makes prosthetics for amputees."

"Got it. Anything else?"

"That's it for tonight. You've earned a few hours off."

"Wow, a whole few hours?" he mocked, making me laugh.

"You know I'll pay you for your time," I said.

"Then I probably shouldn't tell you I love doing this kind of stuff for you and would do it for free."

"You are correct. You shouldn't tell me that."

This time, he laughed. "How's it going down there? Have you caught any werewolves yet?"

"No werewolves but Newt helped me rescue a dog with a broken leg. The poor thing fell into a hole and couldn't get out."

"Aw, poor baby. And good boy, Newt," Devon said, and Newt, hearing it, thumped his tail on the floor.

I thanked Dev again and we disconnected. I should have been tired, should have been sleeping, but I was wide-awake, my brain going in too many different directions at once. The thing with Jon was both distracting and distressing. I forced myself to push those thoughts aside and focus on my case instead. The fact that Lester Hofheyzer was a collector of coins was significant, but I wasn't sure yet exactly what it meant. Was it connected to what was going on out there on Bray Road? Lydia had had those old coins on her when she died. Surely that wasn't a coincidence. Lester Hofheyzer had to be connected in some way. I just had to figure out how.

I took a paper tablet out of my satchel and started writing down what I knew, beginning with Lydia's death, the odd scratches on her car, the coins she had on her when she was killed, the booklet and letter she'd hidden—both of which were fakes—the map that was probably also a fake, the site some distance from where Lydia's body had been found where someone had dug a large hole, and the hairs that looked like they could be Lydia's caught in the wood fence next to this hole.

There was also the creature I'd seen with my own eyes out

there in the cornfield, but I chose to write it in a separate column. First, I needed to understand why Lydia had been out there and then I could look at how she'd died.

I took the Nitti–Capone letter out of my satchel and laid it out on the table so I could read it again. How had Lydia come by it? And if she'd thought it was something of value, had she tried to sell it? Maybe Lester was interested in buying it. But how did the letter tie into the hole in the ground? If I assumed Lydia was the one who had dug the hole, what had led her to that specific spot? I took out the map and laid it out next to the letter. Was there a clue in what the letter said rather than in who had supposedly written it? I read it again, but other than the mention of the taxmen, the substance of it was newsy, everyday stuff. It seemed too random.

Frustrated, I pushed the letter and map off to one side and went back to my list, adding to my second column by writing down Paul McNamara's name and a brief description of what he'd seen the night he was stranded out on Bray Road. As I stared at my notes, the words began to blur as fatigue finally took hold.

Mentally exhausted, I tossed the tablet aside and took Newt out for a last walk, hoping the night air might stimulate my brain. It didn't. When I returned to my room, I took a long, hot shower, put on my jammies, and climbed into bed, hoping a good night's sleep would help.

I woke at the crack of dawn after a restless night of dreams filled with angry, howling dogs, growling wolves sporting fangs dripping with blood, and yipping coyotes baring their teeth. A cup of coffee from the tiny machine in my room didn't help my grumpy mood much and I felt inexplicably irritable. I hoped some fresh air would help.

I donned a jacket and shoes without bothering to get out of my pajamas and slipped outside to walk Newt. When I returned to my room, I walked over to the desk and stared at the papers and notes I'd left out the night before. The writing tablet containing my list was sitting on top of the fake Capone letter, and as I went to pick it up, something caught my eye. My hand froze in midair, and I sucked in an excited breath.

The tablet was positioned in a way that showed only the first letters of the four beginning sentences in the Capone letter lying beneath it. The first sentence began with a capital B, the second with a lowercase r, the third with a lowercase a, and the fourth with a lowercase y. I slid the tablet down lower on the page, so it obscured all but the beginning letters on the rest of the sentences. There was a sentence beginning with a capital R followed by one with a lowercase o, one with a lowercase a, and one with a lowercase d. I shoved the tablet aside and picked up the letter, looking at it from a new perspective. The sentence below the one starting with the letter d began with the word "Every" and since it was the first word in that sentence, the E was capitalized. The line below it, which happened to be the final one in the letter, began with an address where a man the fake Nitti had mentioned supposedly lived, making the beginning of this last sentence the number six.

Excitedly, I grabbed the map, laid it out flat, placed a finger on the letter E in the left margin, and then put another finger on the six in the top margin. Then I dragged my fingers across and down until they met. The spot where they ended up was where the hole was.

The letter was a cipher! I studied it more carefully, dissecting each sentence, looking for an odd turn of phrase, or a word here and there that didn't quite seem to fit, or words where the ink seemed thicker, heavier. Eventually, a pattern began to emerge, and I started another list.

Half an hour later, I looked over what I had written. Owed money was mentioned, supposedly in reference to a particular person by the name of Copper Nabb. It had struck me as an odd name the first time I saw it and now it stood out even more. A quick Google search came up empty, making me wonder if the name was made-up. Could it be a play on words meaning the police were about to nab someone? I sent a quick message to Devon asking him to dig deeper into the name and then moved on.

There was a sentence where Nitti, the supposed writer, mentioned the two treasures in his life—his son, Joseph, and his wife, Anna—and how he was learning to appreciate what was truly important. The word "treasures" looked noticeably darker as if it had been traced over. Another line mentioned how Nitti feared Anna had buried her feelings about adopting their son, and the word "buried" was written not only darker but on a downward slant that left the word below the rest of the line.

My fingers tingled as I held the letter, and I forced myself to slow down and think. Was I reading too much into this? Was I falling prey to a written form of pareidolia, perceiving a meaningful message in the words the way people see familiar images in random patterns like clouds?

I'd already been told the letter was a fake, and if Nitti hadn't written it, who had? Why would someone go to all the trouble of aging paper and leather, drawing a map, and creating an entire ledger of supposed receipts? To what end?

It hit me then. Lydia Palmer had been desperate to find ways to make money so she could create a better life for her son and herself. She believed that the letter, map, and ledger were real and that they provided clues to buried treasure left behind by none other than Al Capone's henchman Frank Nitti. On the surface it seemed absurd and ludicrous. I found it hard to believe anyone of average intelligence would have been duped into believing this could be real. Yet Capone's henchmen did have connections to the area. And while the papers and notebook might have been faked, the coins were very real.

It provided a possible explanation for what Lydia had been doing out there in the middle of the night. She'd needed darkness and solitude so she could dig for buried treasure. That was why the hole was there. Had she found those coins out in the field?

And had something, or even some*one*, killed her before she could find the rest of it?

I desperately wanted to let Devon have a look at Lydia's laptop and phone and I was about to call Wyatt to once again broach the subject when my phone rang and his name came up on the caller ID.

"Wyatt! I was just about to call you. You must have ESP."

"There's been another attack," he said.

"What do you mean?"

"Out on Bray Road. Same general area, but this time the body was left in the woods not far from the road."

"Oh, no. Same kind of injuries?"

"Yes, but much more severe. She's badly ripped up."

"Do you know who it is?"

"Tentatively. There's a car parked alongside the road and the victim has ID on her that matches the car registration. But her face makes visual confirmation difficult, if you get what I mean."

I did and it made me grimace. "Are you there now with the body?"

"Yes."

"I need to see it."

"That's going to be complicated, Morgan. There's a problem."

"What do you mean?"

"The victim had a notebook in her pocket, and it had some names written in it. Yours was at the top of the list."

"What? Hold on. What's the tentative ID on her?"

"The name on her license is Donna Diamond."

Good Lord, it was DeeDee. Something wasn't adding up here. "I'll be there in ten, Wyatt," I said. And with that, I disconnected the call.

CHAPTER 25

I still had to get dressed, so I arrived at the scene fifteen minutes later. There was a crowd of police and emergency vehicles blocking Bray Road from Hospital Road on up as far as I could see. I parked behind one of the cars, leashed Newt, and started walking. As I got closer, I saw several folks hovering around a gray hybrid parked off the side of the road.

Newt and I got some curious stares, but no one tried to stop us until we got close to the rutted path between the two sets of woods, where a deputy sheriff stepped in front of me. "You need to turn around and leave, ma'am. This is a secured area."

I swallowed down my indignation at being called "ma'am" and said, "I'm a consultant working with Detective Moorhead. He's expecting me."

The deputy looked skeptical, his eyes moving back and forth

between me and Newt, indecision stamped on his face. Finally, he used a radio clipped to his shoulder.

"Uh, Wyatt, I got a lady here with a dog who says she's a consultant of yours?"

The deputy's tone left little doubt as to what he thought of my claim, and I feared Wyatt might bust me back to my car. But to my surprise and relief, I heard him let out an exasperated sigh over the deputy's radio and say, "Yeah, let her come through."

"The dog, too?" the deputy said, still eyeing me with suspicion.

"Yeah, the dog, too."

I smiled at the deputy, who didn't smile back. Newt and I moved on, walking around a crime scene investigation van before turning down the rutted lane that led out to the cornfield. Other people we passed—some in uniforms, some in street clothes, some in white jumpsuits—eyed us with wary cordiality as if unsure if we were interlopers or just new members of the team they hadn't met yet.

The big puddle had soaked into the ground, leaving only narrow strips of water in the lowest points of the ruts. It was easy enough to bypass, but the ground felt boggy beneath my feet. I kept Newt tight to my side, eager to ensure he didn't mess up any potential crime scene evidence. We didn't have to go far. I heard Wyatt's voice off to the left in the woods and saw him standing about thirty feet away with a small group of people.

He saw me and waved. "Come through here," he said, indicating a path created by lines of police tape strung between the trees. There was a low murmur of conversation among the people in Wyatt's immediate group, and I tried to hear what they were saying as I approached. But by the time I got close enough to discern specific words, they all suddenly dispersed, leaving Wyatt standing alone.

I was still ten feet away when Newt began to whine. I reassured him and stopped about five feet from the white sheet on the ground. I could see where red stains had seeped through in spots and I swallowed hard, imagining what lay beneath.

Wyatt gave me a chastising look. "You really shouldn't be here," he said, his voice just above a whisper. "I'm going to have a hell of a time explaining you to my boss."

"You should have thought about that before you hired me."

"Care to tell me why this woman has your name written down in a notebook?"

"She's staying at my hotel. I ran into her a couple of times over the past few days. She really liked Newt." At the sound of his name, Newt whined. "We chatted last night while waiting for pizzas at the Domino's in the shopping center."

"Any idea what she was doing out here?"

I shook my head. "None. She said she was in town for the week for a family wedding."

Wyatt held up a plastic evidence bag containing a small pocket-sized spiral notebook. "She also had Paul McNamara's name and Dylan's and Lydia's names written in this notebook, along with their addresses. I'm guessing she wasn't here for a wedding."

I recalled how DeeDee had questioned me about Lydia's death and why I was in town last night. *Oh, you clever girl.*

Things were starting to make sense. "When I went to the library the other day to look at info on the Beast of Bray Road, that fellow Lester was there, and he pulled a file out of a drawer. I commented on how it was right up front, and he said it was because someone else had requested it recently, saying they wanted the info for a documentary."

"Great. That's all we need," Wyatt said, rolling his eyes. "Think it was her?"

I shrugged. "Seems possible." I gestured toward the sheet. "May I?"

Wyatt sighed, removed a pair of gloves from his pocket, and handed them to me. "Put these on."

I did as instructed and told Newt to stay before walking over to what I thought was the head of the body. When I lifted the white sheet, I expected to see DeeDee's pale or bloodied face but instead saw the back of her head. Lifting the sheet higher, I saw ragged tears in her shirt and beneath them deep rivets—four of them—gouging the skin of her back. I looked questioningly at Wyatt.

"We rolled her over before you got here. She has a neck wound similar to what Lydia had, though it's more to the side, and her cheek was also torn apart. Her carotid was severed, and she bled out quickly. There's arterial spray over there."

He pointed toward some trees a few feet away where several people in white jumpsuits were taking pictures and collecting evidence.

"Looks like she was attacked over there initially and staggered here, trying to escape. I think she either turned to see what was behind her or the impact of the back wound spun her around. Then came the slash to her face."

"How long do you think she's been here?"

"Not sure. I'm waiting on the ME. He was in the middle of an autopsy. But I'd guess time of death was around four to six hours ago, during the wee hours of the morning. Rigor has started but isn't complete."

About the same time Lydia had been killed. "Why was she out here?" I said, thinking out loud.

"No idea," Wyatt said.

"You said Dylan's name was in the notebook also?" Wyatt nodded. "Are you planning on talking to him?"

"I am. I suppose you want to come along?"

"I visited him yesterday," I said, sidestepping the question.

"Why?"

I shrugged. "I wanted to talk with him about his mother some more to try to get a better feel for who she was and what she was doing out here."

"And were you enlightened in any way?"

"Not then, no." I started to tell him I had an idea about why Lydia had come out here in the middle of the night but then remembered I hadn't shared the map, the letter, or the ledger with him and decided it wasn't the appropriate time or place to reveal my subterfuge. I needed to be in his good graces a little longer.

Wyatt was eyeing me curiously and I was trying to think up something to change the subject when a woman in a white jumpsuit approached and did it for me.

"We found this over there by the trees with the blood spatter," she said, handing Wyatt a plastic bag containing what appeared to be a gold necklace with two silver capital Ds, one the mirror image of the other. They were positioned back-to-back, their rounded edges slightly overlapping, and there was a small, colorless gem at the center.

"There's blood on the chain, so I'm guessing it belongs to the victim," the woman said.

Wyatt took it and then showed it to me.

"It's for her name," I said. "She told me she goes by DeeDee."

Wyatt returned the bag to the tech. "While we're waiting on a definitive ID, I need to find out why she was out here. I suppose Dylan is the next logical stop. Are you coming?"

I nodded and Wyatt called over a deputy to come and stand guard by the body and wait on the ME's arrival. Then we hiked out to the road, careful to stick to the path created by the police tape.

"My car's way down there," I said, pointing beyond the clutter of official vehicles lining the road. "How about I meet you at Dylan's?"

Wyatt was parked in the street outside Dylan's house and already on the porch, leaning against the railing, when I arrived. I pulled in behind his car and got out, leaving Newt in the back seat for now because Connor's car wasn't in the driveway. Nor was Brittany's car anywhere to be seen. Lydia's car was, however.

"You returned it?" I said, walking up beside the vehicle as Wyatt traversed the ramp to come meet me.

"Yeah, I couldn't really justify keeping it any longer. Lydia's manner of death is now officially accidental due to an animal attack. I had a deputy follow me here first thing this morning when I dropped it off along with the keys."

"I take it no one is home?" I said as I circled the vehicle.

"You got it."

“Are you going to wait?”

“I’m thinking I’ll give it ten minutes. If he isn’t back by then, we can leave. Do you mind hanging for a bit?”

I didn’t and said so, figuring I could walk Newt around in the meantime.

Once I let Newt out of my car, I headed down the driveway toward the backyard and Lydia’s garden, trying to imagine what it might look like when it was in full bloom and properly groomed. Of course, the odds were, it would soon be taken over by weeds. The bird feeder I saw hanging outside the kitchen window was and likely would remain empty of any seed. The mental image of this neglect saddened me. It was clear Lydia had cared deeply about her home, her son, and her life.

My phone chimed and I saw I had a message from Devon letting me know that the name Copper Nabb was a dead end and that all he’d been able to dig up on Connor O’Leary was a history of court cases for unpaid debts and an eviction. It seemed his move hadn’t been as voluntary as Dylan and Lydia had thought.

Before I could contemplate this revelation anymore, a car turned into the driveway. Connor was behind the wheel, Dylan in the passenger seat. Neither of them looked particularly happy to see us.

Dylan opened his door, turning sideways in his seat and lifting his legs out of the car. “What now?” he asked of no one in particular. No one answered him, at least not right away.

Something about him was different but I couldn’t put a finger on what it was. I finally chalked it up to the fact that he was dressed in sweatpants, a sweatshirt, and athletic shoes as opposed to his usual attire of slacks and a button-down shirt. The collapsed wheelchair was in the back seat rather than in the trunk, and while Connor was hauling it out of the car and expanding it, Newt went over to greet Dylan, tail wagging with enthusiasm.

"My dog has taken a definite liking to you," I said.

Dylan smiled and patted Newt on the head before Connor nudged Newt out of the way so he could get the wheelchair in position. Then, in one smooth move, he reached in, lifted Dylan from the car, and pivoted to set him in the wheelchair.

"There has been a development," Wyatt said as we trailed Connor and Dylan up the ramp to the front door.

"Good news, I hope," Dylan said.

Wyatt shot me a look, one that the two men in front of us couldn't see. "Let's talk when we're inside," Wyatt said.

Once we were all in the living room, Wyatt opted to stand rather than take a seat and he got straight down to business. "I'm afraid I have some bad news, Dylan. We found another body out in the woods not far from where your mother was found. It appears she was attacked in the same manner as your mom."

Connor, who was headed for the kitchen and perhaps, I thought, from there to the basement and his computer, froze in the doorway between the two rooms. He turned slowly and looked at Wyatt.

Dylan did the same. "So, what does that mean?" he asked.

"The victim, a woman, had a notebook on her with some names written in it. Yours was in there. So was your mom's, along with your address."

Dylan looked confused. "O-kay," he said slowly. "I guess I still don't understand what it means. Other than the werewolf is apparently a serial killer."

"We think the woman's name is Donna Diamond, but she went by DeeDee. Does the name sound familiar to you at all?"

Connor looked like he was about to say something but then shot a questioning look at Dylan.

"Wasn't that the name of the woman I told you about who came by yesterday?" Dylan asked, looking back at Connor. "Brittany would know. She was here, and I was trying to get some work done, so she answered the door. The woman said she wanted to talk to me about my mom's death, but Brittany told her no and asked her to leave. I think the woman said her name was DeeDee, but I can't be sure. I couldn't even tell you what she looked like because I never saw her."

"Did she say why she wanted to talk to you about your mom?" I asked.

Dylan shook his head. "I assumed she was a curiosity seeker, you know, a crime podcaster or something like that."

Wyatt said. "Do you remember what time it was when she came by?"

Dylan gazed at the ceiling, looking thoughtful. "It would have been around eleven, I think. It was before Connor, Brittany, and I went out to lunch." He lowered his head and looked at me. "And definitely before you came by," he added.

"Where is Brittany?" I asked, eager to hear what she might have to say about DeeDee.

Dylan arched his eyebrows at me. "At home, I imagine, or maybe she's working. She'll be by later."

"Home?" I echoed. "I thought she lived here with you."

Dylan burst into a big grin. "We're thinking about it," he said, a gleam in his eye. "She's been renting a room in a house over on Ridgway Street. I've never been to it because it has stairs and . . . well"—he gestured toward his useless legs—"she doesn't like it there, says the landlord gives her the creeps. And she doesn't really have anywhere else to go. Her mother died of cancer when Brit was six and her father died last year of a heart attack. No grandparents, either. She's been on her own for the last year and it's been hard for her."

Connor, apparently deciding he no longer needed to be a part of this conversation, crossed the room and disappeared down the hall to the bedrooms.

"Can you give me a phone number for Brittany?" Wyatt asked Dylan.

"Sure." Dylan took a cell phone from his pocket, swiped at the screen, and then handed it to Wyatt.

"Where does Brittany work?" I asked.

"At that little coffee shop downtown."

"I thought she did something medical," Wyatt said, handing Dylan back his phone. "Didn't you say you first met her when you were at the rehab hospital?"

"Yep. She was a barista at the hospital coffee shop. We hit it off back then, but when I was discharged and came home, we kind of lost touch. Then we recently reconnected on Instagram, and she moved here."

The smile Dylan had on his face began a slow fade. "Wyatt, do we need to be worried? I mean, first my mom and then this woman who was looking into her death."

"I don't know, Dylan, but I'm going to figure it out."

"You said this DeeDee woman was killed the same way my mother was?"

"It appears so, but an autopsy will tell us more. I'll keep you updated but if you think of anything else that might be helpful, you know how to get ahold of me. In the meantime, you might want to make sure you lock your doors."

CHAPTER 26

Wyatt and I went our separate ways after we left Dylan's. I returned to my motel room and sat on the bed, staring at the wall, trying to make sense of things. I thought I had all the pieces to the puzzle but kept feeling as if I was trying to put them together in the wrong way, as if there was something else, some piece of it I was overlooking or misinterpreting.

I still didn't believe there was a werewolf hanging out on Bray Road, but there was no denying something strange was out there. I'd seen it with my own eyes.

In thinking back to all the things Wyatt had told me about Lydia's case and Paul McNamara's experience, I zeroed in on one piece of it I'd overlooked. Paul had seemed convinced the creature he had seen was eating something and Wyatt thought the something was the farmer's missing dog. Yet now I knew it couldn't have been. Hadn't Wyatt said something about another animal that had gone missing? A goat, wasn't it? One of the farmers on Bray Road was missing a goat.

I knew exactly where the farm in question was because Wyatt had pointed it out to me the first time we drove down Bray Road and I'd been able to see the goats from the road. And the farm was below where all the vehicles had the road blocked off, making for easy access.

When I drove to the goat farm, I saw there were still dozens of official vehicles up ahead lining the road and creating a barrier. There were two women standing in some grass by the end of a driveway, staring down the road at this blockade. They switched their attention to me as I pulled in, stopped, and got out. There were half a dozen goats in a pen at the end of the driveway not far from the house, so I had Newt stay in the car, afraid he might rile the animals. As I approached the women—a tall brunette and a short, stocky blonde—their body language made it clear I was already suspect.

"Hi there," I said, putting on my best smile to hopefully soften them. "My name is Morgan. I'm wondering if I might talk to you about what's going on up the road."

"You with the papers? Or TV?" the brunette woman asked, eyes narrowed and voice laced with suspicion.

"No, I'm not." She looked disappointed by my answer. "I'm part of the investigative team looking into these deaths, both of them." It was essentially the truth, but it earned me a couple of dubious looks.

"Really?" the blond woman said, clearly skeptical. "You a cop?"

"No, more of a consultant."

"Right," Blondie said, rolling her eyes. "Tell us what's going on, then."

I debated what to say, considering what Wyatt would likely have wanted me to say, and then tried to skirt the edges. "A second woman was found dead in the woods up there, not far from where Lydia Palmer was found. She had some, um, unusual injuries."

The two women exchanged looks. I tried to read them but honestly couldn't tell if they were intrigued or put off. They both stared at me for a few seconds, and then the brunette said, "Was it the werewolf?"

"Have you seen one?" I shot back. Nothing. I pushed a little harder. "I understand you're missing a goat. Do you think a werewolf got it?"

"Something got her," the blond woman said. "She's gone and there was blood everywhere. And the other goats were quite worked up."

"Did you see it?"

The blond woman sighed; the brunette looked annoyed. "Do you see the sun at night?" Blondie asked. "Of course you don't, but does that mean it doesn't exist?"

"I know there's something out there. I've seen it," I said.

Brunette gal looked surprised.

Blondie scoffed. "You saw the werewolf?"

"I saw something, though I'm not sure it was a werewolf."

"Then what do you think killed my goat? And these women?" Blondie challenged.

"That's what I'm trying to figure out. And you still haven't answered my question. Have either of you seen it?"

"I have," said the brunette, arms folded over her chest, chin jutted forward. "I saw it a couple nights before the first woman was killed, same night our goat disappeared. If I'd known what was going to happen, I would have gone for my rifle and tried to shoot it then and there. Except I don't know if a plain bullet would have done the job."

I raised my eyebrows in question, wanting to see if she would mention the need for a silver bullet. She didn't.

"It was in the field over there," she went on. She nodded toward an expanse of tall brown grass behind the goat pen. "The full moon was shining down on it bright as could be. It might as well have been daytime. I saw it clear as I can see you."

"Describe it for me."

"Tall, kind of muscular. It stood on two legs and sniffed at the air the way dogs do."

"Any fur?"

"Some. Not a lot, though."

"Could you see its ears?"

She nodded. "They were pointed like a wolf's."

"Did it make any sound?"

"Not then, but after it ran off I heard howls in the distance from the same direction."

"How did it run? On two legs or four?"

"Four."

"Anything else?"

"Yeah, it stunk. I must have been downwind of it because the stench hit me like a punch."

Interesting.

"Did you see it actually attack your goat?"

She cocked her head sideways, looking annoyed. “No, but it was there in the field and afterward my goat was gone. You do the math.”

I nodded. “Thanks. That’s very helpful.”

Sensing I wouldn’t get much more out of them, I turned to go back to my car.

Blondie said, “Are you going to look for Ebony?”

“Ebony?”

“Out goat. She was all black, hence the name,” Blondie explained in a tone that suggested I was an idiot.

“Right.” I eyed the remaining goats, which I noticed were about the same size as Augie, the dog with the broken leg I’d found in the hole. I turned back to the women and smiled apologetically. “I’m sorry,” I said. “I can’t be certain, but I think it’s likely Ebony is dead. Whatever is out there probably ate her.”

Blondie clutched at her pearls, though in this case it was a leather string around her neck with a key on it. The brunette chastised me with a look of disgust. I wasn’t usually this insensitive or blunt, but I was tired and stymied by the latest events, and these women had irritated me with their cagey reluctance and sarcastic remarks. Sensing I’d worn out my welcome, I thanked them for their help and got in my car. I backed out of the driveway onto Bray Road, and as I drove away, I saw them in my rearview mirror staring after me and talking animatedly. I wouldn’t have been at all surprised to learn they were using my name in vain.

The case was really frustrating me. None of it made sense. Clearly people—me included—were seeing something out in these woods and fields. And yes, I had to admit it resembled a werewolf or at least the classic, modern-day image of one. But why had it only now started killing people?

It had all begun with Lydia, at least the deaths had. Paul McNamara had seen his beast a couple of days before Lydia died, but now there were two deaths. Clearly, this wasn't over. And there was Lydia with her secret letters, maps, and codes. She was the key to all of this; I felt certain of it. I needed to focus there. Was it possible a werewolf retained enough human awareness after it had changed form to kill someone over a buried treasure that might not even exist? Or was the possibility of treasure merely a shiny bauble distracting me from the truth of a death that was due to simple bloodlust?

CHAPTER 27

I wanted to talk to Wyatt, to see if he'd talked to Brittany or had learned anything more about DeeDee, but when I called, I got his voicemail. Knowing he'd be busy for a while with DeeDee's death, I opted not to leave a message.

I drove toward town, mulling over the supposed treasure hunt Lydia had been on when she was killed. What had Townsend said about the letter and the ledger? They were fakes but well-done fakes. Who would have had the knowledge and skill to produce something like that? These days, anyone with access to the internet might have been able to pull it off, but I had my sights set on a particular someone who had unlimited resources to pull from.

When I reached the downtown area, I detoured onto some side streets until I was across from the library parking lot, which was located behind the building. After telling Newt to stay and promising to be right back, I went into the library, venturing in only far enough to see Lester Hofheyzer's desk. He was seated there, head bowed over some paperwork. Since I wasn't sure how long it would be, I used the restroom and then went back to my car.

"Get comfy, Newt. We might have a bit of a wait," I said, lowering the windows. I took out a bag of peanuts I had stashed in my glove box and shared it with him.

As luck would have it, it was less than half an hour before Lester exited the building and got into a dark blue SUV in the parking lot. He headed off in the direction opposite me and I pulled a quick U-turn and followed him. We drove through downtown and headed out of town on East Geneva Street, and then, much to my surprise, he made a left onto Bray Road. I watched as he pulled into a driveway half a mile later, parked, and got out. After a second of hesitation, I pulled in behind him and did the same.

Lester had climbed the four brick steps to the porch and had a key in the front door of the house when he became aware of my arrival. I was already out of my car by then and didn't need a psych degree to know he wasn't happy to see me. His body language and perturbed expression said it all.

"I think you and I should have a chat," I said, approaching.

"I'm home for my lunch break. Perhaps another time?" He unlocked the door and started to open it.

"I know you gave Lydia Palmer faked documents. I haven't shared this information with the police yet, but I will." Blurting this out was a gamble but I wanted to stop Lester, to get him to talk to me. It appeared to do the trick because he closed the door, turned around, and sat down on the top step.

"Lydia had a pocket-size ledger with a letter inside it hidden away at her home. She also had a hand-drawn map of the Bray Road area. The letter was supposedly written to Al Capone from one of his closest confidants, Frank Nitti. While all these items appeared to be old, I know for a fact they were fakes, cleverly done but fakes nonetheless. Then there were the coins she had on her when she was killed. Old coins worth some money. Not a lot but maybe enough to help someone like Lydia get a foothold. Or pique her curiosity."

Lester sat there with his forearms on his thighs, head down, staring at his feet. I went up the steps and sat down beside him.

"It got me to wondering who would know how to do something like that and why they would do it. Then it hit me. A librarian would know how or at the very least would have access to books he could learn from. Particularly a librarian who is a numismatist and history buff."

This revelation earned me a surprised look from Lester.

"The part I haven't quite figured out yet," I went on, "is why."

I watched a host of emotions wash over Lester's face so rapidly, it made him look like a morphing shape-shifter. "I don't want to talk about this," he said, his face temporarily settling on anger with a beet red flash of color. "You're trespassing. I think you should leave." He started to get to his feet.

"Did you know someone else was killed last night out near where Lydia died?"

"What?" Lester said sharply. The anger had disappeared from his face in an instant and he looked stricken as he dropped back onto the step.

I nodded, my expression solemn. "It was another woman."

Lester licked his lips. "You're lying," he said.

“I so wish I was, Lester, but you can see for yourself if you just drive a little farther down the road here. It’s all blocked off with official vehicles . . . police, detectives, crime scene techs.”

Lester glanced in the general direction I’d referred to, but we were too far away to see anything. His shoulders sagged with resignation, and he rubbed his palms over his bald head. I noticed that despite the lack of it on his head, the backs of his fingers and hands were quite hairy.

“I never meant for anyone to get hurt,” he said, his voice cracking. He looked like he was about to burst into tears.

“I believe you, Lester. But two people have died, and I need to find out why. Can we go inside and talk?”

He stared at me, eyes brimming with tears. I realized I was asking someone who might well be dangerous—or even a werewolf—to take me into his house, and I heard Jon’s voice inside my head chastising me for once again charging headlong into a situation without thinking it through.

“Or we can just talk out here if you like,” I suggested. “Just you and me.”

Lester nodded.

“Would it be okay if I let my dog out of my car? It’s quite warm today and he’s super friendly.” *And protective of me.*

Lester nodded again. His eyes glazed over, and he sank deeper into himself, defeated.

I let Newt out of the car, curious to see what sort of reaction he would have to Lester. He approached the stairs with typical canine eagerness, tail wagging. But he must have sensed Lester’s mood—or something else—because he stopped at the first step and slunk his way up the rest of them, eventually resting his chin ever so tentatively on Lester's knee.

As Lester reached out to stroke my dog's head, he sighed and I saw his body relax. Newt's superpower.

I settled back in my spot next to Lester. "You created the ledger and the phony letter Lydia had, didn't you?"

Lester didn't look at me. He just kept stroking Newt's head. Eventually, he nodded.

"And the map? That was you as well?"

Another nod.

"I have to say, it was clever and well-done. But I don't understand why."

"I wanted to help her. If I'd known what would happen, I never would have done it." He pulled his hand back and ran a palm over his bald scalp. Newt backed down the stairs and settled on the sidewalk at our feet.

"I believe you, Lester, but I still don't understand why you did it."

"She was going to sell the house and move. I didn't want her to leave, but she said she wanted to live somewhere cheaper where she could perhaps get a better job and more services for Dylan. She said this place had nothing to offer her anymore."

"You created all that fake stuff just to get her to stay?"

He let out an irritated huff. "You don't understand," he said. "Lydia was a very proud woman, someone who would never accept a handout. She worked so hard to better her life, but it seemed like she could never catch a break. I thought if she believed there was treasure buried here, it might convince her to stay."

I was debating whether to tell him Lydia wasn't going to be able to sell the house, but he continued before I could decide.

"In a way, the idea came from her," he went on. "We would talk when she'd come into the library, and she would always share her latest ideas for making money. But no matter what she did it always seemed to go wrong. She even came close to getting arrested once. And then one day, as a joke, she said what she needed was to find a cache of buried treasure."

"You were in love with her, weren't you?" I said, hearing the emotion in his voice.

He didn't answer but he didn't have to.

"How did you come up with the idea of Nitti and Capone?"

Lester shrugged. "That part was easy. This area is rich with Prohibition Era history and stories about speakeasies, secret tunnels, and bootleg liquor. There has been a rumor circulating for nearly a century about a possible stash Capone had one of his men bury in a field around here, hoping to hide it when the taxmen were planning a raid in the area. I'm sure there's nothing to it, but it made for a good starting point."

This jibed with what Bill Townsend had told me. "I heard about it," I said. "There's a lot of Capone lore related to Wisconsin."

"There is. I've always been an avid student of local history, so it didn't take long for me to come up with a feasible plan. I already knew how to age paper and leather. In fact, the ledger Lydia had was one of my test projects from when I first learned how to do it. I gave it a little upgrade, or downgrade really, and then added the entries." He smiled grimly. "Honestly, it was an enjoyable project."

"What about the coins? Did those come from you, too?"

Lester nodded. "They did. I've been a collector since I was a kid. My father owned a five-and-dime shop in town up until twenty years ago. I worked there from when I was eight until I went off to college, running the register, taking money, and making change. One day I found an old-looking penny in the till, a 1909 Indian Head from the San Francisco mint. When I researched it, I discovered it was worth close to a thousand dollars. I've been hunting for coins ever since and have an impressive collection with some prized pieces worth a lot of money." He sighed. "I don't enjoy it as much as I used to and it's getting harder now. Hardly anybody uses real money anymore."

As a store owner myself, I knew this was true.

"Anyway, like I said, Lydia was a proud woman determined to do things on her own. I thought secretly burying some coins and then sending her on a treasure hunt would be a perfect way to help her without her knowing." He paused, biting his lip. "It was supposed to be fun. I thought I'd help her find the spot and we would dig up the treasure together. And then, of course, I would insist she keep whatever we found." He gave a sad shake of his head. "She wasn't supposed to go out there alone."

"Wouldn't it have been simpler, and safer, to just loan her some money?"

He looked over at me, eyes filled with pain. "I would have and could have," he assured me. "I've saved up quite a bit over the years and I inherited a nice sum last year when my mother passed away. But if Lydia felt indebted to me, it would have changed the dynamic between us, and I didn't want that. Besides, I don't think she would have accepted a loan from me."

"And it didn't occur to you Lydia might go out there by herself?"

Lester wagged his head from side to side and let out a little moan. "I honestly didn't think she'd be able to put the whole thing together on her own. Particularly this quickly. I tried to make the clues obscure and cryptic enough that she'd need my help to decipher them. And even if she figured things out on her own, I thought she'd tell me about it and then I'd be able to help her dig it up."

"Weren't you taking a big risk burying loose coins like that on someone else's property?"

Lester shook his head. "I know the farmer who owns that field and knew he planned to leave it fallow for the year. He gave me permission to use a small area by the side fence to bury something. I told him it was for this new geocaching thing that's all the rage now." He looked at me questioningly. "Since you asked about coins, I'm assuming she found them?"

I nodded.

He let out a sigh that sounded disturbingly like a whimper and then clutched at my arm, his fingers digging into my flesh. "You have to believe me," he said, shaking my arm gently, though his grip felt like a vise. "All I wanted to do was keep her from trying to sell the house."

"She wasn't going to," I told him, pulling my arm free. "Apparently she owed more than she could get for it."

Lester stared at me in disbelief for a few seconds before then sucking in a ragged breath and burying his face in his hands.

I gave him a moment to recover before continuing with my questions. "How did Lydia come to have the ledger and map in her possession? From what I know about her, she doesn't sound like a stupid or particularly gullible person. Did you just give them to her?"

"I did."

"And she thought they were real?"

Another sigh, shaky this time. "We get donations at the library all the time when folks clean out their grandparents' or parents' homes and find old books and stuff in the attic. Most of the time it's junk and we toss it, but every once in a while, we discover a real gem. Lydia knows this. . . ." He winced and squeezed his eyes closed. "Lydia *knew* this, and when I told her I'd found the items in a donation that had come in, she believed me."

"If I was Lydia in that situation, the first thing I'd want to know is why you weren't simply keeping these items for yourself and doing your own investigating."

He gave me a wan smile. "She asked me exactly that and I told her I was quite well-off after my inheritance and didn't need any extra money. I knew she could use it and wanted to give it to her as a token of our, um, friendship."

"You never answered my question earlier. You were in love with her, weren't you?"

He stared at his hands in his lap, fingers laced together, thumbs circling each other. It took him a while to respond, and I was about to repeat my question when he spoke.

"She was an amazing woman . . . smart, beautiful, kind, driven. . . ." He sighed. "She had a great personality. And yes, I was quite fond of her."

"What do you think happened to her out there that night?"

Lester turned and gave me a curious look. "The werewolf, of course."

I cocked my head sideways at him and was about to ask if he was serious when I flashed back on something he'd mentioned earlier. "Lester, you said you thought you could help her dig up the treasure. How many coins did you bury?"

"There were six loose ones, plus the box."

"The box?"

He nodded. "It contained the more valuable coins."

"You mean, *more* coins? Not just the loose ones Lydia had on her?"

"Yes," he said. "The loose ones were just to get things started. The coins in the metal box are worth a lot more."

"How much more?"

"A little over ten grand."

I let out a whistle that made Newt perk up.

"Lydia only found three loose coins: a penny, a dime, and a quarter," I said.

"There should be another quarter, another dime, and a Buffalo nickel loose in the dirt."

"Plus coins in a box?" Lester nodded. "What kind of box?"

A wistful smile briefly appeared on Lester's face. "When I was a boy, I buried a time capsule in the backyard here," he said. "I used this metal coin box my dad had, locked it, wrapped it in oilcloth and plastic wrap, dug a hole, and buried it. I was—I don't know—eight, nine at the time. I kept the key to it and dug it up last year when I turned fifty."

"Sounds like a fun project."

"Yeah, it didn't turn out as well as I'd hoped. Water had seeped into the box and ruined the comic books, baseball cards, and newspaper. The other stuff was moldy, and the box itself was all crusted with dirt, rusted, and dented. I tossed everything but the box, and when I came up with the idea of the buried treasure, I realized it would be the perfect thing to use. I put the coins inside a leather drawstring bag I'd made and aged, put it in the box, wrapped the box in the old oilcloth from my time capsule, and then buried it out there in the field."

"How deep?"

He shrugged. "A foot, maybe a foot and a half? Why?"

"Because I don't think Lydia found it."

CHAPTER 28

I thought you said they found the coins with her when she was killed."

"Just three coins, the loose ones. The police didn't find a metal box full of coins. What we did find was a hole about four feet deep with evidence Lydia was the one who dug it."

"Oh." Lester looked up at the sky. "Four feet? That's way too deep. It's probably still out there." He thought a moment and then added, "It's not safe to go find it now."

His voice had changed, taking on a warning tone, and an involuntary shiver shook me. My arms broke out in gooseflesh.

"Do you think werewolves are real, Lester?" I recalled asking him something similar when I'd first chatted with him at the library. He had swiftly denied any such belief, which is why his answer now came as a bit of a shock.

He gave me a Captain Obvious look and then turned away, staring off into the distance. "I do. I saw one with my own eyes back in 1990."

"Really?"

"I was driving home late one night, and when I came around the curve off East Geneva Street onto Bray Road, I saw it there in the field."

"Did you tell anyone?"

He shook his head emphatically. "I didn't want to get drawn into the local circus. There was a general sentiment about town that the people who claimed to see the beast were either crazy or attention seekers. I didn't want to get slapped with any of those labels. I got picked on enough when I was younger."

I felt a twinge of empathy for him. It was easy to picture a younger, thinner, bespectacled Lester being teased to the point of bullying.

"It was ridiculous how much media attention there was back then," Lester went on. "The town fully embraced the beast but only as a lark. A local bakery sold werewolf cookies, a bar offered drinks called Silver Bullet Specials, people made signs and giant cutouts of the beast—it was absurd. Even my father sold T-shirts and the like at his store."

"But you believe what you saw was really a werewolf?"

He wrinkled his face and shrugged one shoulder. "I guess. It was a big, standing, doglike creature with a long snout." He glanced over at me, gauging my reaction. "I admit I was skeptical of the whole thing until I saw it with my own eyes. And recently I started doubting myself after thirty years with no sightings. I thought maybe I'd imagined it or someone had slipped something into my beer that night and I'd hallucinated the whole thing. Believe me, if I'd thought for even a minute that a werewolf was in our community again, I never would have let Lydia go out there, even with me." He took off his glasses and massaged his eyelids with a thumb and forefinger.

"I saw something myself the other night," I told him.

He froze for a second. "Really?" he said, putting his glasses back on and scrutinizing me.

"I'm not convinced it was a werewolf, but there's definitely something out there."

"Do you think it's what attacked Lydia?" He looked sick over the idea.

"I don't know. Honestly, my gut says no, but I don't have a better answer yet. And there was another person, a local, who saw something out there on Bray Road two nights before Lydia was killed."

"I didn't know that."

"You couldn't have."

We sat in silence for a minute and then Lester said, "You know, it's quite fascinating the way people become werewolves."

There was a distinct change in the tone of his voice again. He sounded reverent, respectful, in awe. It was oddly chilling.

"Some think the process is involuntary but that isn't always the case. Nor does there need to be a bite. There are historical references mentioning causes like curses, magic, or even something as mundane as sleeping face up under a full moon or drinking rainwater out of a werewolf's footprint."

I laughed, thinking he was making a joke, but he shot me a chastising look like a parent might give an ignorant child. His entire demeanor had changed, and it made me uncomfortable.

"The change needn't be a permanent thing, either," he said, staring out across his front yard toward Bray Road. He looked like he was in a trance.

"I always figured once a werewolf, always a werewolf," I said jokingly, still hoping to keep things light.

"Not necessarily," he said. "Some think the effects fade with time and age. And 'age' is a relative term because there are those who believe that werewolves are immortal or that becoming a werewolf slows the aging process."

I knew there was a very real psychiatric disorder called lycanthropy, in which a patient believes he is a werewolf and acts out accordingly. Could Lester have been suffering from such a delusion? Could he have killed Lydia in some type of weird werewolf fugue state? Maybe he went out there with her, after all, and when they found the treasure, she kept it and told him to get lost. It made him angry, he snapped, and what . . . clawed her throat out? Lester didn't look the type to do something so vicious but then looks could be deceiving.

And maybe he looks quite different after he changes.

My spine tingled and goose bumps again rose on my arms. My heart started pounding and I felt a familiar tightness in my chest. I knew I was on the verge of a panic attack, and I looked down at Newt, who was calmly dozing on the sidewalk. This reassured me a little and my pulse slowed. When I looked back at Lester, I found him studying me with uncomfortable intensity.

My thoughts must have shown on my face, because Lester said, "Don't worry. I'm not a werewolf."

"I didn't think you were," I lied.

"Do you think Lydia suffered?"

The sudden change of subject threw me, but it also helped calm me. I made a snap decision, one Wyatt might chastise me for later.

"She had a broken neck, most likely from falling and hitting the back of her head on one of the rails in the fence near the hole she'd dug. It paralyzed and killed her almost instantly. The other wounds came later, after she was dead. She wouldn't have felt anything or even had time to be afraid."

This wasn't altogether true because it was possible Lydia hadn't died immediately, but I saw no point in torturing Lester any more than he was already torturing himself.

"How is it you know all that?" he asked.

"I've been working closely with the police on Lydia's case."

"Oh." Lester nodded slowly, looking thoughtful. "The reporter I talked to said that Lydia's throat had been slashed and that she'd been found in the woods."

"You spoke to a reporter?"

"Yes. I mentioned her to you when you asked why the Bray Road file was at the front of the file cabinet drawer."

"Oh, right. The documentarian." DeeDee? "Whoever you spoke to had it partially right. Lydia's body *was* found in the woods, but she died next to the hole by the fence and then her body was dragged into the trees."

Lester grimaced and turned away.

"Lester, do you know the name of this reporter who came to the library?" He shook his head. "Can you describe her?"

He gave me a perfect description of DeeDee, right down to her double-D necklace.

"Am I in trouble for giving Lydia the map and the ledger? Am I an accessory or something like that?"

"I don't think you broke any laws, but I'll need to explain it all to the detective working Lydia's case. He needs to know why she was out there that night. I'll try to paint you in a positive light, but first I need you to swear to me that Lydia never told you she'd figured out the code you hid in the fake Nitti letter or that she planned to go out there to dig."

"*You* know about the code?"

"I figured it out."

Lester looked surprised. And chagrined. "Like I said before, I had no idea she knew. I thought I'd made it obscure enough that only someone very clever could figure it out. Not that Lydia wasn't smart in her own way. She just wasn't much of an intellectual thinker." His brow furrowed in consternation. "Clearly I wasn't as clever as I thought if both you and she were able to figure it out so easily."

"It wasn't that easy," I said, trying not to feel insulted and unwilling to admit I'd only figured it out by accident. Thinking it might be best to leave things there, I stood and said, "I should go, and you probably need to get back to work."

"I'm done for the day," he said, letting me know he'd lied about only being home for lunch. Hopefully it was the only lie he'd told me.

"I'm sorry about how things turned out, Lester. Truly. Lydia sounds like she was a super-nice person."

Lester simply nodded, once again staring off into space.

I stood and Newt opened his eyes, tuned in to me as always. As

I descended the steps I gestured toward the car and Newt got up and followed me, hopping into the rear seat, where I hooked him in. Before I backed out of the driveway, I cast one last look at Lester, a little concerned about his state of mind. I was surprised to see him watching me with an oddly self-satisfied smile on his face.

Had I just been taken in by another master con artist?

CHAPTER 29

As I drove back to my motel, I briefly considered packing it in and heading for home. There were too many roadblocks in the way, both literally and figuratively, and now I at least had an answer to what Lydia had been doing out in the woods in the middle of the night.

Yet the whole werewolf thing nagged at me. I had to know who or what had killed Lydia and DeeDee. I had to know what it was Paul McNamara had seen that night on Bray Road. And I had to know what it was I'd seen standing in the cornfield in the moonlight. Something was out there, and I knew if I left without figuring out what it was, it would nag at me forever.

Then there was the question of the box of rare coins Lester had buried in the field. Was it still out there? If not, where was it?

I had some ideas about how to get the answers I needed but it would mean staying at least one more night—maybe more—and doing the sort of thing Jon wouldn't have liked. I rationalized my concern away by asking myself what difference it made now. Jon was moving on.

The reminder was like a stab to my heart. It literally made me gasp, and I shoved the pain down deep inside.

I'd brought with me to Elkhorn several things that I thought might come in handy, but there was one thing I didn't have and really wanted. I returned to my hotel room and did a quick internet search and made a couple of phone calls. Finally, I found what I needed at a Fleet Farm store in Delavan, fifteen minutes away.

It was a pleasant, bucolic drive to and from Delavan and I lowered the windows to let Newt sniff the country air to his heart's content. Upon returning to Elkhorn, I hit up the nearby Kwik Trip for some snacks for later. Next, I got a salad from Culver's and finally made good on my promise of a cheeseburger for Newt, and the two of us enjoyed a leisurely meal in the room. I spent an hour preparing for my planned excursion, and when that was done, I stretched out on the bed and took a nap.

I awoke as the sun was setting and grabbed the backpack I'd partially prepped earlier. It held some of the toys I'd brought with me—my night vision binoculars with the built-in camera, my Taser, the chemical hand and feet warmers, and a collapsible camp shovel. Even though I didn't think it would work, I checked to make sure I was still wearing my wolfsbane necklace. I'm a pragmatist most of the time, but I have my superstitious moments.

In a more realistic vein, I also had a can of bear spray and an air horn I'd picked up at the Fleet Farm store, both of which I stuffed into my coat pockets. I had a hunting knife with a sheath that I attached to my belt. Then I added my headlamp, a canteen of water, a blanket, the Kwik Trip snacks, and Newt's LED night collar to my backpack inventory. Finally, I made two pots of coffee in the little coffee maker in my room and filled up a thermos.

I pulled on my wool socks and a heavy sweater—a check of the weather had told me it was going to drop to freezing during the night—and donned thick gloves and a knit hat. The last things I grabbed were the metal detector I'd bought at Fleet Farm and my phone, even though I knew it might prove useless.

Two women had died out on Bray Road at night, and I wanted to know how and why. Paul McNamara had seen his creature at night, as I had seen mine. The goat farmer had seen something by the light of a full moon. It made sense to try to find some answers by being out on Bray Road during the dark hours and I intended to stake out the fields and the woods for a night or two in hopes of getting them.

Was this the sort of behavior I needed to be more aware of? Probably, but I wasn't going into it naïvely. I had weapons and a plan. If it turned out werewolves were real, I just had to hope they'd be deterred by a combination of wolfsbane and bear spray. If not, I had a knife and a Taser.

It was a little past nine o'clock when I drove out to Bray Road, and I was relieved to see the police presence was gone and the road was open, though there was a barricade at the entry to the rutted path. I parked, donned my backpack, and walked to the start of the trail between the two sections of woods.

Once I was sure no cars were coming, I scooted around the

barricade and headed down the path, picking my way carefully over the rough ground. Newt stuck close to my side, and while I had a leash for him, I didn't use it. I was wearing my headlamp but didn't want to turn it on until I was fully out of view of the road. However, the darkness in the woods was so complete and the ground so uneven, I caved when I was about a third of the way through after tripping twice. I also put the LED collar on Newt and activated it, creating a fluorescent green glow.

When I reached the cornfield I turned right to walk along the rear tree line to the corner of the plowed field. From there, I followed the fence farther back into the cornfield until I was across from the hole. Then I slipped between the rails.

Newt sniffed and ran around to the far side of the hole where the dirt pile was. Then he began digging.

"Not yet, buddy," I said. "First, we need to do a little reconnaissance work."

Newt ignored me and continued to dig until I told him to stop. I took the metal detector I'd bought at Fleet Farm and started scanning the ground surrounding the hole, walking around it in widening concentric circles, hoping for a hit. The surface dirt was still muddy from the rainstorm and my feet slipped a few times. When I reached the dirt pile where Newt had been digging, I finally scored. The signal was weaker than expected, but I guessed it might have been because the metal box was beneath several feet of dirt rather than the foot or so Lester had said he'd buried it under.

I took out my camp shovel and started digging. Fortunately, the rain had softened the dirt, and Newt had already moved some of it. I didn't have to go far before my headlamp reflected on something shiny. At first, I thought I'd found one of Lester's remaining loose coins but then realized it was a metal button. A minute later I pulled a black jacket from the dirt pile. Lydia's, no doubt. There was one nagging question answered.

I wasn't sure what to do with it and finally decided to wrap it up in some paper towels I'd brought along and stuff it in my backpack. Once the jacket was out of the ground, the metal detector no longer returned a hit for me in that spot. I continued circling the hole until I was about ten feet out and about to call it quits when I got another signal. This time I didn't have to dig. What I'd found was sitting on the surface of the ground and I stared at it, trying to make sense of what I was seeing, my thoughts racing. Newt sniffed at it, wagging his tail. Eventually, I picked it up, wrapped it in a small piece of paper towel, and slipped it inside a pocket of my backpack.

Assuming this hole was where Lydia had found the loose coins she had, the metal box containing ten grand worth of valuable old coins was apparently gone. Could Lester have come out and found it earlier today after my visit with him? I didn't know when the police and evidence team had left but it would have been hard, though not impossible, for him to sneak in here with the police around. I supposed he could have approached the hole from the other direction through the plowed field and then left the same way. But there were no new dig sites, just the original hole, making me think Lester didn't have the box.

The hole did look a little bigger and deeper to me, but the sides of it along with the surrounding dirt were now muddy and slippery. Anyone getting into the hole would have had a hard time getting back out again. I considered getting down on my stomach near the edge and reaching down into the hole while holding the metal detector but decided there was no point. I'd believed Lester when he'd said he hadn't buried his box that deep. So, where was it and who had it? I had an idea thanks to the last item I'd found, but I wasn't ready to leave the area yet.

Ideas began to gel in my mind and the puzzle pieces came together in a way that started to make sense. Minutes later, I thought I had most of it figured out but there was one key piece I still needed. Not to mention proof of my theory.

I gathered up my stuff, slipped between the split rails, and retraced my steps along the fence line on the cornfield side until I reached the woods that went out to the road. It didn't take long to find a suitable spot for what I wanted. There was a large fallen tree close to the back edge of the woods near the fence. I slipped off my backpack, took out the blanket, and laid it over the fallen trunk. Then I turned off my headlamp and Newt's collar, gave him a drink in his collapsible bowl, poured myself a cup of coffee, took my night vision binoculars from my backpack, and settled in to wait.

CHAPTER 30

The location was a good one. A half-moon had risen, and I could see most of the cornfield and a good distance back through the plowed field to the general area where the hole was. It was dark under the trees where I was sitting, but with my binoculars I could see deep into the woods. I knew there was no guarantee I'd spot anything tonight—or any other night—but figured I had to start somewhere.

After thoroughly sniffing the surrounding area, Newt had curled into a comma at my feet, his big head resting on his front legs. He dozed contentedly and boredom overtook me half an hour in. I found myself using the binoculars to scan the fields and look through the woods every few minutes. Nothing stirred over the next hour and then suddenly I heard the distinct sound of a branch breaking underfoot behind me and to my left. Newt heard it, too, and his head popped up, nose to the air, nostrils working overtime. Nervous and excited, I raised the night vision binoculars and scanned the surrounding woods. It didn't take long to find the source: a very pregnant doe carefully working her way among the trees.

Newt made a little *whuff* sound—not quite a growl, not quite a bark—and I shushed him immediately. But it was too late. The doe heard him, me, or both of us and promptly disappeared, bounding off deeper into the woods. I muttered a curse, making Newt cock his head to one side.

"We need to be quiet, buddy," I whispered. Then I held a finger in front of my lips and hoped he understood.

Sometime later, Newt raised his head, sniffed, and looked questioningly at me. I did the finger on the lips again and it seemed he understood because he stayed quiet. This time my binocs caught sight of a rabbit hopping between the trees.

Fearing I might have overestimated my patience for this excursion, I resumed my waiting game. I checked the time on my phone and saw it was nearly one in the morning. I'd been out here going on four hours now and I was cold and had to pee. I got up from the fallen tree trunk and navigated about ten feet deeper into the woods, where there were a bunch of fallen limbs, and did my business. Newt followed me and lifted his leg to water a nearby bush. Having both left our marks, we returned to the fallen tree and I pulled the blanket up around my shoulders.

Another half hour ticked by. Newt was asleep at my feet and my eyelids were growing heavy. I poured a second cup of coffee and began marching in place, holding the mug for warmth, trying to shake off the drowsiness. Newt watched me curiously for a few seconds before sighing and closing his eyes again.

I was on my second sip of coffee when I heard it. It so startled me, I dropped my cup, nearly scalding Newt with hot coffee. It sounded like a baby bawling, and it had come from the general direction of the hole. I grabbed my binoculars and scanned the plowed field, not seeing anything at first. Then I looked over at the cornfield and spotted the same creature I'd seen before. It stood on two legs not far from the fence, waving from side to side as if agitated or upset, its long snout sampling the air, its pointed ears pricked. I adjusted the focus on my binoculars and was startled as the image came into clearer view. The creature looked in my direction and I swore our eyes met and held for a moment. I took a quick picture as the hair on the back of my neck rose. Newt, standing at attention, let out a low growl and I shushed him.

I lowered my binoculars but continued to watch it, able to track its shadowy shape in the moonlight. Once again a distressed cry echoed through the chill night air, but it seemed to be coming from the direction of the hole. Hearing it, the creature dropped to all fours and loped toward the fenced field. I struggled to track it as it seemed to melt into the wooden fence, the rails blocking much of my view.

The sound came again, more of a whimpering, mewling noise this time. I no longer knew where the creature was and felt panic start to rise in me as my eyes searched the darkness. Where had it gone? I started gulping air and knew I was once again on the verge of a panic attack. Newt sensed it, too, and shoved his nose into my hip, whining. I laid my palm on Newt's head, letting the touch calm me. The mewling crescendoed suddenly, becoming louder and more strident until it evolved into a full-throated distress call. Then a mighty roar echoed across the field, bringing with it underlying hints of anguish, ferocity, and fear. It froze me to the spot and every hair on my body rose to attention. Newt tucked his tail between his legs and stood as still as a statue for several seconds. Then he went into protective mode. He barked several times, a fierce, slobbering bark, and took off running into the fenced field.

"Newt! No! Come back!"

He barked again but it sounded distant, and I feared he was chasing the creature. I took my bear spray out of my pocket and checked to make sure I still had the air horn. After turning on my headlamp, I ducked between the fence rails and ventured into the field.

Newt barked again, and with it came the sound of more bawling and another roar. Worry, panic, and determination vied for supremacy as I rapidly navigated the uneven landscape, the muddy clumps of dirt threatening to trip me with every step.

"Newt? Newt! Where are you? Come here, Newt!"

I cursed myself for not turning on his LED collar when I'd first sighted the creature. Then I had a moment of déjà vu—I'd been here before when Newt had found Augie in the hole. Instinct told me it was where I needed to be.

"Newt! Where are you?"

Newt barked in response and this time he kept at it. His steady stream of barks worked like a tractor beam, pulling me ahead. Moments later I came up on him still at it, spittle foaming around his mouth, standing near the hole Augie had fallen into. But his attention wasn't on the hole this time. It was focused off to the side.

I glanced that way, and my heart nearly stopped. The creature was there, standing on all fours, staring at us, its huffing breath steaming in the cold night air. It shook its head menacingly and chuffed at me, shifting its weight from one front leg to the other. Then it rose on its hind legs and roared, a mighty sound meant to scare the crap out of me. It worked. I held the bear spray at the ready and took out the air horn, giving it two quick blasts. The loud, piercing blare ripped through the night air, echoing off the trees and reverberating in the darkness. The creature dropped to all fours, turned tail, and ran.

Newt, also stunned by the sound of the air horn, had stopped barking. I watched until the creature faded into the more distant woods backing on the two fields, and then I turned to focus on the mewling sound coming from the bottom of the hole. Darn if it hadn't trapped another animal. The wet mud on its fur and the claw marks in the slippery sidewalls of the hole showed where this one had tried, and failed, to climb out. I knew I had to help it but also knew the larger creature would be back sooner rather than later. I needed to act fast.

"Newt, come with me," I said, clapping a hand against my thigh.

Newt looked from me to the hole and back to me. I did an about-face and headed for my fallen log in the woods. Newt, reluctantly, fell into step beside me and I paused long enough to reach down and turn on his collar. Once I was back at my camping spot, I returned the air horn and bear spray to my coat pockets where I could grab them quickly, and I took my binoculars, which were hanging around my neck, and tucked them inside my coat. Then I walked over to one of the fallen branches I'd spotted earlier during my potty break. It was a little over six inches in diameter at its widest point, tapering down to about three inches, and about eight feet in length. I hoisted it and slowly began dragging it toward the fence, stopping long enough to don my backpack.

When I got to the edge of the woods, I fed the branch between the rails of the fence and into the plowed field, taking a moment to rest and check my surroundings with the binoculars. Then I climbed through the fence and started dragging again, slogging through the muddy clumps and sweating with the effort. The branch hadn't felt all that heavy initially, but as I moved, it seemed to be gaining weight, as if the mud and dirt clods were tugging at and trapping it. Newt tried to assist by grabbing the other end in his mouth but it made the whole thing go sideways.

"I appreciate the thought but you're not helping, Newt," I said, stopping to rest. "Besides, I need you on watch duty. I don't want that creature sneaking up on me." Newt seemed to understand, and I again used the binoculars to check our surroundings before resuming my trek. Twice more I paused to rest, catch my breath, and scan while Newt kept sniffing the air and scouting around me.

When I finally reached the hole, I carefully eased the larger end of the branch down into it, taking care not to hit the critter at the bottom. It had retreated into a corner, staring at us all big-eyed and trembling. Once I had the lower part of the branch wedged in solidly, I did another scan with the binoculars and told Newt to keep an eye out. Then I used my camp shovel to dig a small trench back from the top edge of the hole so I could nestle the upper end of the branch into it. This both stabilized it and lessened the angle.

The animal at the bottom snugged itself tight into its corner as I worked. Fortunately, it stayed quiet, because had it started bellowing again, I feared its mother would return with a vengeance.

When I was done, Newt and I retreated to the other side of the fence about ten feet away in what I calculated was a downwind position. I squatted behind a post, turned off my headlamp and Newt's collar, and told Newt to lie down and stay quiet.

We didn't have to wait long. Bawling sounds once again emanated from the hole and within minutes the creature returned. She lumbered over on all fours, nose sniffing, head moving side to side. I saw the muscles in her legs, the nearly hairless body, ears so scarred and deformed they looked pointed. And I caught a whiff of her, a foul, pungent odor I knew wasn't normal. I was no longer afraid of her, but I kept the bear spray in hand just in case. Newt stayed perfectly still, never taking his eyes off her.

When I was sure I had a clear view of her in my binoculars, I triggered the camera. I took a couple more shots just to be sure and then watched as she stopped next to the log I'd placed in the hole. She sniffed it and then rose up on her hind legs to look about, before dropping to all fours again with a grunt. Then she stared down into the hole. She growled and grumbled, scratching her front foot in the mud a couple times and waving her head from side to side. The little one in the hole continued to bawl.

The mother creature backed up and then lunged forward, bracing herself on the branch I'd placed there. Seconds later she dragged the smaller creature up and out of the hole by the scruff of its neck, the poor little thing shaking and squalling. They made swift business of their reunion, and in the blink of an eye, the two of them were loping across the field together on all fours, rapidly moving away from us.

Once I was sure they were gone, Newt and I went back to our campsite, where I gathered up the rest of our stuff. It was going on five in the morning by the time I hiked back out to my car and returned to the motel. I saw I had a missed call and a voicemail from Wyatt that had come a little after ten last night, but all his message said was "Call me."

I was eager to do just that and tell him I'd captured the Beast of Bray Road—on film, anyway. But I had my doubts as to whether this beast had been the one that killed Lydia and DeeDee. This beast had a five-fingered claw, not four, and despite the ferocious display it had put on near the pit, I didn't think it would have had the strength, or any reason, to drag Lydia's body from the hole to those woods. I feared that other beast, the deadly one, was more likely of the human variety and much more dangerous.

CHAPTER 31

I took a hot shower and dropped into bed, intending to sleep only a couple of hours, but it was past eleven when I awoke. I took Newt for a walk, grabbed a coffee from Starbucks and a breakfast sandwich from Kwik Trip, and then settled in my room to eat and think things over. There was an email from Devon letting me know he hadn't learned much from Lydia's social media, as most of her posts on Facebook and Instagram were about gardening.

Curious, I got on Facebook and perused Lydia's posts on my own while I ate my breakfast and drank my coffee, trying to shake off the dregs of sleep. Devon was right. Nearly two-thirds of Lydia's posts were about gardening. Strangely, she hardly ever mentioned Dylan.

On Instagram she had a series of photos documenting the creation of the flower beds in both her front yard and backyard over the past few years. The area in front had been cleared and planted before, but she had removed the shrubs that had been there and replaced them with a variety of blooms—bulbs, flowering bushes, perennials, and annuals. In the backyard she'd had to create the flower bed from scratch, removing grass, building it up, and landscaping the area before planting. She had been limited by both time and money and had done it all in stages, taking lots of selfies to document her progress. It was easy to see she had loved gardening and taken pride in what she'd accomplished. Her face, already pretty, positively beamed when she was outside working in the dirt. It was an odd hobby considering her OCD tendencies toward cleanliness in the house.

I was about to close the Instagram page when something in one of Lydia's more recent photos caught my eye. It showed her in the process of expanding and prepping the backyard flower bed for more plantings, and she had bags of soil, mulch, and her gardening tools spread out around her. I enlarged the photo to better see the background because something jumped out at me. It left me racking my brain, trying to remember what I'd seen on my previous trips to her house.

The final pieces of the puzzle clicked into place. The problem was how to prove it. I got up and paced in my room while Newt watched me, and eventually an idea and a plan unfolded. It was time to call Wyatt and share what I'd learned, what I'd found, and what I thought we could do about it.

"Hey, Morgan," Wyatt answered. "Please, don't tell me you're giving up and going home."

"Not yet but soon," I said, "because I think I've got my answers."

"I've got a few myself. It turns out, our latest victim, Donna Diamond, is the sister of Tabitha Diamond, a lab tech who works at the hospital. Tabitha was the one who told DeeDee about Paul McNamara's experience out on Bray Road because he had apparently confided in her. DeeDee runs some kind of conspiracy-theory-podcast site where cryptids are a big thing. That's how the rumors circulated so quickly."

"So, the story she gave me about being in town for a wedding?"

"Utter horsepucky. We found daily notes on her computer. She got wind of you early on, probably from Paul and Tabitha. In fact, she followed us to Paul's house the day you talked to him, and she also followed you out to Bray Road the night you found Augie."

"Remember the gray car that nearly ran me over when we went to see Paul McNamara?"

"Of course."

"I'll bet that was her. And if she was driving a hybrid, it explains why I didn't hear a car engine the night I found Augie."

"I took a picture of some of the tread marks from that night. I'll compare them to DeeDee's tires and see if they're a match."

"Good. In the meantime, I've figured out what Lydia Palmer was doing out there in the middle of the night. And I have the Beast of Bray Road on film. I'm going to contact a friend of mine who will help us capture the actual creature. Or rather creatures, because there are two of them."

"Two? What are you talking about?"

"I'll explain in a minute. I also have some evidence to turn over to you because I found Lydia's missing jacket out by that hole Augie the dog fell into. My guess is, she took her jacket off while she was digging, and it got lost during the attack."

"You think Lydia dug that hole?"

"Some of it. Probably a lot of it. It explains the blisters on her hands and the splinter in her finger. And remember the linear bruise on the bottom of her foot that was mentioned in the autopsy report? I think it was a shovel mark."

"O-kay," Wyatt said slowly. "Yeah, that makes sense. But why was she digging?"

"She was looking for buried treasure. And before I tell you this next part, you have to promise me you won't get mad because I've kept a few things from you."

I heard him emit a weighty sigh. "Yeah, okay. I'm listening."

I told him about finding the ledger and letter in the puzzle box Lydia had in her closet.

"You hid it from me when I was right there?" he said, clearly annoyed.

"Yeah, sorry. I wasn't sure it meant anything at the time."

He made a noise to let me know he wasn't happy. "No comment for now," he said. "If that's all you kept from—"

"There's more," I said.

"Grrrr-eat. Okay, what else?"

I told him about the map I'd found in the tampon box, my trip to Bill Thompson in Lake Geneva, and my subsequent conversation with Lester Hofheyzer.

"Good grief, Morgan, this is more than a few things you've kept from me. And talking to Lester alone was a foolish, impulsive thing to do. But then, you already knew that, didn't you?"

I didn't answer, assuming the question was rhetorical.

"Do I dare ask how you managed to catch pictures of the beast and find Lydia's jacket?"

"You can ask but you probably won't like the answer."

"Great," he muttered again. "I hope I don't get fired over this."

"I spent last night in the woods adjacent to the plowed field."

"You what?"

"It was fine. I had Newt with me, and I went out there prepared with a knife, a Taser, bear spray, and an air horn to scare off any creatures. I even had my wolfsbane necklace on."

"I'm sorry. Say again?"

I supposed I couldn't blame him for being overwhelmed. It was a lot to dump on him all at once. I explained about the necklace, how I'd come to have it, and how I'd been wearing it the whole time I'd been in Elkhorn. Then I told him about my encounter with the beast.

"It's an ordinary black bear," I told him. "Except it's not ordinary because she has a horrible case of mange. It's caused by parasitic mites and it's highly contagious. She could have picked it up from an infected fox, wolf, or coyote or even from a rabbit or raccoon. However it happened, she's had it for a while. In fact, I'm certain the poor thing went into hibernation with it, and it worsened over the winter. She's lost much of her fat and her fur, and her ears are so scarred, they look like they're pointed. It's why she looks more like a dogman than a bear and it's also why she reeks. And she has a cub now, and it might have mange as well. They need immediate medical attention."

"So, the ME was right when he said he thought Lydia's death was due to a bear attack."

"I don't think so. For one thing, the wounds Lydia and DeeDee had don't look right. They're too uniform, too evenly spaced. Same with the scratch marks on the car. Plus, there are only four lines in all the scratches, whereas bears have five claws. Secondly, the poor mama bear is hungry and weak. She can't be long out of hibernation, and she's got a cub to feed. I'm guessing she killed and ate the missing goat from Bray Road and that's what Paul McNamara saw the night he was out there. But I don't believe she attacked a human, much less dragged a body through some fence rails and over a hundred yards of cornfield into some woods. Black bears tend to be shy, and when I blasted my air horn last night, she ran off and didn't come back until she thought we were gone. And then only to rescue her cub."

"Rescue it from what?"

"That damned hole. The poor cub fell into it. It was a little smaller than Augie, and while it didn't appear to be seriously injured, the sides of the hole were too steep and muddy for it to be able to get out on its own. I put a branch down into the hole, hoping it would climb out, and it worked with a little help from Mom."

"Can mange be fatal?"

"It can be if it's not treated. The animals develop lesions, scabs, and crusts that then become infected. I know a guy who can come and capture the bears and take them somewhere for treatment before relocating them. Better to do it sooner rather than later, before one of the farmers out there shoots them."

"Okay. So, if this bear isn't behind Lydia and DeeDee's deaths, what is?"

"Not what. Who. I think something else I found out there answers the question. But to prove it, I'm going to need your help."

"*You're* going to need *my* help?" Wyatt jeered. "This is my case, remember?"

"Of course. Sorry."

Several seconds of silence ticked by and then Wyatt sighed heavily and said, "Fine. I'm listening."

"I'm starving and haven't eaten anything since last evening. Buy me lunch and I'll tell you everything."

"You drive a hard bargain, Morgan Carter. What are you hungry for?"

In the interests of privacy, we decided Wyatt would pick up some fried chicken and coleslaw and bring it to my motel room. While waiting for him, I made a phone call and spoke to Rob, the wildlife specialist I knew who occasionally brought me animal skulls and other items for my store. I told him about the mama bear and her cub, letting him know I would cover the cost of capture, treatment, and relocation. I gave him Wyatt's contact information, and he promised to get to it right away.

When Wyatt arrived, I shared my theory with him as he unpacked the food he'd bought. I showed him Lydia's jacket and the other item I'd found out near the hole. He packaged them up but with a caveat. "If it comes down to it, I probably won't be able to use these as evidence because custody was compromised."

"Yeah, sorry about that. If it helps, I have a plan for how we can secure all the evidence we need. And if need be, I'll be happy to come back and testify."

"I appreciate the offer, but to be honest, a self-proclaimed cryptozoologist doesn't carry the sort of reliable witness traits most prosecutors are looking for."

"I'm going to try to not be offended by your comment."

Wyatt shrugged, grabbing a chicken leg from the box. "It is what it is," he said.

The smell of the chicken had me drooling nearly as much as

Newt. I ate while showing Wyatt the pictures I'd captured with my night vision binoculars and telling him about the arrangements I'd made with Rob.

"You can help smooth the process by contacting the farmers and other folks living in the Bray Road area and letting them know what the beast really is and that Rob might need access to their land. I don't want Rob and his partner getting shot for trespassing."

"I can do that." Wyatt studied a picture of the mama bear standing on two legs. "I have to say, she looks kind of pathetic," he said. "Hardly fitting with her fierce reputation."

"It just goes to show you what vivid imaginations and gossip can accomplish. They are the lifeblood of conspiracy theories, including those centered around cryptids. But even in her weakened state, she's plenty fierce. Don't underestimate the power of a mama bear."

He grabbed another piece of chicken from the box and said, "Okay, let's go over this plan for tonight. I want to make sure we get this right."

We reviewed it all, writing it out step by step on paper. I made some phone calls to ensure I could get the supplies I needed. Then we reviewed the plan a dozen more times, exploring different scenarios, trying to think of what could go wrong, and deciding how we would handle each possible problem. When we were done, Wyatt helped me clean up the mess left from our lunch and then insisted we go over the plan one more time. Clearly, he was nervous. I was quite confident of my conclusions, but I think we both harbored some doubt about how things would play out. Time would tell.

After we finished reviewing the plan for the umpteenth time, I said, "All right. This is it. I'm going to drive to the Walmart in Lake Geneva to get what I need. I'll call or text you when I return to let you know I'm ready."

"Sounds good," Wyatt said. "I'll get my part going and then I'm going out to Bray Road to cover up that damn hole in the ground."

"Be careful," I said. "The beast might still be there. Want to borrow my bear spray?"

He did, and I gave him the air horn, too. Then Newt and I hopped in my car, and I drove to the Lake Geneva Walmart Supercenter. I was in and out in about twenty minutes, and half an hour later, I was back in my motel room. I sent Wyatt a text letting him know I was ready and I settled in to wait for my cue.

CHAPTER 32

I got my go message from Wyatt less than an hour later. Now that it was really happening, doubt began creeping in, making my heart gallop and my thoughts race. Newt sensed my anxiety and stuck close by my side almost to the point of annoyance as I gathered the items I needed and went out to the car. Once he was clipped in the back, I tossed my supply bag in the front passenger seat and then spent a minute gripping and releasing the steering wheel over and over because my hands were shaking. Newt rested his head on my shoulder, and between him and some breathing exercises, I was able to calm my nerves enough to drive.

When I arrived at the Palmer house, there was no sign of Connor's or Brittany's vehicles, though Lydia's was in the driveway. I left Newt in the car, and then, to make sure Dylan was also gone, I followed the ramp to the front door and invested in three knocks and a good five minutes before moving on.

I descended the ramp and headed for the garage. The left-side door was no longer ajar, and I had to wrench it open so I could slip inside. I pulled it closed behind me, making the wall it was hinged to shake so much, the tools propped there fell over with a loud clatter. I stood a moment in the cool darkness before turning on my headlamp.

I removed paper bootees and nitrile gloves from my bag and donned them. Then I walked over to the shelving on the side and took the bucket containing the gardening tools down and set it on the floor. I examined the contents and then snapped a picture of them with my phone before returning it all to the shelf. Next, I removed my Walmart purchase from the bag and prepared to open it but was distracted when the light from my headlamp caught several reflections on the floor a few feet away. They were toward the back of the garage where the power tools were kept, and I bent down and picked one of them up by touching it with the tip of my finger. The item, a tiny sliver of silvery metal, stuck to my glove.

Several more were scattered about, all of them shiny, not dulled with age like I might have expected if they had been left from something Ervin Palmer had been working on four years ago. I snapped more pictures and then returned to the gardening tools to complete my assigned task, checking when I was done to make sure things would work as planned.

When I was ready to leave, I looked down at the tools beside the door that had fallen when I came in. As I went to pick them up, I realized they had multiplied since the last time I was here. I remembered the rakes, the snow shovel, and the hoe, but now there was also a regular shovel in the group. Had it been there before? I didn't think so.

I realized Lydia had likely used this shovel to dig the hole the farmer's dog and the bear cub had fallen into. Then I recalled the small bit of loose dirt I'd seen in the trunk of Lydia's car and thought it had likely come from the shovel. Yet it hadn't been in the trunk on the night she'd been killed. Had she stopped digging and given up on her hunt for buried treasure? Or had she found it? If the latter, where was it and why had she gone back out there?

As I propped the shovel up with the other tools, I noticed the dirt clinging to its blade and squeezed a bit of it between my fingers. It was damp, but according to Wyatt it hadn't rained for weeks prior to my arrival, which meant no rain prior to Lydia's death. If she'd been using this shovel to dig, would the dirt on it have been muddy or damp even if she'd dug down several feet? I doubted it. More likely, somebody had used the shovel since Lydia's death, confirming my theory. I got my phone out and took another picture.

I exited the garage, taking care to close the door as easily as I could, and then I had a look around the backyard for signs of fresh digging. There weren't any and a walk around the entire perimeter of the house produced the same negative result. I hurried back to my car and sent Wyatt a text to let him know I was done. Then I drove back to my motel to face more agonizing hours of waiting time.

Just as I opened the door to my room, a voice behind me said, "Morgan?"

I whirled around, startled. "Jon! What on earth are you doing here?"

"I need to have a serious discussion with you, and I wanted to do it face-to-face. I know this isn't the greatest time for it, but things have happened rather quickly on my end, and I find myself in need of some clarity when it comes to you and me."

Oh, God, he's come to dump me.

I tried to smile and flailed for something positive to say. Nothing came to me except the thought that at least he was decent enough to do it to my face and not over a text. A flood of desperation washed over me.

"Come on in," I said, using the task of opening my door to hide my face. I kept my back to him while I busied myself by refreshing Newt's food and water. Jon sat at the end of the bed and Newt did his best to let him know he'd missed him.

He can't dump me now, not when I've finally made some progress in understanding my behavior. I need to explain it to him. Is it too late?

This last thought prompted me to speak and do it fast. I turned abruptly to face him, and the words burst out of me with all the speed and messiness of a popped can of shaken soda.

"I'm really glad you're here and willing to talk because I've missed you a lot lately and it's given me time to think about things. And oddly enough, this case has helped me to better understand why I feel the way I do and why I act the way I do because Wyatt is a shrink. Did you know that? Did I already tell you? Of course I did, didn't I? But it isn't like Wyatt turned on the light. I saw it myself. I had an epiphany, and he helped me to understand it, to understand myself better and why I do the things I do." I paused my babbling for breath and saw Jon staring at me with wide-eyed surprise.

If he wasn't dumping me before, he will now because I'm acting like a crazy woman!

"I owe you an apology," I said, forcing the words to come out a little slower. "I understand now why I put myself in dangerous situations all the time and how difficult that must be for you. I've been a lousy girlfriend and I'm so very sorry. I hope you'll forgive me and give me a chance to make it up to you. I really, really want to give us another chance."

"Wow," Jon said, rearing back a little. Even Newt gave me a look that suggested he found my behavior a bit over-the-top.

"I know I'm jabbering," I said. "But I've been thinking about all this, about you . . . about *us* a lot these past few months. I know I'm not an easy person to deal with. People expect me to be urbane and wise and cultured because I've traveled all over the world with my parents and lived this incredibly privileged life. But the truth is, I've also lived a very protected life up until three years ago—too protected, if I'm honest—something I came to resent. It grew stifling. And it wasn't that I couldn't understand why my parents behaved the way they did. I knew their money meant I was always at risk of being kidnapped by some yahoo looking for a fast way to make a million bucks or from someone cooking up a blackmail scheme. My parents were constantly bombarded by beggars, charlatans, thieves, and con artists. Trust in anyone was hard to come by and that's not taking into account the fact that they hunted for cryptids, an activity rife with fraudsters, liars, and swindlers." I paused and sat beside Jon on the bed. He stared at me with a blank, expressionless face.

"My parents knew my love life would be complicated by their money because their wealth made the motives of any potential suitor suspect. Men would want to date me and even marry me simply because my family was rich, not because they cared about me. My parents' efforts—particularly my father's—to protect me from such things scared off a lot of guys. It not only angered me. It made me feel defective, like I was something to be avoided at all costs.

"I knew my parents loved me and only wanted the best for me, and I also knew their fears were legitimate. But I felt caged by their hovering interference. And my desperation to break free of it and them was what led me to David Johnson. It left me vulnerable to his lies and manipulations."

I paused again, combing my fingers through my hair, trying to read Jon's face, still clueless as to what he was thinking. "Maybe David killed my parents. Maybe he didn't. I honestly don't know what to believe anymore. He has messed up my head so badly, I don't know if I'll ever recover fully. And my behavior toward my parents during my time with him is something I'm deeply ashamed of. Even if David wasn't the killer, I know on some level I'm responsible for their deaths, and it's a constant struggle to live with the guilt."

Jon's face finally changed, softening into something like pity. Not the emotion I was hoping for but at least it wasn't fear or loathing. Still, I felt judged, though I knew I was my own worst jury. I leaned over and rested my head on Jon's shoulder, wanting to be close to him but not wanting to look him in the eye any longer. I didn't want to see rejection on his face before I finished what I wanted to say.

"The truth is, Jon, I don't know how to survive in the real world very well on my own. I lived almost my entire life in the shadow of my parents, and now that they've gone I've adopted Rita as a surrogate. It's been a struggle. I've had to learn how to run the store and keep the books and pay the bills and order inventory . . . little things, all of which have added up to a lot of extra stress on top of my grieving. And don't even get me started on your uncle and his one-sided investigation."

Jon stayed silent, but at least he hadn't shrugged me off his shoulder. His breathing was slow and even and I took that as a good sign.

"I know this sounds entitled and self-serving. I've heard it all before. I've read the cruel social media comments. 'Boo-hoo, poor little rich girl.' But what happened in New Jersey left me bitter, scarred, and afraid. Afraid of life, afraid of love, afraid of the world in so many ways.

"So, I guess what I'm trying to say is, I know I'm far from perfect when it comes to relationships, especially romantic ones. I don't trust myself or my emotions anymore. David stole that from me." I paused and huffed a humorless laugh. "To show you how messed up I am, I still tell myself my relationship with David had to have been real on some level because it makes me feel less gullible, stupid, and naïve to believe so. Yet I know my ability to identify 'real' was and is severely compromised, and it has impacted my ability to form a healthy, trusting relationship with just about anyone except Newt."

Newt looked up at me when he heard his name. I winked at him, and he lowered his head to his paws again.

"Into the middle of all this self-reflection, angst, and emotional instability came you, this wonderful person I met by chance. You are one of the best things that's happened to me, Jon. You pulled me out of the shell I'd built around myself. You got me back into cryptozoology and I've felt more alive during these cryptid cases than I have at any other time since my parents' deaths." I paused and then blurted out, "I don't want to give it up."

"And I don't want you to," he said.

"But you don't want to be around me when I'm doing it and that's a wall we can't seem to get over. I know you've got issues, too, understandably so. What happened to you was horrifying and I can only imagine the pain you went through after losing your wife and child the way you did. The last thing I want to do is hurt you more, but I don't want to lose you, either. Can't we figure out a way to make this work?"

Jon eased me off his shoulder finally and turned to face me, his hands on my shoulders, a gentle, unreadable smile on his face. "That was quite the speech," he said.

"You're leaving, aren't you?" I blurted out. "I know you put your house on the market and quit your job."

He looked surprised. "How...?" Then understanding settled on his face and he said, "Oh, of course. Devon."

"I suppose I understand why you want to get away. I've struggled a lot with my guilt, the fear, the anxiety . . . all of it. And while I think I'm getting better, I know I'm a work in progress. It's probably not fair of me to ask you to give us another chance but—"

"Morgan, stop," Jon said. He gently placed two fingers on my lips. "Take a breath and let me talk for a bit, okay?"

I nodded and braced myself.

"Yes, my house is on the market, and yes, I resigned from my job. But I'm not going anywhere. I didn't want to say anything until I had a chance to talk to you, but I had no idea how fast things would happen. I only came to this decision a short time ago, after trying for weeks to convince myself I should just walk away. But when I came by your place that day with Wyatt, seeing you was like a breath of fresh air. It confirmed what I'd been feeling. I almost told you what I had in mind right then, but I didn't want to get in the way of your work with Wyatt. I contacted a Realtor that same day, and it turned out, she already had a buyer who'd been looking for something on the island for a while. They made an offer for the asking price before we even had the sign up."

"Wow! That's amazing."

"It is," he agreed. "And I planned to stay in my job until they could find a replacement for me but that, too, happened very quickly."

"But why—"

Jon silenced me with his fingers again. "My turn, remember?" I nodded and he continued. "You're right that it bothered me a great deal to see you putting yourself into dangerous situations. My first instinct was to avoid it at all costs rather than risk experiencing that kind of hurt again, but the idea of never seeing you, of not giving this . . . giving *us* a chance became unbearable. I realized I had to figure out a way to try to make it work."

Oh, my God! These were the words I'd been hoping to hear. I resisted the urge to wrap my arms around him and hug him hard. Instead, I smiled and said, "You have no idea how happy I am to hear you say that. But what—"

"Let me finish. I have a proposal for you."

Whoa! I hadn't seen that coming. Jon saw the panicked look on my face and laughed.

"No, not *that* kind of proposal," he said. "Something a bit different, an idea you gave me in fact. I've already spoken to the sheriff's department on the peninsula and they're willing to hire me on a part-time, as-needed basis. I don't need the money, but I like what I do and want to keep a foot in the door. And the night before you left, you said to me that if you could, you'd take me with you on these cryptid trips all the time. I'd like to propose we do just that. I want to team up with you and work as your partner. I can provide you with some basic security and run interference when it comes to accessing police records and information."

I stared at him, stunned speechless.

"I won't hover over you or tell you what to do," he assured me. "I'll simply assess situations, advise you, and provide you with backup if you need it. And if you don't, we'll simply share in the investigative process, something I know a thing or two about and have enjoyed doing with you in the past."

He paused, watching me with a tentative smile. I tried to imagine it—Jon and me working side by side, hunting for cryptids. The image appealed to me on more than one level. We'd worked well together on the first case he'd brought me, and he'd been involved to some degree in the others. It could work, and the realization that there was hope untangled something taut and knotted inside me. I searched for something poignant and meaningful to say.

"I can't believe you sold your house." Okay, a slight non sequitur but it was what came out.

Jon shrugged. "To be honest, it has always felt a bit temporary. And I think the geographical barriers have contributed to the strain in our relationship. But I'm sticking close by. I found a little cabin right on the water in Gills Rock, about fifteen minutes from your place."

I was stunned. He paused, and I gave it a few beats before jumping in. "You already bought a place on the mainland?"

"Well, I haven't technically bought it yet, but the real estate agent seems confident my offer will be accepted."

"This seems—I don't know—sudden. Are you sure?"

He frowned and leaned back slightly, dropping his hands from my shoulders. He looked concerned and embarrassed. "It's too much too fast, isn't it? I honestly didn't think it would happen so soon but it's not too late. I can undo it all. Have I misread things between us?"

This time it was me putting my fingers to his lips.

"It is sudden, and I need a little time to absorb it all. But a moment ago, I was preparing myself to be dumped, so believe me, I'm happy with this turn of events. Very happy. It feels . . . I don't know." I hesitated, searching for the right words.

Then, at the same exact moment, we both said, "As if it's meant to be."

We both laughed and then Jon said, "I really want to kiss you right now."

"Do you?" I smiled and leaned closer.

"I do," he said, his voice husky. Then his expression turned wary, and he pulled back. "We can continue to take things as slow as you want on the relationship front. No pressure. I know there are no guarantees going forward, and if things don't work out between us, either personally or professionally, we can still go our separate ways."

"Shut up," I said. Then I put my palms on his cheeks, pulled his face to mine, and kissed him gently on the lips. "We can continue this discussion later. Right now, I need to focus on this case, because as soon as Wyatt messages me, we have a killer to catch. Want to come along for the fun, partner? I'll fill you in on the details."

"I would love that."

We kissed again for good measure while Newt thumped his tail in approval.

CHAPTER 33

While waiting for my cue from Wyatt, I filled Jon in on what had happened with the case so far and what we had planned for the night.

"I'm pretty sure I've got some time before Wyatt will message me," I said. "Can I interest you in some dinner while we wait?"

"You can."

I drove us to a place I'd noticed downtown on one of my many drives through. Poor Newt was once again consigned to the car, but he seemed less disappointed than usual. I think he was as happy as I was that Jon was there.

Jon ordered a big bowl of chili while I opted for a baked potato with the works and a side of sautéed veggies. I learned more about the cabin Jon was buying, and he showed me pictures of it on his phone. The living room and master bedroom windows looked out onto Hedgehog Harbor at the north end of Green Bay, where stunning sunsets were a regularity.

We talked about what it would be like to work together on a more regular basis, and while I was generally delighted at this turn of events, I also knew there were potential pitfalls. There were things—like the division of tasks and responsibilities and how to deal with disagreements—that could put a strain on our relationship if they weren't addressed and dealt with either ahead of time or with a plan in place for if and when they did arise. I listened to Jon describe the role he envisioned for himself as more of a reconnaissance man scouting out sites ahead of time, talking with local law enforcement, and perhaps lining up potential witnesses for me to talk to.

"This cryptid stuff is your thing," he assured me. "I'm looking forward to learning more about it, but I'll be leaving the bulk of the cryptozoology role up to you. I'll tag along, keep an eye on things, run interference if I need to, and learn what I can."

"You know, there's no guarantee I'll get another case after this one."

"Then we simply focus on our relationship without any of the pressure. It may be slow in the beginning. That's one of the reasons I still want to have a job. But I'm betting your cryptid business is going to pick up. You already have a reputation here in Wisconsin and I've done a little research and learned this state has more than its fair share of cryptids. Given the reputation your parents had, I suspect there may be other jobs outside the state coming your way once word gets out."

I was beginning to envision the future he had in mind and I liked what I saw. I knew there would still be bumps in the road, but

I was beyond delighted with where things were going. My heart felt pounds lighter.

We were lingering over coffee and a truly amazing piece of caramel-topped cheesecake we had decided to share for dessert when my phone dinged with a text notification from Wyatt.

"We're on," I told Jon while texting Wyatt back with an ETA. "Since you're coming along, why don't you record things on your phone as they're happening? I'm sure Wyatt won't mind."

"I can do that."

After paying our bill, I drove us to Lydia's place. Wyatt's official SUV was already there, parked down the street and out of sight of the house. I pulled in behind it.

"Jon!" Wyatt said when he saw him. "You've decided to join us?"

"I have, assuming you're okay with it."

"Of course. The more the merrier." Wyatt shot me a knowing look and a wink.

"I thought he could record what happens on his phone," I suggested.

"Excellent idea," Wyatt said. He removed some paper shoe covers and nitrile gloves from the back of his car and handed them to us. "Put these in your pockets," he said.

I took doubles of both. "Should I leave Newt in the car or bring him along?" I asked.

"Bring him. It sounds like he was a key part of solving this."

"He was. He kept making me go into the garage."

We all walked up toward the house, past Brittany's car, which was parked in the street, and then down the driveway past Connor's and Lydia's cars. Wyatt led the way up the ramp to the front door, where he knocked with a heavier hand than usual. We waited for a full minute or more and I could tell Wyatt was about to knock again. I tried to peek in through the windows, but the blinds were closed tight. Finally, Connor opened the door. Behind him I saw Dylan in his chair beside the living room couch and Brittany seated in one of the chairs by the fireplace.

"What's going on, Detective?" Dylan asked as we stepped inside. "Did you forget something when we saw you earlier today?" His eyebrows shot up when he saw Jon. "And you brought reinforcements with you?" he said in an amused tone. He looked over at Connor. "They must be afraid of you, dude, because clearly I'm no threat."

"This is Jon Flanders," Wyatt explained. "He works with Morgan."

"Ah, yes, Morgan," Dylan said, turning his gaze my way and then quickly dismissing me and focusing on Wyatt again. "How can I help you, Detective?"

To my delight, Wyatt looked over at me and said, "Morgan, would you like to do the honors?"

"Happy to. I think I know why your mother was out on Bray Road the night she was killed, Dylan. She was looking for buried treasure."

"Buried treasure?" Dylan said, clearly skeptical.

Brittany scoffed and shook her head as if to shake off the madness of such an idea.

"Yes. It turns out, there was something buried out there. And if someone else knew about it, they might have killed her to get their hands on it."

Connor stood in the hall doorway chewing on his lower lip. Brittany started gnawing on a thumbnail. Dylan simply looked amused.

"I was looking at your mom's Instagram posts earlier," I explained. "I saw a picture of her working in the garden and her tools were spread out around her, including a four-tined hand rake. It's essentially a metal claw designed to dig through dirt. As soon as I saw it, I was struck by how closely it resembled the wounds on both your mother and the second victim, not to mention the scratches on the car."

"Okay," Dylan said, his brow wrinkling in thought. "Are you saying my mother was killed with a hand rake to make it look like a werewolf did it?"

"I do think that was the intent," I said. "Your mom died of a broken neck, and the wounds were inflicted afterward, after her body had been dragged from where she'd been digging for the treasure. The second victim had similar injuries, though more of them. And in her case they were fatal. I believe the wounds on both women were meant to appear as if they had been inflicted by a werewolf or some other creature, though they were actually from your mother's hand rake."

Dylan frowned. "You think my mother was wounded by her own hand rake?" he said in a mocking tone.

Brittany tittered a nervous laugh.

"I do," I said. "And we're here to try to find it."

Silence fell over the room, though the air crackled with tension as the trio absorbed the meaning of this while they steadfastly avoided looking at one another.

Finally, Brittany said, "Are you saying you think someone in this house is responsible for these deaths?"

Wyatt said, "It's possible, but we need to get a better look at

Lydia's rake to be sure. It wouldn't be capable of making the wounds our victims had unless it had been altered."

Connor turned to leave the room, but Wyatt stopped him.

"Come in and have a seat, Connor. I'd like all three of you in here for now."

Dylan looked surprised. "Hold on. Are you saying you think Connor has something to do with this?" Then with great conviction he added, "I don't believe that for a minute."

Wyatt ignored him. "Your mother kept her gardening stuff in the garage, right?" he said.

Dylan shrugged. "I guess so. I haven't been in there in years. The door doesn't open wide enough for my chair to get through."

"Mind if we go out there and have a look?"

Dylan shrugged again. "Sure. Whatever you need to do."

"Morgan, will you and Jon go out there and check to see if the hand rake is there?"

"Sure."

"I'll stay here and keep these guys company in the meantime."

Jon and I headed out to the garage. Newt came with us, but I had him sit and stay at the base of the ramp.

We stopped at the garage door to put shoe covers and gloves on.

"Have your phone ready," I said to Jon when we were done. "You'll want to record this." He tapped the screen on his phone and then nodded at me.

We squeezed through the narrow opening into the garage, and I turned on the special flashlight I had picked up at Walmart earlier, aiming it at the floor between us and the shelving on the side wall of the garage. "Look there," I said, pointing to the floor.

"And there." I used the light to trace a path between the shelves and where we stood.

"Nice," Jon said, panning over the glowing footprints with his phone.

"I have my moments. Stay here and I'll go get the bucket."

Jon kept his phone on me as I carefully worked my way around the trail of footprints on the floor, eventually getting to the bucket of tools on the shelf. I picked it up, holding it out from my body, and then took the same route back to the door, leaving a faint trail of my own in my wake.

Jon paused the recording as we squeezed out through the opening and then removed our shoe covers, though I kept my gloves on. Then we made our way back to the house, picking Newt up along the way.

The show was about to begin.

CHAPTER 34

We walked in and I set the bucket down on the floor by the door.

Brittany was still chewing on her thumbnail. Connor was sitting on the edge of his seat, one leg bouncing up and down. Dylan was rocking his chair back and forth. Wyatt was still standing beside the front door where we'd left him, and after I set down the bucket, he bent over to look inside.

"There's a rake in here," I said. I reached in and retrieved the tool, holding it up. "It resembles the one in the picture but there's no way this is sharp enough to inflict the kind of damage we saw on the victims," I added, rubbing my gloved thumb over the blunt ends of the tines.

"We're okay, then?" Brittany said hopefully.

"No," I said, inspecting the rake closely.

Dylan said, "You're welcome to take it and have it analyzed for blood or whatever, but if it's not capable of inflicting the wounds you saw, it can't be what you're looking for, right?"

"That would be true if this was the same hand rake I saw in your mom's Instagram post. But it's not. This one looks quite new. There's some dirt on it, but not much, and it's obviously newer than the other tools in the bucket. The one in the online photo was older, discolored."

"It's almost as if someone put it there purposely to fool us," Wyatt said.

Dylan's face went through a rapid change of expressions.

Brittany dropped the hand she'd had to her mouth and said, "Connor?"

Connor sat across from her, staring straight ahead, looking like the classic deer in the headlights.

"The rake used to create the wounds would have been altered," I said. "The tines would have had to have been ground down to a razor-sharp edge and point."

Dylan said, "This whole idea sounds crazy. Why do you think my mother was looking for buried treasure?"

"Because I found clues to the treasure hidden in her room," I said.

Dylan appeared surprised by this. Brittany and Connor glanced at each other and then quickly looked away.

"Those clues hinted at a stash of cash one of Al Capone's men might have buried out on Bray Road. The coins we found with your mother's body were from that era and worth some money, so she was close to finding it."

Connor sat back in his chair, muttered something under his

breath, and ran a hand over his head. He arched his eyebrows at Brittany in an unvoiced question. She shrugged. I looked from him to her and back again, noting the same pale complexions, blue eyes, red hair, and Cupid's bow lips. How had I not seen it before?

"Oh, my God," I said. "You two are related, aren't you? How? Cousins? Siblings?"

Dylan turned and looked from Brittany to Connor and back to Brittany. Dawning spread over his face. "Good God, is she right? Is that true?"

Connor squeezed his eyes closed.

"Is that why you reconnected with me on Facebook?" Dylan asked Brittany. "Are the two of you in cahoots together?"

Brittany ignored Dylan's questions and instead tossed out one of her own, no doubt hoping to change the direction of things. "Are you suggesting one of us killed Lydia and this other woman?"

"Well, let's see," Wyatt said, stroking a sideburn. "Connor has alibis for both murders. His employer verified he was at work each of those nights, meaning he's in the clear. You, Brittany, have no alibis. Your landlord's cameras have both entrances to the house covered and I've reviewed the footage. You were gone both nights."

"I was here with Dylan," she argued. "The night his mom died, he snuck me in after she'd gone to bed."

"Really?" Wyatt challenged. Brittany nodded adamantly. "Did you hear Lydia leave during the night?"

Brittany thought a moment, forehead furrowed.

"Lydia's car has muffler issues. It's very loud and Dylan's bedroom borders the driveway. It's hard to believe you wouldn't have heard it."

Brittany's facial muscles twitched. "I wasn't feeling well that night. I slept hard."

"Apparently," Wyatt said. "I talked to your employer. You didn't show up for work the next morning. Nor did you call in. In fact, he fired you, didn't he?"

"It wasn't fair. I overslept," Brittany said irritably.

"Actually, I think you were drugged," I said. "Did Dylan give you anything to eat or drink that night before you went to sleep?"

Brittany opened her mouth, presumably to reject this idea, but then she shut it and stared at Dylan.

"How about the night before last?" I asked. "Did you sleep hard then, too? And did Dylan give you something to drink beforehand?"

Brittany's huge eyes grew even bigger. "I wondered why I slept so hard. Did you drug that cocoa you gave me?"

"Don't be ridiculous," Dylan said.

I said, "You have a prescription for cyclobenzaprine, Dylan, a powerful muscle relaxer. And your mother had one for alprazolam, a potent tranquilizer. I'm guessing either one or both would have done the job. I'm curious, Brittany, had Dylan ever invited you to sleep over before the night his mother was killed?"

She shook her head slowly, her expression horrified.

"There's a reason he invited you that night," I said. "He needed a car. I think he knew Lydia had been going out to Bray Road and he knew why. He suspected she'd be going out there again that night and he needed a way to follow her so he'd know the exact spot. Connor was at work. So, Dylan invited you over and drugged you so you wouldn't know he was taking your car."

Dylan scoffed. "How could I even begin to pull off something like that? I can't drive, much less walk around in the woods."

"Can't you?" I asked.

Dylan scowled at me. "Wow, lady, you're seriously deranged."

"Am I, Dylan? The other day when you returned from your therapy visit with Connor, something about you looked different. At first I thought it was your clothing because I'd only seen you in your slacks and dress shirts before, and that day you were in sweats. But it wasn't your clothing at all. It was your nose ring or, rather, the lack of it."

Connor and Brittany both turned to look at Dylan, who reflexively raised a hand to his nose.

"The one you had when I first met you stood out because it was a skull and I'd never seen one like it before. It caught my eye because I have a store back home and thought your nose ring would fit my inventory perfectly. To be honest, I might not have even noticed it was gone because I was so focused on other things by then, except I found it. Want to guess where?"

Dylan stared at me, expressionless. "Let me see if I understand this," he said. "You found my nose ring or one like it, and somehow you think that means I can walk?"

"By itself, it's not proof," I admitted, "though finding it next to where your mother broke her neck is certainly incriminating."

"Give it up, Dylan. They know," Connor said.

I shot a surprised look at Connor. "You know Dylan can walk?"

"I've known for some time now. He managed to hide it from me for nearly a year, walking around the house at night when his mother was at work or asleep or when I was at work. But one night I came home early because I wasn't feeling well, and I caught him."

"Why didn't you say something to someone?" Wyatt asked.

"Because Dylan promised that if I kept my mouth shut, he'd

give me half of whatever settlement he gets from the county. If they knew he wasn't paralyzed, it would blow up the whole case and he wouldn't get anything."

Dylan laughed nervously. "That's a lie. He's making stuff up." He glared at Connor. "What the hell, dude?"

Connor gave Dylan a punishing look.

Wyatt said, "There's a reason I asked you and Connor to come to the station today, Dylan. The conversation you overheard was no accident. We wanted you to hear us talking about how we suspected an altered hand rake was the murder weapon and that we needed to find out if your mother's was still among the tools in the garage in order to rule out people in your household."

Dylan's expression darkened. His hands gripped the wheels of his chair so hard, his knuckles were white.

"We had you followed when you left the sheriff's office," Wyatt continued. "We watched when Brittany came here to pick you up a short time after you got home. You went through the motions of loading your chair into her car and going to the hardware store in Lake Geneva, where you then went inside and purchased an identical hand rake."

"You followed us?" Brittany said.

"We did," Wyatt said. "That's how I know you knew about Dylan's ability to walk." He looked at Dylan. "Going into the hardware store in the wheelchair would have been too memorable, too identifiable on camera if anyone happened to check, right, Dylan? That's why you walked in, obscuring your face from the cameras with the hoodie you were wearing. And the purchase was with cash, meaning no way to trace it if anyone came looking."

"You can't prove any of this," Dylan said defiantly.

"Oh, I think we can," I said, "because I set up a little trap in your garage earlier today while you were at the sheriff's department chatting with Wyatt."

"What are you talking about?" Dylan's righteous anger was fading, as was the color of his complexion.

"A little thing called Glo Germ powder," I said. "It's a nifty little tool used to teach people about the importance of handwashing. I bought some at Walmart earlier today. You sprinkle it on things and have people handle them. Then you tell them to wash their hands well with soap and water. When they're done, you hold a special black light over their hands and anything they've touched. Anywhere the powder remains will glow. Let me demonstrate."

I walked over and turned off the table lamp, leaving just the ambient light from the kitchen and hallway to illuminate the room. Then I turned on my handheld black light, aiming it at the tools in the bucket. Spots on them glowed a fluorescent green. I then aimed the light at my own hands and at the hand rake I'd removed from the bucket and got the same result. Then I turned the beam toward Dylan.

"Well, look at that," I said. "Your hands are glowing green, as are the wheel grips on your chair."

Dylan looked rattled. "That doesn't mean anything. Powder travels. You could have transferred it from your clothes or hands and dropped it here in the room."

"Which is why we have all stayed here by the door," I said. "I was careful to make sure I didn't get the powder anywhere on my body other than my gloves. I sprinkled it on the garage floor, too, but Jon and I covered our shoes with paper booties when we went out there and then removed the covers as soon as we exited." I reversed my light, shining it over myself. Then I briefly lit up Jon, Wyatt, and even Newt. Nothing glowed other than a random speck on the bottom hem of my slacks.

"How about we take a look at the bottom of your shoes, Dylan?" I said.

I expected him to panic but instead he looked surprisingly smug. He reached down, hoisted one of his legs up and pulled the shoe off, tossing it toward me. Then he repeated this action with the other leg and shoe. Sure enough, the bottoms of the shoes didn't glow when I hit them with the black light.

"You changed your shoes," I said.

"Don't be ridiculous." He looked at Wyatt with a woeful shake of his head. "Really, Detective Wyatt, is this the best you can do?"

"Why don't we take a look at the other shoes in your closet?" Wyatt suggested.

"Have you got a search warrant?" Dylan shot back, fully in defiance mode now.

"I have a better idea," I said. I approached Dylan and said, "Would you mind lifting one of your feet again?"

He stared at me, silent.

"Please?" I urged.

"You want to examine my socks now, too?"

"Humor me."

He glared at me but reached down and hauled up his left leg. When I ignored his foot, he looked surprised. I aimed the black light at the foot pedal on his wheelchair instead. The grooved pattern that helped make it skidproof lit up like a Christmas tree.

"Care to tell us how you got that much Glo Germ dust on your foot pedal, Dylan? It didn't come from the shoes you just threw at me, so the only answer is, you were wearing different shoes. Did you change them?"

"He did it when you guys showed up," Brittany said. "He switched them because he was afraid you'd see the mud on them."

"Shut up, you cow," Dylan said.

"Well, we know you were out there in the garage, Dylan, and we also know you had to be standing because as you pointed out, your chair won't fit through the opening. What's more, we were able to capture video of the footprints you left on the floor when you came out."

Jon held his phone up and smiled.

"It must have been Connor or Brittany who left the footprints," Dylan said.

I had to give him one thing: He was quick on his feet with the lies even if they weren't particularly smart.

"Connor wears a size fifteen shoe, Dylan. And Brittany wears about a six, I'm guessing. What size do you wear?"

Thunderclouds rolled across Dylan's face.

"You're the real Beast of Bray Road, Dylan," I said. "Did you find the rest of the treasure your mother was looking for?"

He rolled his eyes. "It was just another one of her stupid, useless ideas," he said, shaking his head. "My father was right about her. She was a mentally disturbed idiot. I'll admit, she had me going with the little booklet and the map. I used to sneak into her room when she wasn't home and go through her stuff until she started hiding things. Then I got into her laptop and looked at her search history and this stupid diary thing she kept on there. That's when I figured out what she was going after, what those things she had might mean." He let out a humorless laugh. "I thought she was really onto something this time, especially when she started sneaking out at night. I should have known better. My mother was a pathetic failure her entire life."

"This time she was right," I said. "There *was* treasure buried out there. It wasn't Capone's but it was very real, to the tune of more than ten grand."

Dylan blinked several times, looking bemused.

Wyatt removed a piece of paper from his inside jacket pocket. "And to answer your earlier question, Dylan, yes, I have a search warrant. Let's see what else we can find, shall we?"

CHAPTER 35

"Should I go rescue Wyatt from Rita's clutches?" I asked Jon. It was a week after the showdown at Lydia's house, and I was happy to be back home. Jon and I were standing next to Henry, my mummified mascot, watching as Rita flitted and fawned over Wyatt, who was seated at a table trying to sign copies of his books.

"I think he's enjoying it," Jon said. "And clearly Rita is."

"I didn't get a chance to talk to Wyatt when he first got here. Did he tell you anything about the case?"

"Some. He said the psychiatric evaluation of Dylan determined he has strong sociopathic tendencies."

"That doesn't surprise me, though his tears seemed genuine," I said.

"Sociopaths are good at faking emotions. Wyatt also said Dylan admitted he was the driver in the accident that killed his father."

"So the gas station witness was right."

Wyatt had finished signing our stock of his books and was hugging Rita, who was flushed beet red once he let her go.

"I think you have a die-hard fan there," I said when Wyatt walked over to us.

He smiled fondly. "She's cute. I'd love a million more just like her."

"Let's go upstairs. Jon and I want an update."

I led the way to my apartment and got us all drinks. Once we were settled in the living room, I said, "Give us the latest."

"Where to begin. . . ." Wyatt said.

"What's going to happen to Connor and Brittany?" I asked.

"Nothing. While they were blackmailing Dylan into sharing his settlement money with them, they knew nothing about the treasure stuff. That was all Dylan. And Connor did provide genuine services to Dylan for nearly two years. It was only when he figured out Dylan's secret that he coerced Brittany into coming down and helping him.

"By the way, Morgan, good catch on the relationship there. Brittany is Connor's half sister. They share a mother, though she's been deceased for years, and both favor her in looks. And while they grew up in separate households, they spent a fair amount of time together growing up because of custody arrangements."

"So, they get to just go on their merry way?" I asked.

"Yep, they already have."

"And what about Dylan?" Jon asked.

"Still an ongoing process. He tried to claim that his mother's death was an accident, that she tripped and broke her neck. But the bruising on Lydia's chest suggests she was pushed hard into that fence."

"It couldn't have been easy for him to drag her body all the way back into the woods," I said.

"No, but lucky for him, Lydia was a small woman. And Dylan has regained pretty much all his strength. His feeling started coming back less than a year after the accident, right around the time he was discharged from the rehab hospital and sent home. He's been doing strengthening exercises on the sly ever since."

"Why did he continue to hide it?" Jon asked.

"Probably money," Wyatt said. "There was talk of a lawsuit early on. Plus, I think he enjoyed the attention and sympathy."

"Do you think he meant to kill himself along with his father in the accident?" I asked.

"I do. He told the prison psychiatrist he intended to die with his father, who had been physically and emotionally abusive to both him and Lydia. It sounds like they were arguing in the car, and in an impulsive moment, Dylan decided to end the abuse and his life then and there. But he also told the psychiatrist he hated his mother for staying with Ervin all those years and putting up with the abuse."

"That might explain how he was able to rip her throat out with the rake, even if she was already dead," I said. "That's cold."

"Yeah, he didn't hold back with DeeDee, either," Wyatt said. "She was a victim of being in the wrong place at the wrong time. After seeing you visit Lydia's home several times, she decided to stake it out that night. When she saw Dylan drive away in Brittany's car, she followed him. It sounds like she either didn't know

Dylan was supposed to be wheelchair-bound or wasn't sure who he was. She just knew a woman from that household had supposedly been killed by the beast and you, the cryptozoologist, kept visiting them. She followed Dylan through the woods and out to the hole and then approached him to ask why he was digging. He gave her some made-up story about trying to catch the werewolf in a trap. They walked back to the road together and I think that's when DeeDee realized she was in trouble. Dylan had the hand rake with him because he had stashed it under the seat in Brittany's car the night he killed his mother. He grabbed it and attacked DeeDee with it. She tried to run from him but fell in the woods, and he killed her in a blind rage."

I shook my head sadly. "If only she'd been honest with me, she might still be alive."

"Do you think Dylan will try for an insanity defense?" Jon asked.

"Doubt it," Wyatt said. "I don't see how he can claim his mother's death was an accident, either. There's a big problem with that."

"The hand rake," I said.

Wyatt nodded. "He went out there that night with the rake already filed and sharpened. That shows premeditation."

"Did you ever find the rake?" Jon asked.

Wyatt nodded, grimacing. "Oh, yeah, and a wicked thing it is. It's essentially four very sharp knives on a handle, an extremely effective weapon."

"Turns the user into Wolverine," Jon said.

Wyatt smiled. "I suppose it did. After he killed DeeDee, Dylan stashed it under the driver's seat in Connor's car, much to Connor's surprise. Smart when you think about it. The handle had been wiped clean of prints, and aside from him not having a serious motive for killing Lydia, the evidence would have pointed at Connor. After all, working with metal is what Connor did for a living."

"I did think Connor might be involved when I saw the metal bits in the garage by the vise and the grinder," I said. "If it hadn't been for his alibis and finding Dylan's nose ring out at the dig site, Connor would have been at the top of my list. And even after I began to suspect Dylan, I thought the two of them might have been in on it together."

"What made you look in the garage in the first place?" Jon asked.

"It was Newt," I said, making my dog lift his head briefly and give a few thumps of his tail. "He drew me to it. He liked Dylan for some reason, and I think he smelled Dylan's scent going into the garage." I shrugged. "That's my best guess, anyway."

"I might be able to shed some light on that," Wyatt said. "In searching the garage, we found bloodied clothes shoved into a bucket in the back corner. There was a pair of black men's pants, a black shirt, and a pair of black athletic shoes. The blood was Lydia's. We also found the clothes Dylan was wearing when he killed DeeDee. They were in the same bucket but inside a plastic bag. My guess is, Newt smelled the blood and that's why he was drawn to the garage."

"That makes sense," I said, choosing to believe this explanation rather than one suggesting my dog had been infatuated with a sociopathic killer.

"Do you think Dylan would have killed Connor given enough time?" Jon asked.

"Absolutely," Wyatt said. "Brittany, too, especially if he had ever found the buried coins. He'd want to eliminate the only people who knew his secret."

"I should have suspected something with Dylan sooner," I said. "You told me his spinal cord had only been bruised in the accident, not severed or permanently damaged."

"It's one of the reasons why the settlement was delayed for so long," Wyatt explained. "The lawyers for the county wanted to see if he'd recover. It's why he was still going to therapy. It was mandated. They tested him periodically by sticking needles in his legs to see if he had any feeling there. The fact that Dylan was able to fool them by ignoring the pain and not reacting shows how determined he was."

"Or how disturbed," I said.

"You never really bought into the werewolf angle, did you?" Wyatt asked me.

"Not really, though I had my moments of doubt. The scratches on the car were suspect. There were too many of them in odd places and they appeared too uniform. Dylan was probably working off old stories about the beast when he made them, and he overdid it. But then there was Paul McNamara's story, which rang true to me, and my own sighting the night I found Augie in the hole. I had no idea that creature was a bear until I saw it up close. Even then it was tough. The poor thing was in rough shape."

Wyatt said, "You'll be happy to know your guy trapped the cub the other day and it didn't take long for the mama bear to show up."

"Yeah, he told me. They're both being treated at a wildlife sanctuary in Canada. Once they're on the mend, they'll be released into the woods up there."

"And this Lester fellow who staged the whole buried-treasure thing, will he get his coins back?" Jon asked.

Wyatt nodded. "Thanks to Morgan here. That was a good catch."

"A lucky guess," I said with a shrug. "After I got to thinking about that box in Lydia's closet, I realized it was much larger than necessary for that one hidden drawer and the jewelry in the top section. Plus, it was quite heavy even after the jewelry was removed. I've had some of those puzzle boxes here in the store before and I knew some of them have multiple hidden spaces. That got me to examining it more closely. It took me a while to find the necessary moves, but eventually I discovered a second secret space. The leather pouch with the coins was in there, including the other loose ones Lester had seeded at the site."

Wyatt said, "We never did find the metal box, but I'm guessing Lydia tossed it in the trash. Her garbage would have been picked up the morning before she was killed."

"I don't understand," Jon said. "If she had already found the box and the coins, why was she still out there digging?"

"It was the loose coins, according to her diary," Wyatt explained.

"Was this the computer diary Dylan mentioned?" Jon said.

"Yep. Dylan was reading it. It turns out, his job at the insurance company finished more than a month ago, and knowing we might want to look at Lydia's laptop after we found her dead, he swapped it with his after wiping all his files off it. Then he downloaded her email and social media apps to his cleaned laptop to make it look like Lydia had been using it and passed it off as hers."

"That was clever of him," Jon said.

Wyatt nodded. "What he didn't transfer was the diary Lydia kept on her computer. It turned out to be quite an eye-opener. In it, she talked a lot about the Capone thing, how she sorted the clues and figured out the map coordinates. But by then she had hidden the map, and without it, Dylan had no way of knowing where the spot was. And even though Lydia had apparently found the box, the presence of the loose coins and the fact that Nitti mentioned in the fake letter that there were two treasures in his life had her convinced there was a second stash buried in that spot."

"What about the laptop I saw in the basement?"

"That really was Connor's," Wyatt said.

"Do you think Lydia knew Dylan's secret?" Jon asked. "Is that why she finally hid the map and the other stuff?"

Wyatt shrugged. "Maybe. I don't think she knew he could walk, but she knew he was snooping in her things."

"With her OCD, it would have been easy for her to tell if something in her room had been moved," I said.

Wyatt nodded. "Based on notes in her diary and some things she confided to a coworker at the hospital, she'd been having doubts about Dylan for a long time. Once he confessed that he was the one driving when he and Ervin had had the accident, she knew something was seriously off with him. She had hoped the paralysis would serve as a wake-up call, a prompt to get his life in order and do something productive. But instead, Dylan picked up where his father left off with the verbal and emotional abuse of his mother."

"That poor woman," I said.

"It's sad, all right," Wyatt said. "I can't help but wonder if she envisioned the settlement from the accident all going to Dylan and the Capone treasure being a way for her to get a new start. I know

Lester and others said she did everything for Dylan, but maybe she was beginning to see she needed to make a life for herself apart from him."

"I guess we'll never know," I said.

We sat in contemplative silence for a minute, each of us lost in our thoughts. Then Wyatt said, "How are things going with you two?"

"Great," Jon said. "My offer on the new place has been accepted and I plan on moving in a few weeks and starting my job with the sheriff's department."

"That is, when he's not working with me on cryptid investigations," I added.

"Nice," Wyatt said with a smile. "And what's happening with the David Johnson thing?"

"Still an open book," Jon said, frowning. "So far we haven't been able to prove or disprove what he says, though Morgan is convinced this New Jersey couple is the same people she saw in the Pine Barrens that weekend. My uncle is inclined to agree with her though neither of them saw them for all that long."

"And David is still out there somewhere," I said, "probably stealing someone else's identity."

"We'll catch him," Jon said. "One of the reasons I want to keep working in law enforcement is so I can have the necessary tools at my disposal to continue the hunt. I've made it my personal mission to find and arrest him."

"Sounds like the guy is quite the slippery chameleon," Wyatt said. "In a way, he's like the ultimate cryptid you need to find."

"You're right," I said. I looked over at Jon and smiled. "And he had better keep looking over his shoulder because Jon and I are in this together now and we're going to make a formidable team."

ACKNOWLEDGMENTS

Whenever I travel to locations to do research for my books, I never have any trouble finding helpful and knowledgeable people who are only too happy to share what they know with me. For this book, special thanks go to Jennifer Wharton at the Matheson Memorial Library in Elkhorn; to Jennifer Melchi, the adult services librarian at the Burlington Public Library; to Julie Eggleston with the Burlington Historical Society; and to Detective Rich Lagle with the Walworth County Sheriff's Office.

I'd also like to say a posthumous thank-you to Linda Godfrey, whose research as a journalist and later as a self-described cryptozoologist investigating the Beast of Bray Road provided for entertaining, thought-provoking, and factual information.

As always, the many people without whose help I wouldn't be able to do what I do deserve thanks as well. First and foremost is my wise and indomitable agent, Adam Chromy, who has steered me through the many ups and downs of my writing career for more than a decade. I may not say it enough, but you are much appreciated. I also need to thank all the amazing folks at Berkley, including my brilliant editor, Tom Colgan, and his editorial assistant, Carly James; my publicity manager, Kaila Mundell-Hill; my marketing manager, Kalie Barnes-Young; and all the other behind-the-scenes folks like copyeditors and cover art designers who are involved in getting my books to the best they can be and into readers' hands. Thanks also to Matie Argiropoulos and Susan Bennett for the production and narration of the audio versions of the books. I am so glad to have all of you on my team.

As always, my family and close friends are due not only thanks but a degree of sympathy and understanding for putting up with me and supporting what I do. Special thanks to Laurie, Cathy, and Amy for keeping me sane and laughing, and to Ryan and Jen for understanding my warped sense of humor. Also, thanks to Winston for being the smartest, most amazing dog ever and the model I use for Newt. You have clearly spoiled us and given us unrealistic expectations for any other dogs, as was recently proven when we added the new little hellion to the household.

And finally, to all the readers who read my books, all the bookstores who sell and promote them, and all the libraries who invite me to visit and yammer away, thanks so much for your support and letting me be a part of your worlds. You are why I do this.